PICKET FENCES

Published by Tidewater Press
New Westminster, BC, Canada
www.tidewaterpress.ca

This is a work of fiction. Names, characters, business, events and incidents
are the products of the author's imagination. Any resemblance to actual
persons, living or dead, or actual events is purely coincidental.

978-1-7770101-4-0 (print)
978-1-7770101-5-7 (e-book)

LIBRARY AND ARCHIVES CANADA CATALOGUING IN PUBLICATION
Title: Picket Fences : a novel / Emma L.R. Hogg.
Names: Hogg, Emma L. R., 1980- author.
Identifiers: Canadiana (print) 20200304623 | Canadiana (ebook)
2020030464X | ISBN 9781777010140
(softcover) | ISBN 9781777010157 (HTML)
Classification: LCC PS8615.O378 P53 2020 | DDC C813/.6—dc23

Printed in Canada

PICKET FENCES

a novel

EMMA L.R. HOGG

TIDEWATER
PRESS

Chapter One

ON THE MORNING of Sloane Sawyer's thirtieth birthday, Roma gifted her daughter a fitness tracker.

"It's as addictive as smoking cigarettes, only it's good for you!" Roma boasted, rolling up her sleeve to show off her own.

Who gives their daughter a fitness tracker? A mother who thinks their daughter is fat.

Roma had been waiting in her car in the driveway for Sloane and Jason to wake up. She would show up like that, driving forty-five minutes from Tippett Valley to Torren Hills without warning. She claimed that if she called first, Sloane would tell her it wasn't a good time. She was probably right.

"This one's for Jason," she said. From her purse, she removed a second wrapped gift—the same shape and size as Sloane's.

It's my birthday—why is anyone else getting a gift?

Roma set the box on the counter. "Something the two of you can do together," she said.

"You mean, like you and Dad?"

It was a mean thing to say. That Roma and Edward would soon be married thirty-two years still amazed her.

"Now that your father's retired, I see enough of him at home," said Roma. "Try it on."

The fitness tracker was the wrong size for Sloane's wrist. Small. She couldn't even get the buckle to meet the last hole. To avoid an argument, she accepted the gift receipt and promised to exchange the band for a larger size.

"Mom, I've got to get ready for work."

Roma sat at the kitchen table. "There's one more thing."

Sloane rolled her eyes. "What?"

"I'm going to China!" Her arms rocketed above her head.

Roma had never been anywhere, had never been on a plane, had

5

never crossed a border, and she had chosen China as her first trip. Come September, she would be out of the country for two weeks. She told Sloane she picked China because of a Greg Brown song of the same name. She didn't care that the lyrics were a metaphor; she was actually going to be in China.

"With Dad?" asked Sloane.

Edward refused to go—not during the NHL pre-season—which was likely the response Roma had expected. Edward was the reason for the trip. Since retiring from the steel plant, he rarely left the house, and the house had always been Roma's space.

"With Vivian. We're applying for visas this afternoon. I need a break from your father. He wants to tell me everything."

"Isn't that a good thing? Couples go to therapy to learn how to be better communicators."

"He's *over* communicating," Roma complained. "I don't need to know everything your father's thinking. I don't need to have each of his movements narrated."

"Narrated? Really, Mom?"

Roma lowered her voice. "'I'm hungry,'" she said. "'I'm going to heat up some soup. I'm going to do that now. Just got to get out of this chair. Oh, the floor is cold. Better put on my slippers. I wonder who won the Leafs game last night. Better look that up to see if it affected my Bruins in the standings. Darn, I forgot to plug the phone in last night. Remember the days when phones just stayed plugged in? Fifty-five seconds for the soup. Last time, I heated for a minute and it was five seconds too long—'"

"Okay, I get it."

"All day, Sloane."

"Is that why you picked China, to get away as far as possible?"

"I've always wanted to go to China."

"No, you haven't."

"How do you know?"

"You've never mentioned it before."

"I don't tell you everything, Sloane. I'm not your father."

"Dad doesn't tell me anything."

"Lucky you."

Sloane dropped it. Roma hummed the Greg Brown tune. Sloane tightened the drawstring of her sweatpants and wondered if her own best friend would go on a trip with her.

"I ran into Joe Harrington yesterday," said Roma. "He was downtown buying glue for his model airplanes. Told me he's looking for help loading some old wood."

Sloane's body tightened. "Their old picket fence?"

"He's finally clearing out his garage. I gave him Jason's number. Joe said he'd pay for the help."

Sloane pushed her glasses into her face. "Jason's not doing odd jobs anymore."

"Sloane, it's the Harringtons."

"Maybe instead of taking the wood to the dump, they should just put the fence back up."

"Why are you being so defensive?"

"I'm not." She was. Sloane backed down.

Around Roma's wrist, her fitness tracker vibrated, alerting her to move. With exaggerated swinging arms, she began walking laps around the kitchen table.

"Will you check in on your father when I'm away? Make sure he's scooping out the ashes from the fireplace, emptying the garbage, eating. I don't want to arrive home to a corpse."

Sloane groaned. "Mom, he's an adult."

"Not a very good one."

"Can you sit down, please? You're making me dizzy."

Roma read the screen on her fitness tracker. "In eighty-four steps," she said.

Sloane pointed to the band on her mom's wrist. "What size is yours?"

"Medium."

"And you thought I was a small?"

"You know I always think of you as my little girl."

"Mom, I'm thirty."

"You haven't grown an inch since thirteen."

In Grade 8 Sloane had been five foot four inches. She hadn't grown in height, but her weight had changed by twenty-five pounds. The last time she had stepped on a scale she weighed in at one hundred sixty-two pounds, seventeen pounds over the ideal weight on the chart pinned to the wall in her doctor's office.

"How was work yesterday?" Roma asked.

"The worst."

"Every day can't be the worst."

"It can if it is."

Roma's face lit up. "Jason!"

Jason Howard walked into the kitchen. His short, spiky hair was wet from a shower and his face clean-shaven. "Hello, Roma," he said, showing off his dimples.

Roma stopped circling the table. With outstretched arms, she crossed the kitchen floor. "I've asked Sloane to check in on Edward when I'm away," she said, placing her hand on Jason's arm. "I'm going to be in China for two weeks in September. She's putting up a fuss about it. Maybe you wouldn't mind?"

"I wasn't putting up a fuss," said Sloane, sounding like a child. "I was merely stating that Dad's an—"

"I can stop by the house on my way to the plant," said Jason.

"Oh, thank you!" Roma swatted his shoulder and then kissed his cheek. Her lips lingered. Jason didn't dodge Roma's kisses or escape from the room when she visited. Sloane knew how important his mom had been to him; how Roma filled the void Roseanne had left when she passed. "Such a big heart," Roma said, rubbing Jason's arm.

Are you flirting with my husband? It briefly occurred to Sloane that Roma might be compensating for her daughter's shortcomings. And maybe Roma found in Jason what was missing in Edward. Sloane's dad wasn't a demonstrative man. He showed his affection for his wife by renovating the house, by purchasing stocks in her name and by not wavering when she came to him with an idea like wanting to go to China with her best friend.

"Sloane?"

"Yes?" Her mind had drifted.

"Great!" Roma beamed. From the doorway, she blew a kiss from her palm. "Happy birthday!" Then just like that, she was gone.

"What did I agree to?"

Jason took Sloane's hands. "Happy birthday."

"Jason, what was it?"

He wrapped his arms around her, holding her tightly. She sucked in her belly so that it wasn't pushing into his.

"You're worried I'm going to run out there."

"Maybe."

When Sloane squirmed free, Jason shot out his arms to block the doorway. She tried to pass and he enfolded his body around hers, playfully clawing at her sides.

"Jason, let me go!" Slapping at his arm, she laughed and snorted. She couldn't catch her breath.

Finally Jason stopped tickling, and Sloane heard Roma's car pull out of the driveway. "There," she said, rotating in her husband's arms. "Tell me now."

Jason didn't let go; he held her close. "Kiss me," he said.

Sloane leaned back. "I haven't brushed my teeth."

"I don't mind your morning breath."

She pecked Jason's cheek.

"Your mom kisses better than that."

Sloane slapped his chest. "You know she has a crush on you." She was only half-joking. *Does she wish she had a son?* "I think you've got a crush on her, too," she added.

"I think we're just both lonely."

Disappointed, you mean.

Disappointment and loneliness were similar. By thirty, Jason had planned to be a video-game developer, not be sitting in a crane all day moving coils of steel so he and Sloane could cover their bills. Each summer he was supposed to be repainting the white picket fence around their house. He was meant to be a father.

"Because it's your birthday," he said, "I'll give you a one-up."

"A what?"

"A do-over. A second chance. A new life."

Sloane sighed, loudly. "A video game term."

He closed his eyes and puckered his lips, waiting.

Sloane didn't want to be inferior to her mom, especially when it came to the kissing of her husband. She ran her tongue over her front teeth and then licked and folded her lips until they held their moisture. Shifting to the balls of her feet, inches in front of Jason, she allowed her mouth to slowly unravel.

The tip of Jason's tongue gently met hers. His head turned and his nose moved around Sloane's as his mouth crawled over her lips. When his hand moved toward the drawstring of her sweatpants, she broke away. "Tell me now. What did I agree to?"

With surprise, Jason's eyes opened.

Angry with herself for ruining the moment, Sloane pushed him away. "Tell me," she ordered, slipping out of his arms.

"Your parents' wedding anniversary is when Roma gets back from China. You agreed to design and submit the announcement for the paper. She's going to send you an e-transfer and email you a photo."

Sloane moaned. Each year, Roma paid for a full-color anniversary announcement in the *Tippett Valley Times*. She kept a scrapbook of the clippings that often made an appearance when guests visited.

"I thought you'd be excited," said Jason. "I haven't seen you design anything lately."

"Because I haven't."

"You used to want to design all the time."

"It's different now."

"Why?"

Why? Are you serious?

"Hey," he said, reaching for her hand. "What is it?"

He looked confused, as if he didn't understand what it was like to have a shitty job, to be debilitated by debt, to be unable to have a baby. To prevent a tear from escaping, she widened her eyes. Now that she was thirty, her disappointments were heavier.

"Nothing," she said. "I better get ready for work."

"Sloane."

On the counter, Sloane's cell phone vibrated. A text message from Stephie.

Can't make 2nite.

"What is it?" asked Jason.

"Nothing."

"Something."

"It's fine."

"Stephie?"

"She canceled, that's all." *On my birthday.*

Jason frowned and placed his hands on Sloane's shoulders. Then he smiled widely. "Now I get to take you out tonight."

"We can't afford to go out."

"It's your birthday. We should celebrate."

Holding back tears, she forced a smile. "Will you pay the hydro bill? It'll be late if it doesn't get paid today. Last thing we need is our lights shut off."

"Wait," said Jason. "Where are you going?"

Halfway up the stairs, she hollered, "To get ready for work."

She entered the bathroom, where she locked the door and reread Stephie's message. Stephie was forgetful; it didn't make her a bad person. *Maybe she forgot it was my birthday.* Sloane texted back.

Another time?

"Sloane?"

The handle of the bathroom door rattled. Jason must have followed her upstairs.

Quickly, she turned on the shower. "My mom got you a gift for my birthday," she shouted.

"What?"

"It's on the counter!"

She didn't get into the shower. Instead, she stared at her phone, waiting for Stephie to reply.

11

Chapter Two

ON THE FIRST day of Grade 8, Sloane slipped on a condom packet that had fallen out of a classmate's backpack, skidding into a wall and tearing a ligament in her ankle. She was on crutches for two weeks and became That Girl Who Broke Her Leg on a Condom. It wasn't how she had planned her first year as a teenager to begin. Any hope of making a friend was gone.

That same week, the Harringtons moved to Tippett Valley. The *Tippett Valley Times* ran a profile piece on Joe Harrington, the new Operations Manager at the steel plant who had come from New Carlton, "the city." Since Sloane was excused from gym, she was assigned to show the new student around. It took her about one second to realize that Joe Harrington's daughter was way too cool to become a friend. She was tall and skinny with long brown hair and a green-eyed glare that could melt skin. Her jeans had rips in the knees and she wore a black t-shirt with a Violent Downfall button pinned to it. Her fingernails looked like they were painted with Wite-Out.

Outside the gymnasium, Sloane struggled to carry her backpack while maintaining control of her crutches. "Hi," she said. "I mean, hey. Stephanie, right?"

"Stephie," said the girl, picking the white from her baby fingernail.

The bell rang and the hallways emptied. In some ways it made being alone with the new girl more intimidating. In other ways it was a relief; if Sloane embarrassed herself there would be no witnesses.

"I'm Sloane," she said. "My mom named me after Sloane Peterson, the girl character in the movie *Ferris Bueller's Day Off.*"

Stephie didn't scrunch up her face the way other girls did.

"Have you seen it?" asked Sloane. "It's a pretty good movie, for an old one, but still. In the movie, Sloane Peterson wears this white rodeo jacket that my mom apparently loved."

Shut up, Sloane.

"It's considered a comedy classic. The movie, I mean. It was released on June 11, 1986. Four years later, I was born on June 11, so that sealed it for my mom. I was meant to be a Sloane, she said."

Shut up.

"My eyes are blue," she rambled on, "but sometimes green. Depending on the light. It's the only cool thing about me."

"You keep the condom?"

Sloane teetered on her crutches. "What?"

"You slipped on a condom, right? That's why you're on crutches."

"You heard about that?" The new girl was already making fun of Sloane. "It's not even right, what they're calling me," she said, defensively. "It's a torn ligament and the condom was in a packet."

"You got it?" she pressed.

"What, the—" Sloane lowered her voice "—the condom?"

"Did you keep it?"

At first, Sloane considered lying, but then she wondered if Stephie was serious. She nodded, too embarrassed to admit that she had stuffed the shiny purple packet into her pocket. It looked so much like the lotion samples that arrived each month in her mom's magazines. She hid it in a ring box inside a dresser drawer.

"Can I have it?" asked Stephie, in the school hallway.

"You want it?"

Stephie asked for it like she was asking for a stick of gum, but it was a condom. *For sex?* Stephie squinted and half her eyes disappeared, which somehow made her seem even more powerful.

"I'll bring it to school tomorrow," said Sloane, afraid to say no.

She was now guaranteed to talk to the new girl again. It was exciting and terrifying, depending on how fast Stephie got in with the popular clique.

"Stephie!"

A boy, clearly younger than Sloane, practically ran into Stephie. She shoved him hard and he stumbled back, knocking a crutch. The rubber bottom skidded along the floor and Sloane almost fell. A *Sweet Valley High* book dropped from her backpack. She quickly snatched it up. No way would Stephie read *Sweet Valley High*. Maybe she didn't read at all. She probably had real friends.

"Watch it," Stephie snapped. "You almost knocked over a disabled person."

"Sorry," he said, glancing up at Sloane, and then back at Stephie. "See you after school, right?" Panic crossed his face. "You promised Mom."

Kevin Morgan, the sixth-grader presumably assigned to show Stephie's brother around, caught up to him. "Come on, Benji," he said.

"What if I can't remember the way home?"

Stephie shrugged, seemingly unsympathetic. "Guess you should've been paying attention on the way here." She looked at Sloane. "Aren't you supposed to be showing me around?"

Stephie didn't wait for Sloane's reply. She walked away and Sloane hobbled to catch up.

"See you after school!" Benji hollered.

"You have a brother," said Sloane, nearly ramming into Stephie when she stopped suddenly.

"You smoke?"

"What?"

"Cigarettes. Do you smoke?"

"No. Do you?"

From her pocket, Stephie revealed a single cigarette. "I'm going to skip the tour. I'll find my own way. It's not that big around here."

"Where are you going?"

"Can't smoke inside."

She wasn't supposed to smoke outside either.

In the empty hallway, Sloane swayed on one foot and stared

at the door closing behind Stephie. *I should tell a teacher. Maybe the principal.* She squeezed the handles of her crutches. What would Stephie do if she found out Sloane tattled?

Sloane considered hiding out in the washroom until the end of period, when she would be no longer responsible. As if to prevent herself from escaping, she pressed a crutch down on her toes. If thirteen was going to be different, then she was going to have to be different. She followed Stephie outside.

"Over here," she said, directing the new girl to behind a garbage receptacle where older students smoked.

Sloane sat on the pavement beside Stephie, watching her light the cigarette. On school property. During school hours. When she took a drag, she didn't cough and the cigarette maintained its cylinder shape, her lips clamping down with just the right pressure. Her fingers were in perfect control, as ashes fell gracefully into the narrow circumference of a lipstick lid. When Stephie offered her a drag, Sloane shook her head. She didn't speak, afraid she would say the wrong thing. Stephie didn't say anything either, but Sloane was pretty sure it wasn't because she was afraid. The two of them sat together until the bell rang.

"Thanks for the tour," said Stephie, standing.

"You're welcome." Sloane cringed, realizing too late that Stephie was being sarcastic. "What class do you have next?"

"Art."

"I hate art."

"It's the only class I like."

"I didn't mean I hated it. I meant I'm not very good at it. I'm good at typing. I can type really fast and accurately." *Shut up, Sloane.* "I can show you to the art room."

"I don't need a babysitter."

Stephie walked ahead, too fast for Sloane to keep up on crutches.

The next day, Sloane gave the condom to Stephie in the girls' washroom. She slipped it into her front pocket. Sloane didn't dare ask what she was going to do with it.

"I don't really hate art," said Sloane, picking up their conversation from yesterday. She had worried all night that she had offended the new girl. "I like designing things," she said. "Like posters and title pages for projects. I'm just not good at drawing realistic things, but art has a wide definition."

"You're really smart, aren't you."

Sloane shrugged. *Wide definition.* She couldn't believe she said that.

"Straight As?" pressed Stephie.

Sloane dropped her head. Last year, she had even gotten an A in gym, only because she tried really hard. "Do you have another cigarette?" she asked. "I want to try it this time."

"I can get more."

"How?"

"I steal them from my dad."

"My parents don't smoke."

"Too bad."

"You'll bring one to school tomorrow?"

Stephie nodded.

For the second day in a row, Sloane had arranged to meet with Stephie.

It turned out Stephie didn't want the condom for sex. In art class, she sculpted a clay figurine of a girl and then rolled the condom over top of it. She said it symbolized the imprisonment of life and was sent to the principal's office for "using inappropriate materials in the classroom." After that, everyone in school stopped talking about how Sloane Sawyer broke her leg on a condom and started talking about how Stephie Harrington had used the condom in an art project.

Stephie was admired and feared by everyone, but she rejected the established school cliques. Like Sloane, she was a loner, but on the cool end of the spectrum. The best thing about her was that she didn't seem to mind Sloane hanging around.

Still, Sloane wasn't certain she and Stephie were friends until the day Sloane was paired with Gina Anderson for a profile drawing assignment in art. Gina had drawn Sloane's ear to look like a fetus. When the teacher pointed out the assignment was realism, Gina held her drawing up beside Sloane to show the class how accurate her rendition was.

"Look," she said, pointing to Sloane's ear. "You can see the arms and legs right there."

Word of Sloane's fetus ears traveled quickly through the school. It was so much worse than being known as That Girl Who Broke Her Leg on a Condom.

The next day, when Sloane reluctantly entered the art classroom, she discovered the ear had been cut out of Gina's drawing. When Sloane told Stephie, she replied, "Gina's a terrible artist."

"It was you?"

Stephie shrugged like it wasn't a big deal, but no one else would have defended Sloane's honor like that.

That was when Sloane knew for sure. *We're friends. Best friends.*

Chapter Three

SITTING AT HER desk, staring at the digital clock on her phone's display screen and urging the last five minutes of her workday to pass more quickly than the rules of time, Sloane noticed her sweater was inside out. Her reaction attracted the attention of her boss, whose glass office was just five steps behind Sloane's cubicle. As if to dig out the piercing sound, Joan Dawes inserted an index finger into each ear. Like gophers, the heads of account managers popped up over cubicle walls, their focus on the Director of Account Services.

Sloane smiled as if everything was fine as if the long, shrill intake of breath had passed through someone else's throat. Jason had once described her shriek as the audio version of an exclamation mark. But she knew it was more like the squeal of a knife scratching a plate embedded with a microphone. Sloane pointed to the ceiling and shrugged, implying that the sound might have come from the flickering florescent light, vibrating and popping overhead. Through her glass wall, Joan glared out to the office floor, and heads lowered. With just over a week remaining in the month, and the department yet to reach its September revenue target, no account manager wanted attention, especially when the agency was in danger of losing their best client.

The Kaye Agency managed advertising campaigns for large companies. It was owned by Regina Kaye, now in her seventies, a trailblazer of her time who was no longer involved in the day-to-day operation but remained highly respected. Last month, one of her first clients, Lionel Brownwood, had retired and his son Daniel had become the CEO of Brownwood Industries. He wanted to "bring the company into the twenty-first century" by shifting the company's focus away from developing low-rise family housing in favor of high-rise condos aimed at a younger demographic. New Carlton, with its population of one million, was becoming unaffordable, and young couples were increasingly willing to trade an hour-long commute by train for homeowner-ship. Daniel had made it clear that he was considering retaining an agency in the city to handle the rebranding.

Sloane imagined her hot cheeks were pumping like flashing sirens as she clamped her hand over the tag waving from her ribs like a miniature flag. She tried ripping it off, but it hung on like a leech, refusing to let go. With her left hand, she practiced opening and closing a pair of scissors, then aimed for her ribs. It was a risk, using her non-dominant hand, and she couldn't get her arm twisted far enough around to reach the tag anyway.

To hide the inside seams of her sweater—the stitches so obvious now she couldn't comprehend how it was possible she hadn't noticed earlier—she pressed her arms against her body. Maybe the snickering Sloane had overheard between account managers earlier in the day had been about her and not about Joan, as Sloane had assumed—"Joan" and "Sloane" sounded similar. Maybe everyone had noticed. Why hadn't anyone said anything? Adele would have, but she had canceled lunch.

When Sloane had applied for a job in the agency, her seventy-five-word-a-minute-zero-error typing average and stellar recommendation from her previous employer earned her the position of Joan Dawes' assistant. It was supposed to be her "in" for the role she really wanted: graphic designer.

Did the designers notice my sweater was inside out? Did Gary Goldman? Sloane covertly looked around the department; not one set of eyes met hers. Maybe it wasn't so mortifying if no one noticed her anyway. No matter how well she performed her job, half the time she felt invisible.

If she hurried to the washroom with only five minutes remaining in her workday, Joan might assume she was leaving early and make a note in her file. Joan didn't believe in relative definitions; every action either contributed to revenue or took away from it, and it was part of Joan's job to manage the ledger. For last

19

quarter's review, Sloane had turned Joan's meticulous notes into a graph illustrating the number of times an employee in Account Services arrived late or left early. When an account manager asked Joan how many minutes each data point represented, she responded, "You can build a telephone pole out of toothpicks." Two weeks later, he was gone.

As a distraction, Sloane calculated the cost to the agency if she left five minutes early: $2.33. If all eleven employees in Account Services left five minutes early each day, using Sloane's wage of $28 per hour, the lowest salary for any role in the department, that worked out to $25.63 per day, which was $128.15 per week, which was $6,663.80 per year. That didn't include the yearly cost of potential lost revenue from 195 total hours of nine account managers not selling. The math temporarily ignited Sloane. Toothpicks could add up to telephone poles. Maybe one day, by saving their change, she and Jason would own a house. But their combined student loan debt couldn't be reduced to the size of a single telephone pole.

It was an excruciating exercise to stare at a clock. Under her desk, Sloane's knees bounced. Her thighs jiggled and the extra flesh around her belly spilled over the waist of her pants. She shifted her focus to her hips, spreading over the edges of her chair. Fashion magazines labeled the shape of her body "hour-glass," and claimed her silhouette was coveted. But Sloane's hips were wider than the seat of some chairs, proof that society built its architecture around the lean figure. Why were chairs made to accommodate the average body size when half the population wouldn't comfortably fit? Rather than redefining the dimensions for a standard chair, the onus was on people to redesign their bodies. What if she kept gaining weight? What if one day she couldn't even sit in an average chair? On Thursday, all the chairs in Account Services were being replaced with ergonomic models, the last step in a long-overdue renovation partly undertaken to impress Daniel Brownwood. What if her hips didn't fit past the armrests of her new chair?

Maybe there was something wrong with the clock; the time seemed stuck at 4:59 p.m. Sloane wiggled the phone cord in its jack and then stabbed the phone's digital screen with the end of a pen. She quietly opened her desk drawer, where she kept her personal cell phone. It also showed 4:59 p.m. And she had two new text messages from Roma.

  10,023!

  How many steps?

Halfway around the world, vacationing in China, Roma regularly updated her daughter on her daily step count.

Sloane surreptitiously texted a reply. She didn't want to get caught on her personal phone during work hours.

  9,043, almost there!

A pang of guilt gripped her chest. She still hadn't exchanged the fitness tracker her mom had given her three months ago.

Sloane fiddled with the name plaque attached to her cubicle wall: SLOANE SAWYER, EXECUTIVE MANAGER, ACCOUNT SERVICES. A big title for a glorified secretarial position. Sloane answered the phone, took messages, booked meeting rooms and put together reports and PowerPoints that Joan requested by email in the middle of the night. Typically, it took Sloane only a couple of hours to complete the list, which meant she had to spend the rest of the day looking busy, which was a hundred times worse than actually being busy.

The light above her desk flickered, like radiance coughing. If she blocked out the activity from the department, she could hear the hum of electricity. Sometimes, she would concentrate on the sound, tuning out the ringing phones, clacking keyboards and hum of client calls, to give the impression she was racking her brain on something work-related. She could convince herself that the buzzing sound was soothing and pleasant, rather than disturbing and irritating. She pushed her glasses over her forehead. When the frames dropped to her nose, the time was still 4:59 p.m.

Lenore Robinson, the account manager for Brownwood Industries, hurried past. In his first week, Daniel had replaced

Brownwood's long-time marketing manager, and Lenore's key contact for day-to-day business, with a "millennial"—Lenore's label. She had looked tense ever since.

When the time finally changed to 5:00 p.m. Sloane catapulted to her feet, turned her computer off, grabbed her cell phone from the drawer, scooped her jacket and purse off the back of her chair and took off for the washroom.

In a stall, she pulled her sweater over her head, flipped it right side out and stuffed her body back into it, hitting her hand on the toilet paper dispenser. Static caused strands of hair to dance around her head like sunrays, and her skin was moist with sweat, but she wouldn't bother drying off. She just wanted to get home. Tonight was Stephie's birthday.

Sloane removed her wedding rings and ran cold water over her tender hand. She checked her reflection in the mirror. Familiar flushed blotches patterned her face and neck, but she didn't feel like she was looking at her own reflection. She had lost the connection to herself. Even her prescription eyeglasses seemed like a prop. The big, red, round spectacles that had once made her feel hip and cool, now made her feel like a fraud and a fake. *What happened to me?* She was supposed to have kids, a successful career as a graphic designer, a shelf full of design awards that her two kids begged to touch, and a house with a white picket fence—not for the cliché, but because she really did like the look.

Lifting her shirt in the mirror, she filled her belly with air. *Does Jason pretend, too?* Alone, in front of a mirror, did he mime pushing a buggy or rocking a baby in his arms? Did he still think about becoming a father? He had stopped talking about it. Worse, he didn't seem upset. It irritated Sloane how content he was with failure. How she had to carry the weight of not only her disappointments but also theirs.

She sucked in her belly, trying to look thin. The irony wasn't lost on her. When a high school classmate had called her fat, it triggered a new awareness in Sloane. She started to spend unhealthy amounts of time in front of mirrors, analyzing. She didn't have a sister to compare to, just Stephie—who had been nicknamed "Bones" in gym and had been the recipient of several stares when anorexia was taught in health class. Looking back, Sloane hadn't been fat, but she'd felt fat. Now she tilted to the side and watched in the mirror as the skin over her ribs buckled like a Slinky.

The door to the washroom swung open, and Sloane shrieked for the second time that day. She quickly pushed down her sweater and covered her face, crushing her glasses. Peeking between her fingers, she saw Adele Mack.

"Sorry," said Sloane, her chin rising. The sound of her shriek was still echoing off the concrete walls. With the cuff of her sweater, she cleaned the lenses of her glasses.

After five years of working with Adele, Sloane had learned her moods. A heavy sigh, followed by the dramatic flipping of her long dark hair, and then the slap of her palm on the counter meant that she was upset, and Sloane could guess why. In seven days, Adele would turn thirty, and her boyfriend had yet to propose.

"Something the matter?" asked Sloane, conscious of her tone. It always took a few minutes for her to dispel the envy that Adele's presence created. Since starting with the agency on the same day as Sloane, Adele had been promoted to Deputy Human Resources Manager. She had her own office now, while Sloane hadn't moved from her cubicle and had been turned down twice for a transfer to Creative Services. Adele and her boss, Gary Goldman, were friends, and Sloane was jealous she didn't have a similar relationship with her boss. On top of her career success, Adele had bought a house, found a suitable candidate to marry before her thirtieth birthday, and hadn't gained a pound. She was the definition of success.

"Lawrence cheated," she said.

Sloane pulled her sweater away from her skin. "On his taxes?"

"On me."

Sloane stopped pinching her sweater. "Oh."

23

For the past year, Adele had been dating Lawrence, who sold used cars at his family's auto shop and whose principal appeal seemed to be impeccable posture. He slept practically sitting up, Adele told Sloane, and even preferred having sex upright, which was why his car wasn't a bad option, even though Adele had suffered minor injuries from banging her head against the sun visor and getting her elbow caught in the steering wheel. Lawrence was saving to buy a share in the business, so he lived with a roommate even though he was thirty-four. It didn't matter to Adele because he had a driver's license (she didn't drive), he wanted to be a dad (a deal-breaker if he didn't), and he didn't cheat (Adele had firsthand experience with cheating and never wanted to go through it again).

Sloane had only seen Lawrence once, when she had left her lunch in her car. Crossing the parking lot, she had spotted Adele getting out of a red sports car with the license plate AVERYS. Lawrence was tall and clean-cut, with rosy cheeks and shiny shoes, and yes, perfect posture. To get his legs back into the car, he had to press each knee into his chest and guide each foot to the pedals. He had honked his horn when he drove off.

"I bet she has cats."

"Cats?"

"Like four of them, that shit all over her apartment." Adele scratched and picked at the birthmark on her chest, another sure sign of stress. "She probably only changes her toothbrush after a dentist appointment, and she's likely one of those people who think turning on the shower counts as washing the tub. I bet she doesn't look at the expiry date stamped onto food labels either. I can just imagine her waking up in the middle of the night to eat ice cream because she doesn't have air conditioning and if she doesn't cool herself down she'll be swimming in her own sweat. I know Lawrence doesn't like to get wet. He takes the shortest showers, avoids going anywhere in the rain, and uses hand sanitizer because it dries faster. It won't be long before he realizes he made a big mistake."

"Who are you—"

"Trish."

"She's the woman who—"

"Yes."

"You know her?"

"I bet I described her perfectly."

Sloane wanted to grab Adele's wrist to stop her from treating her birthmark like a removable sticker.

"He told you?" asked Sloane.

"He doesn't know yet that I know."

"How'd you find out?"

"He pocket-dialed me. It went to my voicemail. I heard them. I've listened to it a hundred times."

So that's why you canceled lunch. "What were they saying?" asked Sloane.

"They weren't *saying* anything."

"Nothing?"

"Nothing."

"What did you hear then?"

"Panting. Grunting. Lawrence calling out Trish's name." She sucked in a quick breath, and then released it slowly.

"You sure?" said Sloane.

"I'm sure. Listen."

Adele played the voicemail. It sounded exactly how she described it: solid evidence of Lawrence's infidelity.

"It wasn't as if I was going to marry him," she said.

But it was. She had been adamant with Sloane that if she wasn't at least engaged by thirty she would accept she was destined to live a single life. For months, Lawrence's pending proposal was all Adele talked about.

Sloane didn't know what to say. She felt guilty for feeling a sliver of pleasure that Adele was getting a taste of failure—a familiar flavor for Sloane.

Adele applied lipstick, a red so bright it stung Sloane's eyes.

"My sweater was inside out all day," said Sloane.

25

With her eyebrows perched high on her forehead, Adele dabbed her mouth with a tissue.

"You knew?" said Sloane. "When did you notice?"

"I saw you this morning."

"You didn't say anything."

Adele shrugged. "It was obvious."

"I wouldn't choose to wear my sweater inside out!" Sloane hadn't meant to shout.

"It wouldn't be the first weird thing you've worn."

"What's that supposed to mean?"

"The purple scarf?"

Sloane's chin dropped. The purple scarf. A gift from her mom who said it was all the rage in Paris, as if she had traveled there, as if she hadn't spent her entire life in Tippett Valley. Roma had been so excited as she wound all ten feet of it around her daughter's neck. Sloane had looked to Jason for a second opinion. "Beautiful," he said and kissed her forehead. It seemed his lips barely reached with the scarf between them.

Sloane wore it to work, thinking maybe she would get noticed, that she would look like a graphic designer, obviously misplaced within the unofficial black and white dress code of account managers. (Joan once told an account manager in a red dress, "If you want to get noticed, exceed your target.") Slowly, Sloane walked past the graphic designers, desperately wanting to be a part of their colorful team. *See! I'm like you!* The scarf prevented her from lowering her chin and she blindly walked into a box of photocopy paper that had been left on the floor. If it hadn't been for Irving Paulson catching her arm, she might have fallen into the machine. The designers cringed at the sound of her shriek. Sloane never wore the scarf again.

"The sequined pumps?" said Adele, leaning into the mirror. Her eyes met Sloane's reflection. "The sweater with the horse pattern? The blue jumper?"

"Okay, I get it." Sloane's fashion attempts had been a disaster.

Another failure to add to the list. It didn't matter anymore; she had stopped walking past Creative Services.

Adele dropped her lipstick into her purse. "See you tomorrow."

"Wait," said Sloane. "Are you going to—?"

Adele spun around. "What? Go over to Lawrence's house and slap him in the face?"

Sloane's mouth popped open.

"Go over to Trish's house and slap her in the face?" Adele's shoulders slumped. "Neither will change the fact that on Sunday I'll be thirty."

Sloane wondered if Adele's palm could even reach Lawrence's face. Maybe Trish was the more realistic option. Sloane considered inviting Adele out for Stephie's birthday, but that would make a third wheel, and she worried it would be her. It wasn't as if Adele was a real friend, as if they did anything together outside of the agency—they hadn't even exchanged personal phone numbers. Besides, it was tradition to celebrate Stephie's birthday just the two of them, and no amount of sympathy for Adele would trump what Sloane felt for Stephie.

Adele's phone rang.

"Is it Lawrence?" asked Sloane.

Adele shook her head. "Travis."

Travis Wright. Sloane couldn't understand why Adele was still friendly with her ex-boyfriend and his girlfriend who had broken them up over ten years ago. It was a puzzle Sloane didn't have all the pieces to, and it seemed too personal to push for answers. Sloane didn't want to encourage Adele to inquire about her own teenage years.

Adele shrugged. "Don't forget your rings," she said, on her way out.

Alone, Sloane checked her phone. She had one new text message from Jason.

Everything okay?

On my way.

Via The Discount? You promised.

She'll notice you're not wearing it.

Sloane wanted to text back, "So what, it's a stupid fitness tracker!" but she didn't. Jason wasn't finished.

It's been 3 months.

He didn't wear Roma's gift either. If he did it would just make her look worse.

It's Stephie's birthday.

There's time.

I'm certain my mom isn't thinking about it all the way in China.

She was, and Sloane knew it.

You're making excuses.

Tiny explosions of emotion burst inside Sloane. *What do you care so much anyway?* Before she could reply, Jason texted again.

It matters to your mom.

If all it takes to make her happy is to exchange a gift, then why not?

Sloane bit her bottom lip.

Fine.

She grumbled as she slipped on her wedding rings. Swiping her cheek with the sleeve of her jacket, she dropped her phone into her purse. *Your mom asked for so much more from me.*

Chapter Four

IT WAS UNLIKELY that Sloane and Adele would have established weekly lunches if they hadn't started with the agency on the same day, or if different employees had attended the orientation session. Sloane was sure Adele had chosen the seat beside hers only because the other options in the room appeared worse. There was an older woman with blond hair and gray roots who Sloane learned had been on medical leave for long enough that the corporate policy required her to reorient. She cleared her throat constantly and repetitively counted the money in her wallet. Sitting in front of Sloane was acne-laden, tooth-braced Irving Paulson, who looked so young that Adele whispered a comment about child labor. He smelled like the banana-flavored cough syrup Sloane remembered from childhood and was so nervous he was barely able to introduce himself, stammering over his own name.

"What kind of name is Irving anyway?" whispered Adele.

The presenter was Gary Goldman, the incredibly attractive Human Resources Manager. He was fit—muscular and defined—with light brown hair that highlighted his blue eyes, thick eyebrows and a clean-shaven face. His freckled nose wasn't a flaw; it was a unique characteristic, setting him apart from other incredibly attractive men. He was almost too perfect, like the male love interest in a Harlequin novel; Sloane had read a dozen of the steamy romances over the summer before turning thirteen. She guessed Gary was in his thirties, maybe early forties, and he didn't wear a wedding ring. Even his voice was attractive, smoky and articulate, and his smile remained fixed as he talked. "Anyway," he said, shuffling papers, "let's get started."

A laptop was connected to a large TV projecting a PowerPoint slide. Gary started on company benefits.

Adele shifted her chair closer to Sloane. "What'd you get hired for?" she asked.

Sloane waited for Gary to look at the screen before answering, "Executive Manager." It sounded so much more important than her previous job titles: Cashier, Secretary. Her career was finally taking off. At least moving in the right direction. "Account Services," she said. "You?"

"Human Resources. I'll be working with him." She threw her chin at Gary as if he weren't the most attractive man in the building. She shifted her gaze to Irving. "Wonder what department he was hired for."

Sloane was embarrassed to be talking about Irving when he was sitting in front of her. A banana was hanging out of his pocket. Sloane imagined telling Jason all about her first day with the agency and having to explain that it was no joke. *I literally saw a banana in the new guy's pocket.*

"IT, I bet," whispered Adele. "Definitely more comfortable talking to a machine."

Sloane hoped Irving hadn't heard that and that Adele would stop talking.

She wondered what title Adele would have guessed for her if she hadn't volunteered the information. She hoped her big red glasses, the stylish blouse with the wide cuffs, and the way she wore her hair pulled back loose in a tiny bun with a strand hanging over each ear suggested graphic designer.

"Graphic designer," said Adele.

Sloane's eyes popped. Then she realized Adele was referring to Irving. She was hovering over his shoulder, snooping at the paperwork in his lap.

A pang of jealousy hit Sloane, right in the pit of her belly. Irving Paulson had been awarded her job. He didn't even look like a graphic designer; there was nothing cool or hip about him. His outfit spanned two colors: navy blue and dark gray. How was he to be trusted with creating a million-dollar advertising campaign?

Sloane turned to Adele, scanning her new colleague as if she were a barcode. Adele's hair was brown and straight, shoulder-length like Sloane's, and sparkling in one spot, as if she had knocked her head on a glittered surface. Like a map, her cheeks had faint contour lines from the fracturing of a thick layer of foundation. With so much makeup masking the clues, it was difficult to speculate, but Sloane guessed Adele was close to her age. Adele was thin and lacked any significant curves, except for her breasts, which were noticeably unlevel. They weren't that big either, but they were accentuated by the narrowness of her waist, her hips, her neck, her shoulders. Sloane's breasts were bigger, but they didn't scream, "Look at me!" Sloane wondered if Jason would think Adele was pretty.

At the front of the room, Gary lifted his knee and his pant leg rode up his calf. Even his socks were cool. He moved on to talking about vacation entitlement.

"You're married," whispered Adele, her gaze locking on Sloane's rings. "How long?"

To break Adele's stare, Sloane slipped her hand beneath her thigh. "Just last year," she said.

Clamped between the seat of her chair and her leg, her rings sunk painfully into the flesh of her thigh. She didn't adjust her hand. With Gary in the room, it was a good reminder. Not that she actually wanted to be with Gary. Sloane loved Jason. She was going to have his baby.

"Got kids?" asked Adele.

Sloane shook her head, even though she and Jason had recently started trying. She wouldn't tell anyone at the agency, not until she was pregnant and not until she was showing. She didn't want her pregnancy affecting her promotion to graphic designer.

"What about you?" she whispered. "Married?"

Adele's cheeks twitched. "Soon," she said.

"You're engaged?"

"Not yet." With pressed lips, Adele crossed her fingers and

glanced at the ceiling. "I'm almost twenty-five," she said. Same age as Sloane. "If I'm not married soon . . ." She gripped the edge of her seat.

"Then what?" asked Sloane.

"I'm destined to be a spinster."

In front of Sloane, Irving squirmed.

"You're a little young to be worrying about that, aren't you?" whispered Sloane, unsure if Adele was joking.

Adele's eyes narrowed to slits. "My parents got married at twenty-one. Four years younger than I am now."

"So?"

"How old are you?"

"I turned twenty-five in June."

"So you were twenty-four when you married?"

Sloane nodded.

"When did you meet your husband?"

"First-year university."

"Exactly."

"Exactly what?"

"*Exactly,*" said Adele.

Gary caught Sloane and Adele whispering. Sloane ducked guiltily behind Irving, but Adele sat up straight and met Gary's gaze. It reminded Sloane of Stephie back in high school.

"I can only make policy so exciting," he said, smiling. Then he started talking about the agency's emergency procedure during a fire alarm.

Relieved, Sloane slipped her hand out from beneath her thigh. A mesh design had imprinted on her palms, and her leg throbbed. She dangled her arm at her side, swaying it like a pendulum, her fingers almost knocking the banana right out of Irving's pocket.

"Your parents still together?" Sloane whispered.

"Your guess is as good as mine," replied Adele. "I moved out when I was sixteen. Haven't seen or talked to them since."

"Oh. I'm sorry."

"Don't be. We were terrible to each other."

Sloane thought of her own parents. Roma was often annoyed with Edward, and while he had never said it, Sloane was sure her dad found her mom overbearing. She certainly did.

At the front of the room, the TV suddenly went dark. Gary fiddled with the cord and, when that didn't work, rolled up his sleeve. His forearm was tanned and burly, and it disappeared behind the screen. Sloane was concerned his arm would get stuck. Part of her hoped that it would and that she would be the one to free it.

With her eyes on Gary, Sloane whispered to Adele. "It's the twenty-first century. You could ask your boyfriend to marry you."

"I don't have a boyfriend," said Adele.

The temperature quickly rose in Sloane's cheeks. "I didn't mean to presume," she said. "A girlfriend?"

Adele sunk into her chair. "Single," she said, in a tone generally reserved for words like cancer.

Sloane pulled on her loose chunks of hair. If Gary needed her help, she would have to get close, and she didn't want him to see the shape of her ears.

"I was engaged once," whispered Adele. "At nineteen."

"As a teenager."

"Travis was my first boyfriend. We called it off."

"What happened?"

"Eva."

"She was the reason you broke up?"

"Yeah," said Adele. "She lives with Travis now. Anyway, I don't want to talk about the past. I'd like to get as far away as possible from that version of me. I'm a different person now."

In front of Sloane, Irving shifted in his chair, causing the banana in his pocket to drop to the floor. He didn't notice and Sloane worried he would step on it and lose his balance. He would become That Guy. He would always be That Guy.

Sloane retrieved Irving's banana from the floor. "Here," she whispered, tapping his shoulder with it.

Irving twisted around looking frightened.

"It fell out of your pocket," she said.

Irving's cheeks flushed.

"It's a banana," said Adele. "It's not as if she's handing you a tampon."

She said it so factually that Sloane wondered if it wasn't intended to be mean. A blast of air passed through Adele's teeth, sounding like a tire deflating. When Adele released a second blast of air, Sloane realized she was sneezing, not hissing. Before Sloane could explain, the TV screen lit up at the front of the room.

"There," said Gary.

To Sloane's disappointment, he easily slipped his arm out from behind the screen.

"Any questions?"

Adele shot her hand up in the air. "I've got one." She stood, and even though Gary was more than a dozen feet away, he took a step back. Adele's chin lifted. "How many employees work here, thirty-five?" It wasn't a question. "Looking at your map of the office, three of the four fire escapes are located on the same side of the office." She pointed to the diagram on the TV screen. "What happens if the fire occurs on *that* side of the office?" Again, not a question. "It eliminates three of the four fire escapes, leaving only one alternative way out of the building. I passed that exit, by the washroom there, this morning, and there's a stack of boxes blocking half the hallway. If a fire starts on *that* side,"—she stabbed her finger into the air—"most of us will likely burn or be crushed by falling boxes."

For a moment, the room was quiet, except for the hum of the laptop and the woman in the back clearing her throat and counting her money. Sloane stared at Adele. She was confident, assertive, fearless and unapologetic for her boldness. The way Stephie had once been.

Gary smiled. "Thank you, Adele," he said. "A prime example that we hire only the best. When we're finished here, we'll address the box situation."

Sloane wanted to be a prime example. She wanted to be

noticed, to be talked about, to be known. Once she was transferred to Creative Services, she could go on parental leave and raise her two hypothetical children. She and Jason would buy a house with a white picket fence, and Jason could quit his job at the steel plant and work on developing a video game. Their lives would be perfect. Soon.

"Want to have lunch together?" asked Adele. The question pulled Sloane back into the present. Gary had returned to his slides.

Sloane whispered, "I better leave it open for Joan. She'll probably want to have lunch with me today, so we can get to know each other better."

Chapter Five

DISCOUNT ELECTRONICS IN Torren Hills was only a few blocks from the agency. Sloane could exchange the fitness tracker and still get home with enough time to have dinner and pack a bag before meeting Stephie in Tippett Valley. Jason would finally stop guilting her into being a better daughter, and Sloane could stop texting her mom fake step counts, or at least wear the band when Roma visited.

On the way over, Sloane couldn't stop thinking about Adele, imagining her repeatedly listening to her future husband breathing heavily and calling out another woman's name. She regretted not inviting her out, but it was too late now; outside the agency, Sloane didn't have a way to reach her. Besides, Sloane wanted Stephie all to herself tonight. Did that make her a terrible person? Or a loyal friend? Sloane and Stephie rarely talked anymore, but sleeping over on her birthday had been a tradition since sixteen, and Sloane was determined to uphold it.

Sloane wondered how Adele would be spending her evening. Not with Lawrence, unless she really was planning to show up at his place. Adele didn't have many friends, or if she did, she didn't talk about them with Sloane. Except for Travis and Eva. Adele spent a lot of her weekends with them, and even some holidays. As an only child, estranged from her parents, she said that Travis and Eva were the closest she had to a family.

Working the counter at Discount Electronics was a young girl with a long braid and sunken cheeks that looked like potholes. Spoiling her grin was a crooked tooth she attempted to cover with her tongue. Her nametag labeled her Stephanie M., which was probably why Sloane thought she looked a bit like Stephie—the high school version, minus the crooked tooth.

"My best friend's a Stephanie," said Sloane, approaching the counter. Sloane smiled, as if the two of them had become instant friends. "Do you go by Stephie, too?"

Stephanie M.'s eyebrows lifted and her mouth closed over her teeth. She smiled a locked-lip smile. The way a teenager smiles at an old person. "I go by Stephanie M.," she said.

Onto the counter, Sloane plopped down the fitness tracker, the gift receipt taped to the box. "I'd like to exchange this please," she said, "for a larger size."

Stephanie M. examined the receipt. "It was bought three months ago."

Sloane nodded. "You can see it's never been worn. Look, the sticker is still on the screen."

Stephanie M. tore the gift receipt from the box. "I can't exchange it if it was bought more than thirty days ago," she said, and then lowered her voice. "I can make an exception though, if it looks like it was bought recently and the customer doesn't have a receipt. It counts as a sale for me."

Sloane stuffed the receipt into her purse. "Thanks."

To determine the correct size, Stephanie M. offered to measure Sloane's wrist. Sloane rolled up her sleeve and held out an arm. Moist with sweat, it stuck to the counter.

When Stephanie M. popped back up from below the cash register, her nose wrinkled. "I can't find the measuring tape," she said.

Sloane wondered if the girl had caught sight of the eczema on the inside of her forearm. She quickly rolled down her sleeve. "It's not contagious," she mumbled. "It's just dry skin."

"What?"

"Nothing."

Stephanie M. pointed behind Sloane to the fitness trackers on display. "We're out of medium," she said. "Just large and extra-large." Her tongue slithered over her crooked tooth.

If Stephie had been there, she might have grabbed the girl's braid and yanked until she begged for mercy and measured Sloane's wrist. Stephie used to do things like that, or threaten to do things like that. Since she was very believable, she rarely had to follow through.

37

If Jason had been there, he might have asked for the manager. Then later, in the car, he would talk to Sloane about something else, and by the time they arrived home, she wouldn't feel so terrible.

But Sloane was on her own. She blindly grabbed a box from the display while Stephanie M. squeezed a big glob of hand sanitizer into her palm. She rubbed her hands together and then squirted the bottle over the counter, wiping the glass with a tissue.

From the parking lot, Sloane texted Stephie.

See you tonight!

Chapter Six

EVERYONE WHO LIVED in Tippett Valley called it Tippy. Living in a valley meant a lot of the basements flooded whenever it rained and pollution constantly hung in the air. Half the residents were employed by the steel plant on the outskirts of town. The single-screen movie theatre was rundown and there were more antique and secondhand stores in the downtown than any other type of business. Tippett Valley's best feature was the baseball diamonds, groomed and maintained like a palace lawn. That hadn't mattered much to Sloane and Stephie, who only went to the park for the concession booth and the make-out shed, where nearly every teenager experienced their first kiss. It was such a popular spot there was often a wait. At night, after the lights shut off, the town's teenagers gathered under the bleachers. Cigarette butts mixed with gravel mixed with chewed gum stuck to the bottom of shoes. Hundreds of initials were carved into the underside of the benches. Not Stephie's though—to rebel against the rebellious—so not Sloane's either.

Throughout Grade 8, Sloane had spent most of her free time at the Harringtons'. She and Stephie kept mostly to Stephie's bedroom, where the door had a lock to ensure privacy. Stephie played music on her CD player and drew in her sketchpad while smoking a cigarette by the opened window. She would tell Sloane about the boys she kissed and groped behind the make-out shed at the diamonds, the latest hiding spot for her weed stash, and how as soon as she finished high school she was going to get out of "this shithole of a town" and become an artist, maybe go to art school. Stephie was a C-minus student who smoked pot, drank alcohol, did things with boys that shocked Sloane and dismissed her brother, not kindly, whenever he asked to be included. By contrast, Sloane worked hard in school, didn't smoke or do drugs or drink alcohol, was still exploring her own sexuality and was nice to Benji. They balanced each other out.

In Grade 9, a year after the Harringtons' moved to Tippett Valley, Sloane was hanging out with Stephie in her room, when Stephie asked, "Why do you like me?"

Sloane looked up from *Great Expectations,* the book she was reading for Grade 9 English. Stephie was supposed to be reading it too, but she preferred to wait for Sloane's synopsis. Sloane blew on her fingernails, recently painted with Wite-Out. "I don't know," she said.

"You never think about it?"

"No. Not really. Do you?"

"People aren't friends for no reason, Sloane. Think about it." It sounded like a dare. "It's not like we have anything in common."

"Yes, we do. We both live in Tippy."

"We don't like anything the same."

"You like to draw and I like to design. It's both art. We decided so, remember?"

"Can you think of anything else?"

Sloane couldn't. Not on the spot. "Sometimes opposites attract," she said.

Stephie rolled her eyes and opened her sketchpad. "That's such a cliché."

"It doesn't mean it's not true," said Sloane, holding her book open with her elbow. "You're nice to me."

"Not really."

"You don't let anyone be mean to me."

"Except me."

Encouraging her fingernails to dry, Sloane waved her hands. "Well, why do you like me?"

Instead of answering, Stephie drew something in her sketchpad. Sloane started to panic, but then Stephie said, "You don't tell me the truth."

Sloane's shoulders pulled back. "I don't have any secrets from you."

"I don't mean you're keeping secrets. I mean, you don't tell me the truth."

"What truth?"

"That I'm an awful person."

"You're not awful. Everyone likes you."

"They don't like me. They're scared of me."

"*I* like you."

"Sometimes I think that makes me worse."

"What's that supposed to mean?"

"You forgive me for everything, no matter how terrible I am."

"You're not terrible."

"I stole ten dollars from your locker."

"You did?"

"I swear you saw me take it. I don't know why I did it. I didn't need the money. I didn't even spend it. It's right there. Take it." She eyed the ten-dollar bill on her dresser.

Sloane stuffed the bill into her pocket; it was her allowance for the week. "If you were awful," she said, "you wouldn't have told me. You would've spent it."

"See? You're not telling me the truth."

"I am. You're a good person, Stephie."

"You really believe that, don't you?"

"You're my best friend."

Sloane didn't want to go back to being the studious, shy girl who spent her weekends with her mom. Her life was a thousand times better with the Harringtons in Tippett Valley. Stephie tolerated her, for whatever reason, and Sloane was grateful.

"You should make other friends," said Stephie. "I don't mean characters in books, Sloane. They don't count."

"Did my mom say something to you?"

"We weren't supposed to become friends. I didn't want one when I moved to Tippy."

Sloane's elbow slipped and her book snapped shut like a

mousetrap. It wasn't the first time Stephie had tried to push her away.

"I had a best friend in New Carlton," she said. "Kendra Jamieson." Stephie didn't talk much about her life before moving to Tippett Valley, and she certainly had never mentioned a previous best friend. "We're not friends anymore," she added.

"I don't ever want us to not be best friends," said Sloane.

Stephie started to count the cigarettes she had stolen from her dad and stored in a clear cassette case.

"What happened?" asked Sloane. "With Kendra."

Stephie moved to the window. "She didn't have a dad and her mom worked a lot. Her older brother had parties at her house so we started hanging out with his friends."

"Cool," said Sloane. In Grade 7, she spent her nights playing gin rummy with her mom.

Stephie snapped shut the cassette tape. "We thought so. Then this guy," she said, angrily, "Tyler Patinkin, started to give Kendra a lot of attention. She was crazy about him." Stephie slipped the cassette tape under her mattress. Sitting on her bed, she shoved a blue pencil into a sharpener and shavings fell into her lap. "My dad had an interview for the Operations Manager job here in Tippy," she went on, surprising Sloane with her openness. "My mom decided she'd go with him, to see the town and check out houses. I convinced her that they should go out for dinner too, make a night of it, that Benji and I'd be fine, that I was old enough to babysit. I wasn't allowed to have anyone over, but I knew they'd be late, so I invited Kendra. Benji promised not to tell. But Kendra showed up with Tyler and a few other people.

"Tyler and Kendra disappeared for a while. When they came back, she was really upset. Said Tyler tried to make her do things."

Sloane gasped. "Did they have sex?"

Stephie squinted and bit her lip. "You don't have to have sex for it to be sexual assault, Sloane."

Was that what she was talking about? "I know," Sloane said

42

quickly, but she really didn't. Outside of health class, this was the first time she had actually heard someone use the term.

"Tyler bragged to his friends. He was in Grade 9, so."

Sloane's heart pumped fast. "What did you do?"

The pencil slipped from Stephie's fingers. "I didn't believe her," she said, her hand forming a fist. Her knee bounced. "I didn't understand then that thinking you want something and actually wanting it can be two different things."

No means no. It had been repeated a dozen times in health class.

Stephie's leg stilled. "She was really glad Benji walked in."

"He saw Kendra and Tyler?"

Stephie nodded.

"What did you do?"

"I told her she shouldn't have gone upstairs with him." She returned to the window. It had started to rain. "At school, someone scratched 'slut' into her locker. I told her it didn't matter what anyone thought of her, but it did. It mattered what I thought. I was her best friend."

Stephie paced, finally returning to her bed where she tore the pencil shavings into smaller pieces.

"Benji never told your parents?"

Stephie stared up at the ceiling. "He eventually did. He told my mom he thought he heard me crying in my room. When he opened the door, he saw Kendra's underwear and it was blue."

"Oh my god."

"My mom freaked out and called Kendra's mom. By then Kendra and I hadn't talked for a month."

"It wasn't your fault what happened to her."

"It was my fault for not believing her and for not standing up for her." Her voice cracked.

"Did you tell her you were sorry?"

"She avoided me at school, and since I was grounded for the rest of the school year it was hard to try to meet up with her outside of school. When we eventually talked she said I'd been right, that she shouldn't have gone upstairs with him. I told her we could go to the principal or the cops or somebody. She said it was too late. She was already The Slut.

"At the end of summer, my dad accepted the Operations Manager job in Tippy. My mom was glad that we were leaving the city, that I would start Grade 8 in a new school, make some 'more appropriate' friends and stop 'acting out.'"

Stephie was quiet for a long moment. "I'll kill you if you tell anyone." Her glare was like a physical force, pushing Sloane back.

"I won't," she promised. As awful as the story was, Stephie had trusted Sloane with it.

Kendra Jamieson never came up again.

On Stephie's sixteenth birthday, Sloane showed up to the Harringtons' with a set of colored pencils and a blank sketchpad—the same gift she had given Stephie for the past three years. She walked alongside the fence, her hand tracing the top of each picket, her arm rising and falling. Following the cobblestone pathway, Sloane made it to the front door, decorated with a balloon for the occasion.

Stephie's brother answered the door.

"I made the cake," he said, showing off his braces. "Chocolate. Her favorite." His hair was long, reaching past his shoulders, and his dark gray glasses were the same color as Sloane's.

"Hi, Benjamin."

Since starting high school, he was no longer Benji. He was Benjamin now.

"She upstairs?"

"She's *always* upstairs. Will you come for my birthday on Monday?"

Benjamin's birthday was just four days after Stephie's.

"Maybe," said Sloane. If Stephie were made to attend.

Benjamin followed her upstairs, where she knocked on Stephie's bedroom door. "It's me," she said.

The door opened just long enough for Stephie to grab Sloane's shoulder and pull her inside. It slammed shut as Benjamin was asking, "Can I listen to music with—"

"Not even on your birthday?" said Sloane, feeling bad for Benjamin.

Stephie shrugged. She was wearing tight jeans with rips that exposed her boney knees. Covering most of her hands were the cuffs of her long-sleeve shirt, her fingertips peeking out. Her lipstick was plum red and smeared in the corners of her mouth, and her bangs were tickling her eyelashes, causing her to blink more than usual.

Sloane handed Stephie her gift. "Happy birthday," she said.

Stephie tossed it onto her bed and said nothing. The two of them had planned to have dinner with Stephie's family and then Stephie's dad, Joe, was going to drive them to the bowling alley in Torren Hills. Of course, the plan wasn't to actually bowl, but to meet up with Rachel and Rahul and sneak through the back entrance of a bar named the Maverick where Violent Downfall was performing. Sloane wasn't usually allowed to sleep over on a school night, but both Jasmine and Roma had agreed to an exception.

"Is something the matter?" asked Sloane.

The Harringtons' telephone rang. Stephie tucked her hair behind her ears and lit a cigarette, crouching in front of the window. Like a curtain, her bangs closed over her forehead. The ringing stopped.

"What is it?" pressed Sloane.

"Just wait," Stephie said, calmly blowing smoke out the cracked window.

From downstairs, Jasmine's voice shouted. "Stephie!"

Sloane heard footsteps on the stairs and then banging on Stephie's locked door.

"Open this door right now," Jasmine demanded.

Stephie pressed her index finger against her plum-colored lips, warning Sloane to remain quiet.

"I've had enough!"

45

Sloane mouthed the words, "Enough of what?"

"Your principal has had enough, too," shouted Jasmine. "You're suspended. Two days."

Sloane's mouth popped open. Stephie casually took a drag from her cigarette and smiled.

"Did you hear me? Open this door!"

From her lip, Stephie picked off a flake of tobacco and flicked it onto the rug.

"You're grounded," said Jasmine. "Starting right now."

"But it's your birthday," Sloane mouthed.

"Sloane, are you in there? Open the door."

Stephie cautioned Sloane with a glare.

"Are you smoking in there?"

Sloane waved her arms, moving smoke away from the door.

"Don't even think about leaving your room." Giving up, Jasmine stomped downstairs.

"What did you do?" Sloane asked, uneasy.

"Nothing," said Stephie.

"You got suspended."

Stephie shrugged. "Guess so."

"You're grounded on your birthday. Why?"

On the window ledge, Stephie stubbed out her cigarette. "Mrs. Ashton caught me drawing on the washroom wall."

Sloane's arms flew out to the side. "When Kate got caught, she just had to wash it off during detention. It's not fair you got suspended."

"It won't wash off. I used permanent marker."

Sloane's shoulders dropped. "What did you draw?"

"A black rainbow."

"You mean, a big black arc? Why?"

Stephie flopped onto her bed.

"You called Kate a cliché for writing on the washroom wall," Sloane reminded her.

"This was different."

"Did it have something to do with an art project?"

"You don't have to stay."

Something sank inside Sloane. "You want me to go?"

"I'll just be in here all night. Doesn't sound like much fun."

"It's your birthday."

"So."

"So, you shouldn't spend your birthday alone."

Stephie shrugged. She was acting weird. Sloane would have expected her to be more upset about missing her favorite band, for being suspended from school, for being grounded on her birthday.

Sloane didn't want to go to the Violent Downfall show anyway. She was worried the two of them would get caught sneaking into the bar, and then, on the drive back, Joe would agonize over whether to tell Jasmine or spare his wife's distress and let Stephie off the hook. Sloane was pretty sure Joe would keep it to himself, which was why she didn't worry about Roma finding out. But spending a night with her best friend all to herself was even better.

"I'm staying," she said.

That night, Sloane and Stephie talked and laughed and listened to music and painted their toenails and made prank phone calls to random numbers. Outside Stephie's door, Benjamin left two slices of birthday cake, which Stephie permitted Sloane to retrieve only after Benjamin stopped loitering. Just before falling asleep, Stephie told Sloane it was cool of her to have stayed. For Sloane, the night couldn't have been more perfect.

"We should do this every birthday," she said.

The next day at school, Sloane found Stephie's black rainbow. She could tell by the puddle of soapy water on the floor that someone had already tried to wash it off. To remove it, the bricks would have to be sandblasted. To disguise it, the entire wall would have to be painted black. With Stephie at home, Sloane didn't have anything better to do than try to figure out what it meant, what it stood for. Why a black arc? It took five minutes of staring to recognize a letter faintly peeking through the dark ink. She moved closer to the wall, the tip of her nose grazing the bricks. Something had been written underneath. Squinting, she spelled out the hidden words: *Benjamin Harrington is a fag.*

Chapter Seven

WHEN SLOANE GOT home, she discovered she had picked an XL fitness tracker. The band was so long that it slid halfway up her arm, but she wasn't about to exchange it again. Jason was pleased she had made the effort, which was the point anyway. She put it back into the box.

The XL printed on the packaging mesmerized Sloane. Was this who she had become: Sloane Sawyer, XL? Just last week, she had purchased size XL sweatpants. They were the only pair remaining on the sale rack and dropped to the floor without the drawstring pulled tight, but still. At least they didn't get stuck on her hips, and if she continued to gain weight, she could just loosen the drawstring. She wouldn't have to go out and buy another pair. She removed the tag so Jason wouldn't see the size when it was his week to do laundry.

Across the table, Jason twirled his utensils, winding spaghetti around a fork pressed into a spoon. Not having to work tonight, he was probably looking forward to having the house to himself. "What are you thinking?" he asked.

"Nothing."

"Something. Come on, it can't be that bad."

Sloane's chin shot forward. *It can be that bad. It is that bad.*

"Tell me," he said, reaching for her hand, his sleeve absorbing dribbles of tomato sauce. "You worried about tonight, with Stephie?"

Sloane moved her hands into her lap. "No." *Yes.* "I was thinking the fashion industry should change their sizes to something that doesn't contain 'extra' or 'plus.' As if there's something about someone's body that isn't supposed to be there. What is it 'in addition' to?" She pointed to the letter X printed on the packaging of the fitness tracker. "Look," she said. "Do they have to use such a negative letter? It's written on tests for wrong answers. It crosses out words to indicate a mistake. It's used in symbols to mean 'No' or 'Don't.'"

"People vote using an X. That's positive." A strand of spaghetti hung from Jason's lips. He reeled it in like fishing line.

Sloane slapped her palm on the table. "Next thing you know, they'll be charging more for larger sizes. More material, more stitches, more work, more cost. That's what they'll say."

Jason swallowed and then swiped the back of his hand across his mouth. "They should label sizes by color," he said. "Size red. Size blue. Size yellow. You can't rank primary colors. Each is equally necessary. No hierarchy. Different, not better or worse. Just like bodies."

Like uninvited guests, demoralizing thoughts crashed Sloane's mind. She poked at her thighs, her belly, her hips. Roma had told her she would be grateful for them one day, when she was ready to have her own kids. "Childbirth will be easy-peasy," she said. But getting pregnant hadn't been.

"Sloane?" Jason stacked his hands on top of hers, which had subconsciously made their way back onto the table. She accepted his sympathy only for a moment, and then gathered the empty dinner plates.

At the sink, Jason moved in behind her. He gently pushed his chin into the back of her head. "X is the symbol for a hug," he said, squeezing her ribs.

Sloane tensed. How could he want to touch her?

"I've got to get ready for Stephie's birthday," she said, slipping out of his grasp.

Escaping upstairs, she imagined Jason heading down to the basement, where he would play video games or write source code for the remainder of the night, grateful for the solitude.

She texted Stephie.

On my way!

As the message sent, a feeling of uneasiness spread through her. So much had changed since high school. The only thing that had survived was Stephie's birthday tradition. Even in adulthood, Sloane slept over, and the two would talk and laugh and stay up late. One night of the year, Sloane didn't have to compete for Stephie's attention and actually felt like her best friend.

Chapter Eight

SLOANE DIDN'T GET invited to parties; Stephie did, and Sloane tagged along.

Tina Johnson's parents were out of town and her cousin was visiting, which meant she was having a party. Tina lived in Wilson, a seven-minute drive from Tippett Valley. Sloane had just earned her full driver's license so she borrowed her dad's car and volunteered to be the designated driver.

When Sloane arrived at the Harringtons', the white picket fence had been taken down so that construction on a new pool could begin. The wood had been stacked in the garage and small orange flags marked the holes left by the posts. The house looked naked, but Sloane looked forward to spending even more time at Stephie's this summer.

Inside the house, Stephie was tying the laces of her boots and yelling at Benjamin.

"Get your own life and let me have mine!"

"Stephie," shouted Jasmine, "he's your brother. He's part of your life."

"Can I at least have my own room?" she responded, sarcastically. "And does he have to keep his hair long like that? It's like he wants to look like me. It's not healthy, Mom."

"I'm sorry," said Benjamin, sounding genuine. "I shouldn't have gone into your room without your permission." With flushed cheeks, he glanced at Sloane and then back at Stephie. "And I shouldn't have taken what I took. I'll put it back."

"Keep it," said Stephie. "Come on, Sloane, let's go."

"Take your brother with you," said Jasmine.

"No."

"You're going to the same party, you can all drive there together. Make sure he gets home tonight, too," said Jasmine, firmly.

"I told you, I'm staying at Sloane's."

"After you get your brother home. Your dad and I will be out late."

"Benji can take care of himself."

"Benjamin," he said, quietly.

"Stephie," warned Jasmine, "I'm not going to tell you again."

"Whatever."

"Home by ten tomorrow. In the morning the grass needs to be cut."

In the car, Stephie turned the volume up on the CD player and rolled down her window. Benjamin's hair was blowing like a windsock. As soon as Sloane parked, Stephie was out of the car and heading toward the house. Benjamin grabbed his backpack and Sloane heard the familiar chime of bottles.

"Thanks for the ride," said Benjamin, patting down his hair. He smiled fiercely. His braces had recently come off and he suddenly had a perfect smile.

"See you inside," said Sloane.

In Tina Johnson's house, Sloane filled a red plastic cup with Coke and sat on the couch beside Stephie who was drinking gin and tonic and had already filled her cup twice. Without effort, she drew a crowd. Stephie didn't say much, but when she spoke, everyone listened. It had been almost five years since the Harringtons moved to Tippett Valley and Sloane still couldn't believe that Stephie was her friend. Before Stephie, she never thought she would be at a party.

"What did you think about Mr. Fresne's math test?" Ashley with the red hair asked the group gathered in the living room.

"That test was *hard*," someone said.

"Totally," said Sloane.

"What are you talking about?" scoffed Ashley, her face scrunched. "You'll get an A. You always do."

To disguise her flushed cheeks, Sloane took a sip of Coke.

"She'll get an A because she studied her ass off," said Stephie, filling her cup again. She glared at Ashley. "You don't know what hard is." She swung her arm, punching at the air. Ashley faded into the corner, clearly unwilling to challenge Stephie Harrington. Sloane noticed just how far away everyone was sitting. Even the boys didn't come close to Stephie. Not for a conversation. Not when she was sober. People feared her, just as much as they were intrigued by her. If it weren't for Sloane, she might be sitting on the couch alone.

Benjamin had his own group of friends, the Grade 10s, which included Tina's brother, and Sloane periodically glanced in his direction. Both the Harringtons were getting noticeably drunk.

When Stephie went outside to smoke a cigarette, Sloane took the opportunity to use the bathroom. A girl Sloane didn't recognize, likely Tina's cousin, was already waiting. At the end of the hallway, through the glass patio doors, Sloane saw Stephie shove a boy from their class.

"Sloane!"

She spun around. "Oh, hey," she said. It was only Benjamin.

Tina's cousin entered the vacated bathroom.

"I scared you," said Benjamin, reaching for the wall.

Sloane grabbed his arm, which was surprisingly solid. Benjamin was fifteen, not a little kid anymore. His face had cleared of acne and his voice had dropped. On his jawline was a shadow of stubble, and his murky blue eyes were unobstructed by the glasses he usually wore. His long hair was shiny and stayed tucked behind his ears, something Sloane's never did. Not that she wore her hair back anymore. Not since she learned her ears looked like fetuses. For the first time, Sloane considered that Stephie's brother was . . . cute. "You okay?" she asked, releasing him.

"I'm *greeeeeat!*"

"You're drunk."

Benjamin nodded.

"Stephie's gonna kill you."

He nodded again, and then closed his eyes and moved his face closer.

Sloane jerked back. "What are you doing?"

His voice softened and slowed. "Kissing you?"

Sloane laughed. "Why?"

"I like you."

She looked away, embarrassed.

"It would make me really happy," he said.

"You already look really happy."

"Really happy-*errrr*."

It scared Sloane that she wanted to say yes. "What about—"

At first contact, Benjamin's lips were hard, but then his mouth softened and opened. Forgetting where she was and who she was and who he was, she kissed him back. The side of her nose touched his, and it wasn't awkward; unlike her first kiss at the make-out shed. Benjamin was gentler, slower, softer. Unhurriedly, he peeled his lips away from hers, but remained close, staring into her eyes. Sloane stared back, not knowing what to say or what to do. Then where she was and who she was and who he was came rushing back. *Oh, no.* Kissing your best friend's younger brother had to be in some codebook of what *not* to do.

Sloane squinted down the hallway toward the patio doors. To her relief, Stephie was no longer outside on the porch. She hadn't seen. Without a word, Sloane fled to the safety of the living room. Maybe Benjamin wouldn't remember the kiss. At the pace he was drinking, he likely wouldn't remember much. *But what if he does? What if he tells Stephie? What if someone else does?*

"Where were you?"

Sloane turned. "Stephie!"

Stephie glared and Sloane panicked. *I just kissed your brother.* Wasn't it better she heard it from Sloane?

"Bathroom," she said. She still had to pee.

"Did you take something?" Stephie's face zoomed in on Sloane's.

"What? No." Sloane gently pushed Stephie away. "I'm driving, remember?"

"You look crazy, in a good way."

"I didn't take anything."

"Here, take this then." Stephie held out her hand, a pill in her palm.

"What is it?"

"Robbie stole it from his mom."

"His mom has cancer."

Stephie popped the pill. "You might've been roofied."

"What?"

"Your cheeks are all red."

Because I kissed your brother.

Whatever Stephie took, it hit her hard and fast. Sloane tried to keep an eye on her, but she was distracted by Benjamin. He repeatedly tucked his long hair behind his ears and punched his hands into the pockets of his hoodie. His smile was contagious. He kept close to his sister and Sloane, but Stephie kept shooing him away.

Stephie and Benjamin got drunker while Sloane stayed sober. Benjamin could barely stand upright; Stephie made out with two different boys and kicked over a floor lamp. Maybe it was on purpose.

"We should go," said Sloane, nudging Stephie's arm. "Your brother can barely stand."

"It's not even midnight," said Stephie, petting Sloane's shoulder.

"Look at him. If we don't leave now, he might pass out and we'll have to carry him."

"I'm not leaving."

Sloane wanted to stay with Stephie but she was worried about Benjamin. Besides, if she didn't get him home tonight, then Stephie would be in trouble again. "I'll be back, okay?"

Sloane couldn't be sure if Stephie heard. She was shouting something at her brother.

Benjamin slept most of the way back to Tippett Valley. When his eyes fluttered open, Sloane tested his memory.

"About what happened," she said. "At Tina's. Between us. Do you remember?"

Benjamin smiled. "I love you," he said. He closed his eyes and his forehead fell against the window.

Sloane panicked briefly, but then remembered he was drunk and barely coherent. She pulled over in front of the Harringtons'.

"You need to sober up before your parents get home," she said. "Or you and Stephie are both going to be in trouble. Take a shower, okay? Promise me you will."

He nodded and smiled. "Thanks, Sloane."

She could feel her cheeks heating. *What's wrong with me? He's Stephie's little brother.*

She watched him struggle with the door handle and stumble into the house. As soon as he was inside, she took off back to Wilson. Back to Stephie.

Chapter Nine

IN TIPPETT VALLEY, Stephie Harrington and Randy Goff shared the top floor of a townhouse owned by Randy's parents. Sloane tolerated Randy only because he had become a permanent fixture in Stephie's life. He played guitar in a metal band, worked seemingly random hours for an events company named Oasis Rentals, and had girlfriends that never stuck around—like Stephie, he was apparently averse to love. He was also just as bad at remembering to pay bills, cleaning up after himself and eating proper meals, relying on the food truck parked up the street. He did weird things like paint his nails black, sport a handlebar mustache and use a head of broccoli as a brush to scrub his hands after a day at work. He made Stephie's life seem normal and seemed okay with all her irresponsibility. When Stephie skipped a therapy session, he didn't chide her for it; instead, he paid her therapist's bill— with money Sloane was sure he had gotten from his parents—to keep her timeslot.

"You can't force someone to accept therapy," he had said when Sloane asked why he didn't encourage her to actually go to her session. "But you can give them the opportunity when they're ready."

Stephie swung open her front door.

"Happy birthday!" said Sloane, relieved that Stephie was home. "Is Randy here?"

"No."

Good.

Stephie hadn't tidied up for Sloane's visit. Dirty dishes collaged the two coffee tables, DVDs were spread out on the floor below the TV, an ashtray was overflowing and crumbs lined the seams of the couch like stitches. Sloane was grateful for the incense stick burning on the window ledge.

Stephie had lost weight, which Sloane didn't think was possible. Her shirt kept falling off her shoulder and it wasn't a shirt that was supposed to do that. Her hair was short and uneven, longer in some spots—*Did you cut it yourself?*—and the rips in her jeans exposed her kneecaps. She was holding her jacket.

"Going somewhere?" joked Sloane.

Stephie pulled her shirt over her shoulder. "The Stairway. Gotta pick up my cheque." She worked at the bar as a server four nights a week.

Sloane's breath caught. "But it's tradition to stay in. Just us."

"You don't have to come."

"No, I'll come." It would be a quick stop, in and out, barely a blip in the birthday tradition. "I'll have to change first."

"No one will notice what you're wearing."

"I'm at least changing out of my sweatpants."

Stephie moved Randy's guitar off the couch and sat dramatically, as if she had been shoved. A stack of teetering books tumbled. Sloane read the titles scattered on the floor: *Beyond Good and Evil, Being and Nothingness, Zen and the Art of Motorcycle Maintenance*—Randy's. She wondered if he gave synopses to Stephie like she used to.

Sloane moved into Stephie's bedroom to change into the black pants she had packed for the morning. Her work wardrobe had shifted from colorful and hip to dark and bland. As she struggled with her zipper, Sloane hollered, "Did your parents call?"

Stephie mumbled from the couch. "Why would they?"

"To wish you a happy birthday."

"You know I haven't talked to them in years."

"Not even on your birthday?"

"Birthdays aren't exceptions for everyone."

Sloane emerged from the bedroom and handed Stephie her birthday gift: thirty colored pencils—for Stephie's thirtieth birthday—and a sketchpad. Stephie accepted the gift but didn't open it.

"Do I look okay?" asked Sloane, holding out her arms.

Stephie stood. "Like I said, no one'll notice." She walked over to the island between the kitchen and entranceway and placed her hands around the one-gallon fishbowl sitting on the ledge. "Hey," she cooed to a black and yellow goldfish. "What you saying, Bee?" Not only did he look like a bumblebee, he acted like one, swimming around excitedly and ramming his nose into the glass when Stephie gently tapped his bowl.

Sloane was embarrassed to be jealous of a goldfish, the only thing in Stephie's life she didn't neglect. Randy had said a goldfish like Bee could live anywhere between six months and five years. It had already been two years and Randy had been warned by the pet store that this one had been in the tank for a while. So Bee had to be reaching the end of his life. Miraculously, he seemed perfectly happy as far as Sloane could tell, though she wondered if she would notice if Bee was unhappy.

"I told you my mom's in China?" said Sloane. She had told Stephie twice. "It's kind of been nice. Too expensive to call."

Stephie released her hands from the fishbowl. "I slept with Randy."

Sloane's jaw dropped.

Dismissively, Stephie shrugged. "We both agreed it didn't count. Neither of us got off."

"You don't even like him that way," said Sloane, shocked. "He's just a friend."

"It won't happen again. Neither of us sleeps with the same person more than three times. Good thing this morning didn't count."

"You slept with him twice before?" *You didn't tell me.*

"Come on, you ready? I'll drive. There's employee parking."

The Stairway in Wilson was a one-hour walk or a seven-minute drive from Randy and Stephie's townhouse in Tippett Valley. Years ago, Sloane and Stephie had walked home once and Sloane considered them lucky for not getting mugged.

Both were quiet on the drive. Sloane was still processing the fact that her best friend had slept with her roommate three times. If Stephie and Randy were going to be a couple, then Sloane worried Stephie would grow even more distant. Randy was already interfering; as a boyfriend, it would only get worse. Or maybe intimacy would tear them apart and Sloane's relationship with Stephie would strengthen. Stephie would have to move out— it was Randy's parents' townhouse—and then maybe she could stay with Sloane and Jason in Torren Hills for a while until she found her own place. It would be just like Sloane had planned it in high school. At least the living together part.

The Stairway was crowded and loud and dark, even on a Monday. It was a popular bar with students, especially those underage, so everyone inside seemed young. When Stephie had first been hired, Sloane would sit at the bar and watch her work whenever she was home from university. She enjoyed seeing Stephie smile, even though she was only doing it for tips.

Sloane backed away when the bar's staff swarmed Stephie. One of the servers brought over a round of shots and the group sang an off-key version of "Happy Birthday." Then another round of shots showed up. It didn't take long for Stephie to be drunk, and it didn't stop her from drinking more. Sloane kept trying to get her to leave. When Stephie said, "You're the one who insisted I celebrate my birthday," Sloane admitted defeat and accepted a shot. Then two more. They would have to take a cab home.

Ignored at the table, Sloane wondered how Adele was doing. She was about to turn thirty without a fiancé. *I should've invited her.*

Sloane didn't think the night could get worse until someone spilled a drink on her. She jumped up and hurried to the washroom, where she dabbed at the stain on her pants with an unsteady hand. *I should just go home.* She clumsily texted Jason—he would come get her.

> Hey.
> Watcha doing?
> You home?

Of course he was home. When he wasn't working, he was in the basement playing video games, often deaf to the sound of his phone vibrating in the real world. Sloane understood because it was the same for her when she was reading a good book or designing a poster. When he focused on a screen, it was as if the external world didn't exist.

Sloane returned to the table where Stephie and her co-workers were handing out another round of shots. It dawned on her then that celebrating Stephie's birthday at the Stairway had been Stephie's plan all along. Stephie slid into the chair next to Sloane and began petting her shoulder. When she was drunk, Stephie treated everyone like a cat. "You want to go," she said.

"Yes."

The collar of Stephie's shirt fell almost to her elbow. Below her chin, her collarbone jutted out like a drawn sword. "Just one more," she said. Sloane didn't want another shot, but if it would get Stephie to leave the Stairway, then she would pay the price.

Stephie must have had special status with Wilson Taxi because a cab pulled up to the curb almost right away. Sloane got into the backseat and Stephie shimmied in beside her. *Finally.* Shifting closer, Stephie knocked into Sloane, making room for a man she was pulling into the cab.

"What are you doing?" hissed Sloane.

Stephie walked her fingers up the man's thigh. "Tippy," she said to the driver. "65 Ranger Street." The car rolled forward.

Sloane pulled on Stephie's knee. "Do you even know him?"

The man grinned. "Nasser," he said.

"He's Nasssssaah . . ." Stephie laughed. "He's been to the moon!"

"What about Randy?" Not that Sloane cared about Randy, but if it got Nasser out of the car . . . "This morning, you," she lowered her voice, "you slept with him."

Stephie smiled, her eyes only half-open. The lipstick had come off her bottom lip, but the color was still visible on the top. "I told you, it didn't count. And so what? I can't sleep with two people on the same day? You don't mind, do you?" Before Nasser could have an opinion, she turned and planted her lips on his mouth.

Stephie and Nasser kissed and groped all the way to Tippett Valley while Sloane tried to focus on her phone. Jason hadn't yet texted back.

> I know you're in the basement.
> Probably saving a kidnapped princess from a monster.
> Holding her hostage in her own castle.
> But in real life, I need you to save ME. Be my Super Mario!
> Hello?
> Helllllloooooo!

When the cab stopped, Stephie dragged Nasser inside, leaving Sloane to pay the fare. She considered asking the driver to take her back to Torren Hills, but it would cost a small fortune she didn't have, and she would have to ask Jason for money—again. She considered whether she was sober enough to drive home. She wasn't. She inhaled deeply, regrouping. If she left earlier than she originally planned in the morning, then she could go home to shower and change before work. She just had to make it to morning. Besides, it was tradition to sleep over on Stephie's birthday. Sloane's eyes rolled. Tradition.

When Sloane entered the house, Stephie and Nasser were almost in Stephie's bedroom. Stephie looked over her shoulder. "Take Randy's room," she said as the door closed behind them.

Sloane considered sleeping on the couch, but books still covered two of the cushions and it would take her the remainder of the night to pick out the crumbs embedded into the seams. She peaked into Randy's room. At least his bed was made. She wanted to change out of her stained pants and scrub off the layer of vodka coating her teeth like glue. Then she realized her tote bag was trapped in Stephie's room. She checked her phone. Still no reply from Jason.

In Randy's bedroom, Sloane cracked the window, revolted by a smell both fruity and foul. At least a dozen cigarette butts had been stubbed into the ledge. A box of powdered laundry detergent had fallen off a shelf; clusters of white particles infused the carpet. A pair of work boots smelled so bad she was sure they were emitting gas. On a desk, an open bottle of nail polish remover had tipped over; a pool of blue liquid was slowly soaking a pay stub from Oasis Rentals. She considered cleaning up the spill with a tissue, or with one of the dozen black t-shirts bunched up in the corner on the floor, but she worried if she moved around too much she would find something worse. *Just get through the night.* She shivered as she got onto Randy's bed, refusing to get under the covers.

Outside the window, a car alarm went off. Lights flashed. The blinking reminded Sloane of her university apartment in Torren Hills. The building was across from a club with a giant sign that flickered *Open! Open! Open! Girls! Girls! Girls!* in red lights. She had imagined seeking out the club's manager to insist that, at the very least, the sign was changed to *Women! Women! Women!* She had planned to do it when Stephie visited, but that never happened.

Lying in Randy's bed, Sloane brooded over the night. It was Randy's fault. If he hadn't slept with Stephie that morning —or the two times before—then maybe Stephie wouldn't have needed to get drunk and sleep with Nasser. She and Sloane would have spent the night talking and laughing and upholding the birthday tradition. Shivering, Sloane grudgingly slipped her socked feet under the blankets. *Just get through the night.*

Chapter Ten

AFTER TINA JOHNSON's party, Stephie slept over at Sloane's as planned. Roma was out of town visiting Vivian and Edward didn't enforce a curfew, so no parent was waiting at the front door when Sloane arrived home late and with a drunk best friend.

Stephie still had alcohol in her bag and insisted Sloane catch up. Now that she had fulfilled her responsibilities as the designated driver, she didn't have an excuse not to. Besides, if she were a little tipsy it might be easier to tell Stephie about the kiss.

In her bedroom, Sloane took a sip of gin and cringed at the taste. "Thanks for sticking up for me," she said. "At the party. With Ashley. She never liked me."

Getting comfortable on the bed, Stephie concentrated on separating strands of hair from her bangs.

"Your brother was pretty drunk."

"Shit, my brother," Stephie slurred.

"He got home," Sloane assured her.

Stephie placed her palms on her forehead and tipped back. Tomorrow, when she sobered up, maybe she would thank Sloane for driving Benjamin home and sparing her from a grounding.

"Why do you find Benjamin so annoying anyway?" asked Sloane.

"Everyone annoys me."

"Me too?"

"The most."

Sloane laughed and took another sip of gin. "I was thinking. After high school, we should start a business together. We could design posters for bands like Violent Downfall. I could do the graphic design and you could do the drawings."

"Maybe," said Stephie, uninterested.

Sloane's shoulders dropped. "My mom insists I get a university degree, but graphic design is a diploma."

"Both are just pieces of paper."

"I don't get why my parents think it's so important when neither of them got a degree. My dad didn't even finish high school!"

"Maybe that's exactly why."

"Maybe my mom thinks I wouldn't be a good graphic designer."

"Trust me," said Stephie, "your mom believes you can do anything. She's nothing like mine."

"Do you think I can do it?"

"Have you ever failed at anything you tried?"

Yeah. Before you, making friends. Fitting in. "If you go to the art school in Torren Hills and I go to the university, we could get an apartment together."

"Torren Hills is *way* too close to Tippy."

"Where do you want to go?"

"Far away from here."

"Back to New Carlton?"

"Further."

"Wherever you go, I want to go with you, okay?"

Stephie was playing with her hair again.

"Stephie, okay?" Sloane needed to hear her say it.

"Yeah."

"I saw you with Rick at the party. Why did you make out with him? You don't even like him." Rick wore his hair greased back and his shirts half-unbuttoned, exposing his chest. He was a lot like Jeremiah, who Stephie had slept with at the beginning of Grade 12. He was even greasier than Rick.

Stephie shrugged. "I don't know."

"I also saw you shove Greg, but I know you think he's okay. You don't want a boyfriend?" Not that Sloane was complaining. She didn't want Stephie to have a boyfriend, either. Not even a nice one. "I don't get why you would make out with Rick and be mean to Greg."

Sloane wondered if it was because Stephie felt like she didn't deserve someone like Greg. Maybe kissing Rick made her feel in control over the worst kinds of boys, like Tyler Patinkin.

"Tiny hearts break easily," she said. "Better to not hand mine over to some nice guy. They eat tiny hearts for breakfast."

The more Sloane drank, the more compelled she was to tell her best friend about the kiss. Finally, she was ready.

"I have to tell you something," she said, her voice turning serious.

On Sloane's bed, Stephie was curled up into a ball, her eyes closed.

"Something happened tonight. With your brother and me at Tina's."

"Benji," whispered Stephie, half unconscious.

Squeezing the gin bottle, Sloane took a deep breath and cringed. "We kissed." *Don't be mad, don't be mad, please don't be mad.*

When nothing happened, she slowly opened her eyes.

"Stephie, did you hear what I said?"

She had fallen asleep.

I'll tell her tomorrow.

Sloane woke up with a headache. She could only imagine how much worse it was for Stephie, who could barely open her eyes.

Roma had arrived home. Sloane could hear her mom's voice traveling upstairs.

"I'll go out the back," said Stephie, her voice gravelly.

It was a good idea since it was nearly impossible to escape the Sawyers' without Roma inquiring about a million different things. From the top of the staircase, Sloane listened for her mom to move into the living room. "Now," she relayed to Stephie, waving her forward.

Stephie quietly descended the stairs but stopped halfway. Looking up, she said, "I'm glad we're friends."

Sloane smiled at the unexpected proclamation. "I won't

tell anyone," she joked. Then she remembered she had kissed Benjamin and maybe Stephie wouldn't have said that if she knew. "See you later today," she whispered. "I've something to tell you."

Sloane arrived at the Harringtons' a couple of hours later. During the walk over, she practiced her speech. *I kissed your brother. Last night. At the party.* Maybe Stephie wouldn't think it was a big deal. Maybe she wouldn't care. She had kissed a dozen boys. *What if Benjamin told her already?* Sloane quickened her pace.

In daylight, the missing fence around the Harringtons' made it seem like the house wasn't their home anymore. She wasn't surprised to see the grass hadn't been cut; neither Stephie nor Benjamin was in any condition to operate a lawnmower. Two police cars were parked out front. Her heartbeat quickened.

A police officer answered the Harringtons' door. Disoriented, Sloane stumbled off the step.

"Who are you?" asked the officer.

Despite the kindness in the woman's voice, Sloane's hands shook. She was afraid Stephie had been arrested for underage drinking and now she was going to be busted, too. Fearing her breath still smelled of alcohol, she pressed her lips tightly together.

"You're a friend of Stephanie's?"

"Stephie's," said Sloane. "What's going on?"

The officer seemed to hesitate. "Wait here," she said, turning back into the house.

Sloane peered inside. A second officer was sitting at the kitchen table with waxed versions of Joe and Jasmine: still and unmoving. Stephie had to have been caught for something way worse than drinking. *The stash of weed under her bed? The pregnancy test she had wrapped in tinfoil and discarded? That wasn't illegal. Besides, it was negative. Oh no, not the sunglasses from the Pharma Mart! It was an accident, really. The arm had gotten caught on the strap of Stephie's bag. She didn't even know she had stolen them.*

Sloane entered but remained at the door. Stephie's parents

looked like their souls had been taken from their bodies. Jasmine's pale cheeks shone with tears and her hands were beginning to shake. The flesh of Joe's face was gray and sagging.

Sloane didn't know what to say.

Joe's vacant eyes didn't move. "Benjamin's dead," he said, his voice monotone.

Jasmine's chair slid back and her forehead slammed hard onto her folded arms. As she wept, the officer placed a hand on her heaving shoulder. Joe stared straight ahead.

Benjamin's dead? Sloane was slow to understand. *He can't be dead. I just saw him last night. He was fine. Everything was fine.*

The officer who had answered the door returned. "Stephanie's in her room."

"Stephie," breathed Sloane.

"She says you can go up. I'm sure she'd appreciate a friend right now."

"How'd it happen?" Sloane's voice was barely audible.

"He fell. Hit his head."

Hot droplets of sweat traveled down Sloane's neck as she climbed the stairs. It felt like the tip of a knife was slowly cutting her open. *How can Benjamin be dead? He fell. Hit his head.* She squeezed her hands into fists and gently knocked on Stephie's door. It swung open, unexpectedly unlocked.

Stephie was in her bed, lying on her side, facing the wall.

"Hey," said Sloane, quietly, "you okay?" Of course she wasn't okay. Her brother was dead. It didn't seem like it could be true.

Uncertain, Sloane hovered over her best friend. Finally, she sat, her weight causing the mattress to sink. Stephie's body rotated, opening up. Her face was pale, her lips cracked, the corners of her mouth crusted. Her bloodshot eyes seemed stuck half-open, like a jammed garage door.

"There wasn't any blood," she said.

"What?"

"In the bathroom, there was no evidence. No clues."

Benjamin fell in the bathroom?

69

"This morning, before I knew, I just walked right in there. You'd think I'd have felt something."

"Like what?" asked Sloane.

"I don't know, his spirit?" Stephie laughed—she *laughed*. "I might've puked all over it."

Sitting up, she stabbed a pencil into her dresser, sending shards of wood and graphite flying. Sloane squinted to protect her eyes, or maybe because she felt the same way. Like her organs were exploding. *I was his last kiss. Was I his first?* She wouldn't tell Stephie. It didn't matter anymore.

Over the next few days, Stephie's aunt brought over cases of Gatorade and left them in Stephie's room. "Ironic, wouldn't it be?" she said to Sloane. "With the way that girl lives her life if we lost her to dehydration?"

She laughed and then apologized. No one knew what to do, what to say. No one could be prepared for the loss of a fifteen-year-old, especially not Benjamin Harrington, a good kid who earned top grades, had made the junior basketball team, was well-liked and got along with his parents. It didn't make sense that he was the one who was gone.

When word got out, the Harringtons' house filled with flowers and sympathy cards and casseroles that spoiled in the fridge. Stephie's uncle flew in from the east coast to handle the funeral arrangements. Other family members arrived and loitered around the house, taking up space. The phone rang a dozen times a day. The construction crew showed up; Jasmine sent them away. A week after the funeral, when everyone was gone, the house felt hollow. It was as if Sloane were entering a cave. Jasmine refused to turn on a light and the temperature seemed to drop.

Both the door to the upstairs bathroom and to Benjamin's bedroom were now permanently closed. No one talked about the tragedy and Sloane didn't ask. Joe took a leave-of-absence from the plant and developed an interest in building model airplanes.

Even the toxic fumes from the glue couldn't eliminate the stench of sadness. The weeks following, employees from the steel plant took a turn to help the grieving family. Stephie stopped eating. She said it wasn't that she didn't want to eat, she just couldn't. Like she had forgotten how to be hungry. She also stopped going to school, putting graduation at risk.

Sloane wasn't sure if she had a right to mourn with the family, but she visited her best friend every day, lying beside Stephie on her bed and telling her everything that had happened at school. The tragedy had overwritten Stephie's reputation—she was no longer the cool, rebellious, popular girl, but the sister of Benjamin Harrington who died. As long as she stayed in the town, she would always be The Sister. Sloane showed her photos of the "RIP Benjamin" posters the Student Council had put up in the hallways of the high school. Eventually, the posters dropped off the walls and footprints patterned the signs. Sloane didn't take any pictures of that.

Stephie never asked questions. Before leaving, Sloane would gather up the empty Gatorade bottles and take them home for recycling, replacing them with things Stephie liked before the tragedy—licorice nibs, the new Violent Downfall CD, a sketchpad and a set of pencils. Stephie spoke, often for the first time since Sloane arrived: "You'll come tomorrow?"

One day Sloane walked into Stephie's bedroom to find her smoking a cigarette while Violent Downfall blasted from the CD player. A surge of hope ignited her until she noticed pieces of paper scattered on the floor, the logo of the Tippett Valley Police letterhead visible. Drawings on pages torn from the sketchpad littered the bed. Piecing together the scene, Sloane concluded that the police had finally released their report on Benjamin's death, and Stephie had turned it into an art project.

When Sloane turned down the volume on the CD player, Stephie didn't react. Hesitantly, she approached the bed, where eight pencil sketches depicted Benjamin's death from different perspectives. He had died in the bathtub.

Sloane suddenly felt cold. According to the sketches, Benjamin had entered the bathroom, turned on the shower and fallen, his neck all scrunched up, his face pressed against the tub's bottom. His hair had clogged the drain. *Is that even possible?* How much artistic license had Stephie taken?

Sloane reached for the wall. *I told him to take a shower. If I hadn't kissed him, would I have taken him inside, made sure he got to bed?* She turned up the volume on the CD player, as far as the dial would rotate, but the music wasn't loud enough to silence her thoughts. She stared at Stephie, who lit another cigarette. *It's my fault your brother's dead.*

That summer Sloane's secret ate at her constantly. Stephie, once the fuel for her confidence, became a constant reminder of her guilt. To please her parents, Sloane enrolled at the university in Torren Hills, agonizing about whether to commute and live at home rent-free or take out student loans to cover the cost of living in residence. She finally decided she would stay in Torren Hills during the week and take the bus back to Tippett Valley on weekends.

She was getting out, but not with Stephie, who was four credits short of graduation. Stephie had finally left her room to hang out under the bleachers at the baseball diamonds. She became a regular at the Stairway.

Sloane insisted she spend her last night in Tippett Valley with Stephie. She was going to the Stairway, which meant so was Sloane. Watching her on the dance floor, Sloane barely recognized her best friend. She had dyed her hair jet black and cut it short in the back, leaving the front long. She chewed the ends of her bangs as if the strands were licorice sticks, the dye turning her tongue black. She wore colored contacts that made her look alien and baggy clothes that flopped around her like a parachute.

On the dance floor, a woman tripped and slid into Stephie, her stiletto heel penetrating Stephie's ankle like a dagger. Sloane shrieked and hurried to fetch a towel from the bartender.

Collapsed on the floor, Stephie rolled her ankle, wringing her flesh like a sponge, as if to encourage the loss of even more blood. Afraid of being caught serving minors, the manager had one of the bouncers drive them to the hospital, where Stephie received five stitches and a set of crutches. Joe and Jasmine picked them up, neither asking any questions.

"Remember when I was on crutches?" asked Sloane, breaking the silence on the drive back to the Stairway to pick up her dad's car.

Stephie didn't respond.

"In Grade 8, remember?"

Slowly, Stephie turned her head. "They talk about him like he's not a person anymore. He's a tragic story."

Chapter Eleven

SLOANE WOKE UP disoriented, kicking to release her feet from the blankets that bound her ankles. It all came back to her in a flash—Stephie's birthday, the Stairway, Nasser, and why she was in Randy Goff's bedroom. Sleep had taken her by surprise.

She fumbled with her phone. Three texts from Jason and the time was 8:08 a.m. *Shit!* She had to be at the agency in fifty-two minutes. With morning traffic, the drive from Tippett Valley to Torren Hills could take an hour. There wasn't time to stop at home. *I can't be late for work.* As much as she hated her job, unemployment would be worse.

When she entered the living room, Nasser was at the front door tying a shoe. "Sneaking out?" she said. She wasn't condemning him for it. He might actually be a nice guy, someone who might be good for Stephie, but she would only disappoint him. Sloane was sure Stephie would say something like, "I've got Randy and Bee," as if she didn't need anyone else. Not Nasser. Not even Sloane. It was a guilty thought, but sometimes she wished Randy would fall in love and Bee would die.

"Got work to get to," said Nasser. "You?"

Sloane nodded. In daylight, his youth was a surprise. *Twenty-one?*

"Cool fish," he said.

"That's Bee."

He dipped his finger into the fishbowl and stirred the water. "Like a bumblebee, right?" Bee swam in circles and then hid behind the plant at the bottom of his bowl.

"Stop it," snapped Sloane. "Probably feels like a hurricane to him."

Nasser dried his hand on his pants. "Let Gloria know I'll call?"

"Gloria?"

He waved a torn piece of paper like a sugar packet. "I got her number." He shoved it into his pocket.

Stephie had probably given him Jasmine and Joe's phone number. According to Roma, who ran into Jasmine at the grocery store, multiple men had called asking for various women, the persistent ones accurately describing Stephie. When Sloane told Randy, he said she was probably subconsciously telling her parents they were right to believe the fates had made a mistake, that the wrong Harrington child had been taken.

"Stephie's parents would never think that," Sloane refuted.

"It doesn't matter," said Randy. "It's what she believes."

"How could she think that?"

"We can convince ourselves of anything. It doesn't always have to be rational."

Nasser headed for the door. "See you around," he said.

Doubt it.

Refocusing, Sloane quickly checked her phone: 8:11 a.m. Jason had texted again, but there wasn't time to reply. She had to get to the agency. She went to retrieve her tote bag and found Stephie face down on her bed, sprawled out like a starfish, her ribs and veins visible beneath her skin, the scar on the back of her ankle a white line. Sloane tossed a blanket over her and scribbled a note onto a page in a blank sketchpad: "Text me when you wake up." Grabbing her bag, she hurried out. She was late for work.

Chapter Twelve

SLOANE'S FIRST WEEK at university seemed to fly by, and yet when she arrived back in Tippett Valley that Friday night, it was as if months had passed. For the first time, she noticed the smell of the steel plant. Roma picked her up at the bus depot, embracing her as if she'd been gone for months.

"Mom, you're hurting me."

Roma gave her daughter one more squeeze before letting go. "You look older," she said. "More mature."

"It's been six days, Mom."

"Do I look any different to you?"

"You look the same."

"I got my haircut. Your father didn't notice either."

Sloane got into the car, where Roma drilled her with questions about her classes, the campus, her closet-size room. "You can still change your mind," she said. "I haven't changed a thing in your bedroom."

"I like my residence room," said Sloane, which wasn't completely true. There was nothing likable about it, except that it wasn't in Tippett Valley.

"Have you made any friends? How about joining a club?"

Sloane looked out the window. As they passed the Harringtons', she asked, "Have you seen Stephie?"

"Ran into her aunt at the post office."

"Did she tell you about the abduction?"

"The what?"

"She answered Stephie's phone when I called. She told me Stephie hadn't left her room in three days and she had stopped eating again. I should've stayed in Tippy."

"That family has been through so much."

"She broke her stitches," said Sloane, "from the accident at the

Stairway. Stephie's aunt said they snapped because Stephie kept rotating her ankle, like she wanted them to break."

"Poor girl."

"So she abducted Stephie."

"Abducted?"

"Practically. Took her to a group therapy session for teenagers."

"Oh. Maybe that's a good thing, right?"

"Maybe."

Roma pulled into the Sawyers' driveway.

"Can I take the car?" asked Sloane.

"To where?"

"Stephie's."

"You just got here."

"I need to see her."

"You haven't even entered the house yet."

"I could walk if you'd prefer."

Roma sighed. "No, take the car. But be home in time for dinner. We need to see you, too."

"You want to see me. Stephie *needs* to."

When Sloane arrived at the Harringtons', Jasmine answered the door. She used to be one of those young-looking moms who everyone thought had her kids as a teenager. Now her cheeks were sunken and her skin had lost its luster. The lower curve of each eye was dark, reminding Sloane of athletes managing sun glare. She had lost at least thirty pounds, but she hadn't bothered to change her wardrobe. Her clothes hung loosely, threatening to drop to the floor.

"Hi," said Sloane. After five months, she still didn't know how to act around the Harringtons. She didn't want to add to the lingering sadness, but cheerfulness seemed insulting.

"She's upstairs," said Jasmine, walking away.

Sloane passed Stephie's dad in the living room. Joe half-grinned—never a full smile, never with teeth—and Sloane waved as if he were a mile away. He was, in a way.

Climbing the stairs, Sloane didn't know what to expect. After the conversation with Stephie's aunt, she had texted Stephie repeatedly about the therapy session. Finally, Stephie had replied. It was ok.

Sloane hadn't been able to tell if the reply was genuine or sarcastic, hopeful or apathetic.

Stephie's bedroom door was wide open. No need to lock it anymore. Sitting cross-legged beside Stephie on her bed was a boy.

"Oh. Hi," said Sloane, her voice dropping. "Who are you?"

He didn't avoid her, but he didn't make an effort to meet her eyes either. "Randy," he said.

He was different from the greasy, muscular boys Stephie was typically interested in. He looked a couple of years older, skinny with a lip ring. His right arm was the canvas for an entire sleeve of tattoos. His left arm was bare except for the inside of his forearm, which had *Anna 1992 - 2008* freshly tattooed in black ink. His jeans were as ripped as Stephie's and his shirt hadn't been white for a while. Sloane wondered if he reminded Stephie of her brother; Randy's hair was as long as Benjamin's had been.

"He's in my therapy group," said Stephie.

So he had lost someone, too. Anna. Randy understood what Sloane could only imagine. *Is he why Stephie's okay?* Jealousy nibbled at her heart.

"You live in Tippy?" she asked, attempting composure.

Randy nodded.

"He just moved here," said Stephie, "from Torren Hills."

"Who's Anna?"

Stephie answered. "His sister."

"You work at the steel plant?"

Randy shook his head. From his pocket, he removed a bag of marijuana and rolling papers. Stephie moved her crutches out of the way to give him more room.

"Were you just leaving?" asked Sloane, hoping Randy would take his drugs and go.

Stephie glared at Sloane. "No, he isn't," she said.

Randy rolled a joint. On the bed, his knee almost touched Stephie's. There was no room for Sloane; Randy was in her spot. Stephie kept sweeping his hair out of the way so it wouldn't get rolled into the joint. She laughed—Stephie *laughed*—and Sloane almost cried. Wasn't that what she wanted, for Stephie to be herself again? *Not because of him.*

"How's your ankle?" asked Sloane.

"Fine."

Stephie hobbled across the room to open the window. Randy followed and the two of them plopped down together on the floor.

"Your parents are just downstairs," said Sloane.

Stephie shrugged. "They don't care about anything anymore." She accepted the joint, blowing smoke out the window. An inch closer and she would be kissing Randy. His knuckles grazed hers and she didn't pull away or take a swing at him. Maybe she would sleep with him. The sooner the better: once she did, she would get bored, and Randy wouldn't be hanging out in her room anymore.

Sloane declined the offered joint. "Maybe I should go," she said. Stephie didn't argue, and Sloane held back tears. "I should visit my parents anyway."

As Stephie exhaled, she placed the joint between Randy's lips, holding it in place. The two of them were acting as if they had known each other for a lot longer than two days.

"Want to come over for dinner tonight?" asked Sloane. "Stephie, I mean." *Not you, Randy. Obviously.*

Stephie met Randy's eyes. "I think we're going to hang out."

He smiled. Not unkindly or boastfully, but worse: indifferently. Like he didn't care that Stephie had chosen him. It was then Sloane suspected there was something different about him.

"Are you . . ." she started. "Are you two . . ."

"Friends, Sloane."

"Right." In some ways, that was worse. "I guess I'll see you later then." *Without Randy.* She turned to go. Stephie didn't stop her.

This would never have happened if Sloane had stayed in Tippett Valley. She had promised she would visit every weekend, but she should have known it wouldn't be enough. Stephie hadn't even made it a week. Sloane could have taken extra high school credits—a victory lap, some called it—or gotten a job to save for university the following year, after Stephie graduated and they could leave together. Or she could have commuted the forty-five minutes to campus, like her parents expected. If Sloane had stayed, Stephie wouldn't need another friend.

At the top of the stairs, Sloane lingered, staring at Benjamin's closed bedroom door. As she approached it, she expected an alarm to sound or Jasmine and Joe to hurry upstairs or Stephie to stop her, but none of that happened. Not even when her palm landed on the doorknob. Not even when she turned it and the door clicked open. Not even when she entered Benjamin's room.

The space had a musty smell—not that much different from the rest of the house. Some of Benjamin's clothes were on the floor and his bed was unmade. A bottle of glasses cleaner sat poised on a bedpost and a half full—half empty?—glass of water had been left on the dresser. Dust had settled on everything.

Memories of Benjamin flooded back. She remembered how he had always wanted to join her and Stephie, promising to be quiet, to just sit in the same room, but Stephie never allowed it. As an only child, Sloane had learned the complicated relationship of siblings from the Harringtons—how a sister and brother could be so cruel despite loving each other; how one emotion was expressed regularly and the other rarely, and yet were both so passionately experienced, sometimes within a single day.

Catching Sloane's attention was a shoebox, half hidden under the bed. Inside was a collection of A+ school tests, notes from friends, a baseball, a yellow highlighter, gum wrappers, movie tickets and an oval-shaped drawing. At first she thought nothing of it, but then she realized what it was. It was her ear, drawn by Gina Anderson in Grade 8 art and later cut out by Stephie. *How'd Benjamin get this?*

Sloane suddenly realized how wrong it was to be in Benjamin's room, looking through a box of his memories. *I'm the reason he's dead.* The thought surfaced like an unexpected wave—sudden and explosive. She hurried downstairs. No one reacted as she bolted out of the house.

Chapter Thirteen

WITH ONE HAND on the steering wheel, Sloane reached into her tote bag and found a tube of toothpaste. She squirted a glob directly into her mouth and then used her tongue and index finger to spread it over her teeth. She swished from the water bottle she had left in the car overnight and decided swallowing was the least offensive option. She found her deodorant and dabbed it right onto her pants over the stain. She couldn't get to her hairbrush, but did the best she could with her fingers, arranging the strands to cover her ears. With a tissue, she cleaned her glasses without taking them off, all the while keeping an eye on the road. After yesterday's fashion mishap, she repeatedly examined the seams of her shirt. She blindly answered her vibrating phone.

"Hello?"

"Sloane?"

Jason. "Hi," she said, her voice laced with subtle irritation.

"Am I on speaker?" he asked.

"I'm driving."

"You didn't return my texts." He sounded rattled.

"*I* didn't return *your* texts?"

"I was worried," he said, missing her sarcasm.

Sloane squeezed the steering wheel. If he had looked at his phone earlier last night then she wouldn't have had to sleep in Randy Goff's bed. "I'm late for work."

"You okay?"

No.

Sloane checked herself. None of it was Jason's fault. She changed her tone. "Just tired," she said. "How was your night?"

"I missed you."

If you missed me, you would've checked your phone. "I texted," she said. "Like six times."

"I guess I got distracted."

"I know. Playing video games."

"I still missed you."

"You missed me while you were playing video games?"

"I miss you whenever you're not home."

Right.

"How's Stephie?" he asked.

"She's Stephie. I'm almost at work. Can we talk tonight?"

"Afternoon shift. Overtime, remember?"

"Oh. Right."

Afternoon shift started at three and ended at eleven, which meant she wouldn't be seeing her husband until tomorrow morning.

"Thought I'd stop in on your dad on my way to the plant," he said. "Make sure he's living up to your mom's standard while she's away. The Bruins are having a good start to the pre-season, so I'm sure he's doing fine."

"Okay. Good. Thanks."

"You could wait up for me tonight."

"I didn't get much sleep last night."

"You used to wait up, remember?"

It had been different then. She had been fifteen pounds lighter, hadn't been passed over for a transfer to Creative Services, still thought she could get pregnant and was looking forward to buying a house. When she used to wait up for Jason, she hadn't failed.

"I'm pulling into the lot," she said.

"Sloane, wait."

"What is it?"

She could hear him breathing. For a passing moment, she thought he might say something important. There were so many things that hadn't been said between them lately that the possibilities rolled through her mind like a grocery receipt printing.

"Jason?"

"We're out of coffee," he said.

Sloane folded her lips into each other. "I'll pick some up on my way home," she said. "It's garbage day tomorrow. Your turn."

"I'll put it out before I leave for work. Sloane?"

"Yeah?" She tapped her pass and the garage door slowly opened. It was 9:01 a.m. She prayed for a parking space close to the building's entrance.

"I—"

"Jason?"

Underground, the call had disconnected.

I love you.

Chapter Fourteen

IT WAS WEDNESDAY night, so Sloane was in her residence room studying when Stephie called.

"Stay on campus," she said.

"What?"

"Don't visit Tippy this weekend. Not for me."

Sloane put Stephie on speakerphone. "What would you do without me?" she joked.

"I've got Randy." Six months, and he was still there.

Sloane sucked in a quick inhale of breath. "Well, I don't have anyone here."

"You would," said Stephie, "if you didn't come back to Tippy every weekend."

"I like Tippy."

"You hate Tippy."

"So do you."

"Which is why I don't get why you keep coming back."

"Because *you're* in Tippy."

"So?"

"*So?*"

Stephie was in a mood, which meant she especially needed a visit.

"I'm coming," said Sloane.

"*Don't.*"

Sloane stilled. "Don't what?"

"Don't get on the bus on Friday." Stephie's voice had stiffened. "Stay in Torren Hills. Spend the weekend on campus."

You're serious? "There's nothing here for me to stay for," said Sloane.

"Don't you get it? There could be if you didn't spend your weekends in Tippy."

"You mean if I didn't spend my weekends with you." A tickle ignited the inside of her nose, causing her eyes to water. "You're my best friend."

"If you believe that, then that's the saddest thing I've ever heard."

That couldn't be true. Last year, she had learned her fifteen-year-old brother was dead. "Did you get high with Randy?" said Sloane. "Did you take something?"

"Geez, Sloane."

"We're best friends, Stephie."

"We *were* best friends. We're not kids anymore."

Sloane picked up her phone and pressed the receiver snug against her ear. "But I want to see you," she said.

"I'm moving in with Randy."

"What?"

"Don't take the bus to Tippy on Friday."

"Stephie," Sloane breathed. "Stephie?"

The line was dead.

Sloane waited for Stephie to call back. She was likely high on something she had gotten from Randy. When she sobered up or came down, she would call back to apologize. Or maybe she wouldn't remember anything she had said. Either way, everything would be okay. Even if Stephie was moving in with Randy.

Panic set in on Thursday night when Stephie still hadn't called. What did people do on campus without classes? She was fine spending her evenings studying as long as there was an end to them every Friday night. Getting her homework done during the week meant it didn't interfere with weekends in Tippett Valley. But an entire weekend by herself in Torren Hills? What would she do? *She'll call. She will.*

Making friends had never been easy and Sloane hadn't made much effort to meet anyone in residence. Last semester, Elizabeth down the hall had invited her to a party, but Sloane had declined in favor of going home to Tippett Valley. She hadn't invited her anywhere since. On Friday afternoon, Sloane noticed Elizabeth's door was open.

"Hey," she said, pretending to be just walking by.

Elizabeth looked over from her computer. "Hey," she said, in a way Sloane interpreted as awkward.

Oh, God. "Sorry," said Sloane, moving on.

Elizabeth caught up to her in the hallway. "Hey, you need something?"

"I was just saying hi."

"Oh. Hey then."

"Hey."

Elizabeth was as short as Sloane and just as wide, but more proportionate. Her face was pretty—clear skin, blue eyes, thick eyelashes—and her lip was pierced like Randy's, except her ring was off-center to the right instead of off-center to the left.

"I might be staying on campus this weekend," said Sloane.

It looked as if Elizabeth were trying to thread her tongue through her lip ring. "Oh. Okay."

"I don't know, maybe we could, maybe . . . I don't know."

Shut up, Sloane. "I might still be going back to Tippy tonight, so."

"If you do end up staying on campus and need a break from studying, knock on my door."

"Okay."

Before she could come off any more desperate, Sloane entered her room. She had three new voicemails, all from Roma.

Despite Stephie's warning, Sloane considered getting on the Friday bus. But if Stephie refused to see her in Tippett Valley she would be stuck spending the weekend with her parents. If she stayed in Torren Hills, maybe she and Elizabeth could do something together. Sloane finally decided she would go to the student center with her packed bag. She could watch the buses pulling in and out and be ready when Stephie called.

The café was full of worn furniture crammed so closely

together that students had to leap over couches and chairs to get a seat in front of one of the dozen TVs. Coffee stains patterned the cushions and the carpet, and the windows were streaked with soot. Sloane claimed the couch closest to the window, with a view of the bus stop.

When the bus to Tippett Valley departed, Sloane was stunned. She called home to let her mom know she wouldn't be visiting this weekend. Roma offered to drive to Torren Hills and spend the night.

"Mom, you can't. I think it's illegal. I swear I read that somewhere in the residence rules. Besides, shouldn't I spend a weekend on campus?" *No. I should be taking the bus to Tippy.*

Sloane hid in her room, reading. Over the weekend her phone rang a dozen times; each time it was Roma, never Stephie, encouraging her to go for a walk, to attend a campus event, to talk to someone. She finally summoned the courage to knock on Elizabeth's door, but there was no answer. She didn't try a second time.

The following Friday, Sloane again watched buses come and go, her bag at her feet. Stephie hadn't texted or called for nine days. It had to be a record in their friendship. Eventually Sloane had to call Roma to let her know she was staying another weekend on campus. It wasn't any less startling the second time. "It's fine, Mom. I want to." Tears welled in her eyes. "Have you seen Stephie around?"

Roma hadn't. "Promise me you'll talk to at least one person," she said.

Sloane kept her promise. When she went down for lunch in the residence cafeteria, she noticed the cashier had a copy of *The Hunger Games* beside her register. The book had just been published last September; Roma had given it to Sloane as a going away gift and she had read it over three nights. "I wish I was half as brave as Katniss," she said, loudly.

The cashier smiled. "Me too."

Sloane kept up the Friday night routine for a third week. In the café, she tried to read *Gulliver's Travels* for her second semester Satire in Literature class, but instead her eyes volleyed from the window to her phone, not wanting to miss activity from either. Behind her, two guys plugged in a game console and shared a couch. The soundtrack from the video game had a hypnotic quality, music that might have put Sloane to sleep except that every few minutes the player wearing a ball cap would drive his controller into the cushion or jab it toward his opponent, depending on whether he lost or won. Each time, Sloane turned around, but it was his opponent who captured Sloane's interest. He smiled, calm and focused, neither a sore loser nor a boastful winner. His hair was dark, short and spiked, naturally jutting out from his scalp. He had thick eyebrows, and when he smiled an M&M candy could fit into each dimple.

"Excuse me."

Sloane turned. It was him.

"Hi," he said, as animated as he had been since Sloane had noticed him.

She looked around, not sure he was talking to her.

"Can I ask you a favor?" he said.

"Me?"

He smiled. "Can you play a round in my turn? I'll be right back."

"Can't you just pause it?"

He shook his head. "I don't trust him." His opponent was tugging on his shirt, fanning himself. Beads of perspiration hugged the hairs flaring out beneath his cap.

"I don't know anything about video games," said Sloane.

"You just have to press this red button," he explained, demonstrating. "As fast as you can." He encouraged her to take the controller.

"That's it?"

"That's it."

"What if I lose?"

"You'll rack up more points than if he plays without me."

Sloane hesitated, and then accepted the controller. It was warm and damp, almost greasy, but not in a gross way, more in a massage oil kind of way. *Oh, God.*

He stood. "I'm Jason, by the way."

Like spooling thread, Sloane quickly wound strands of hair around each index finger, then released the curls to fall over her ears. "Sloane," she said.

He flung his chin at his opponent. "That's Brad. He's not to be trusted." Jason smiled and Sloane looked away. "I'll be right back. As soon as you see him start, you press the red button."

"As fast as I can."

"You got it."

Sloane twisted completely around. She leaned over the back of the couch, her knees sinking into the cushion, focused on Brad's hands. He pressed a thin black button and then started going wild on the red one. Sloane jabbed her index finger as fast as she could on her own red button. On the TV, balls or bullets shot out of some kind of a gun and all kinds of other things started flying around, shrapnel maybe. Sloane couldn't follow what was going on, so she concentrated on the controller. When one finger tired, she just switched to another, each finger equally strong and accurate. She had won the typing competition each year of high school. It was her advantage over Brad.

It took much more exertion than she expected. Her body heated and she worried she was starting to look like Brad, with his flushed cheeks and sweaty shirt. Then he drove his controller into the cushion hard enough to lose his grip. It rebounded, hitting him in the face. Without a word, he left the café, passing Jason on his way out.

"What happened?" asked Sloane, when Jason returned. "Did I do okay?"

He read the TV screen. "More than okay," he said, looking impressed. "You won."

"Really?"

When Sloane tried to return the controller, Jason wouldn't take it. "Oh, no," he said. "I want to see this." He picked up Brad's controller. "You can sit here if you'd like," he said, patting the cushion beside him.

Sloane hesitated.

"Unless you want to get back to your reading."

"I wasn't really reading," Sloane admitted.

Jason stood. "Can I get you something to drink?"

Sloane cleared her throat. "Oh. A water, I guess," she said. "Thanks."

While Jason was at the café counter, Sloane stuffed her book and phone into her bag, and then clambered onto the couch in front of the TV. She wanted to be the first to sit, leaving it to Jason to determine how close they would be. That would tell her a lot.

Jason returned with two bottles of water and sat. Close to Sloane. So close that, if she weren't careful, her thigh could slide into his.

As he settled, he asked, "What's your major?"

"English," she answered. "You?"

"Computer Science. First year?"

Sloane nodded. "You?"

"Same. First year. Ready?"

Sloane aimed her index finger at the red button. "Ready."

She was used to typing without looking, so she studied Jason while she jabbed at the controller and he focused on the TV screen. The left leg of his jeans was wrinkled at the ankle; he probably tucked his pant leg into his sock so it wouldn't get caught in a bicycle chain. Stubble peppered his chin and jawline, but his cheeks were bare of any shadow. She was curious what his hair felt like, if it was sharp like a thousand sewing needles or soft like fur. Maybe it was something in between, like floor carpet. The muscles in his arms pulsated as his thumbs pressed the buttons on the controller. He didn't seem to care who won or lost the game; when the game ended, he just started another.

"Were you going somewhere tonight?" he asked, eyeing her bag.

"I was, but not anymore."

"Home for the weekend?"

Sloane nodded.

"Decided to stay?"

"Something like that."

"Fight with the folks?"

"Fight with the best friend."

"Want to tell me about it?"

"No."

"Okay. Tell me something else then."

"Like what?"

"What book were you reading?"

"Just *Gulliver's Travels*. For class."

"Not a book you'd chose to read?"

Sloane shrugged. "It's okay. I prefer contemporary fiction."

"You have a favorite book?"

"I couldn't pick just one. I really like Miriam Toews. Have you read anything by her? *A Complicated Kindness*?"

Jason shook his head. "Where did you grow up?"

"Tippy. Tippett Valley."

The next thing Sloane knew, she was describing to Jason what it was like growing up in a small town with an overbearing mother and a father who worked a lot of overtime at a steel plant. Then somehow she started telling him about her recent—though surely temporary—falling out with her best friend. For the story to make sense, she had to explain who Stephie Harrington was, and how the two of them had been best friends since Grade 8. Then unexpectedly, Sloane said, "Her brother died last year. It changed her. It changed us." She met Jason's attentive eyes. Embarrassed, she looked away. "I can't believe I told you that." *What's wrong with me?*

"Go on," he encouraged.

"We were supposed to leave Tippy together," she said. "But

she had to stay, to finish high school. She's moving out of her parents'. She's just probably really busy with that right now." Sloane's palms were sweating. "Tell me something about you." *Please.*

"My mom raised me on her own." He smiled, and his dimples stole Sloane's attention. "She's kind of a superhero." Jason grew up in a basement apartment in a small town several hours away. He fell in love with video games at eleven, when his mom bought an Atari 2600 with Pac-Man taped to it at a yard sale. Moving to Torren Hills had been a hard decision, but the Computer Science program was one of only a few that offered a focus in game design, and his mom had encouraged him to follow his dream. "Like I said, superhero."

"You have a favorite?" asked Sloane. "Video game, I mean."

Jason smiled. "I couldn't pick just one. I just bought Dead Space. It's awesome."

Sloane pointed to the TV. "Is it like this one?"

"Nah. This is vintage. Not that there aren't great aspects of older games. I still play the classics but better technology has allowed for some really cool capabilities."

He told Sloane the history of game consoles, listing brands she had never heard of, and described all the different game genres—action, role-playing, simulation, strategy, sports, puzzle, and more. He told her the back story for Dead Space, something about trying to survive on a futuristic spaceship with aliens.

"Am I boring you?"

"No. Go on," she said. His passion was genuinely entertaining.

Sloane suddenly realized Jason wasn't holding a controller, and neither was she. They had abandoned the game long ago. She checked her phone and discovered she had spent the past two hours with Jason. Six times Roma had called, likely because Sloane had neglected to let her mom know she wouldn't be on the bus to Tippett Valley.

"I have to go," she said, gathering her bag.

Jason ran his fingers through his short hair. "Would you want to do this again?" he asked.

"I don't usually play video games."

"It doesn't have to be that. We could do something else."

Sloane froze. "Oh, um." *Are you asking me on a date?*

"It was really nice talking with you," he said.

"Really?"

He unplugged the game console from the TV and started winding the cord. "We can meet here," he said. "Tomorrow night?"

"Okay." She cleared her throat and said it again louder, so Jason could actually hear.

"Seven o'clock?"

Sloane nodded.

"You live on campus? I can walk you if you'd like."

Sloane flung her bag over her shoulder so hard that the momentum pushed her forward. She almost grabbed onto Jason's arm but caught the armrest of a couch instead. "I'm just across the path," she said, recovering.

"Still, if you'd like."

"It'd be like fifteen steps."

"In the dark."

Sloane looked out the window. "Okay. Thanks."

Chapter Fifteen

ON TUESDAY MORNING, Sloane sat down at her desk at 9:06 a.m., tired and hungry with a pounding headache. She regretted drinking on a work night. Dark circles discolored the pits of her shirt, but there was no time to regroup in a washroom stall—she had already cost the agency six minutes and she didn't want to contribute more to the spike in Joan's graph. She yanked her shirt over her thighs to cover the stain on her pants and turned on her computer. Finally settled, she turned around, bracing for Joan's glare.

But Joan wasn't in her office. Sloane relaxed, but only for a moment. Something wasn't right: the lights in her office were off. Joan had a reputation for being the first to arrive and the last to leave and almost never scheduled personal appointments during business hours. Not once had she been late or called in sick or even taken a vacation day. Sloane had never been at her desk without the lights from Joan's office illuminating her back.

She checked her voicemail: a few hang-ups but no messages. She checked her email next. One message from Irving, sent last night: "Closes tomorrow." Attached was the job posting for the open graphic designer position. It was the third time Irving had sent it to her. Like the previous two times, she fired off a quick thank you, adding, "Loved your Langley Jewellers ad. Perfect use of whitespace."

Not one email from Joan. *What if something's happened?* Sloane suddenly regretted her negative thoughts, all the times she was upset because Joan hadn't thanked her for her work or noticed the extra effort she had put into a task. Joan could have been in a car accident; she could have fallen down the stairs; she could have been kidnapped and was being held for ransom. *Or maybe this is a test.*

One of Sloane's responsibilities was to track attendance. If an employee was two hours late and hadn't contacted their department's Executive Manager, then policy dictated that the Executive Manager was to call the employee. If the employee couldn't be reached, their emergency contact was to be tried. It was 9:11 a.m. Joan wasn't answering her phone and she was more than two hours behind her normal arrival time. Sloane couldn't begin to calculate *that* cost.

The agency had a single file for emergency contacts that was managed by Human Resources and shared with each department's Executive Manager. Scrolling through the list, Sloane found Joan Dawes. Her emergency contact was . . . *Joan Dawes?* A typo, it had to be. Maybe it was supposed to be John Dawes. Or maybe Joan was named after her mother. If Joan really didn't have an emergency contact, then Sloane wouldn't be all that surprised. Joan practically lived at the agency, was feared by most of her staff and intimidated most of her colleagues. As far as Sloane could tell, Joan had no interest in anything unrelated to revenue.

Sloane dialed the number on file and was connected to a voice messaging service in Joan's familiar voice. She hung up. To ensure she passed the test—if it was a test—she dialed the number again and left a message this time, informing Joan Dawes that Joan Dawes hadn't arrived for work, nor had she called to confirm her whereabouts. "On behalf of the Kaye Agency," said Sloane, in her most professional voice, "we're concerned." She left her direct line for Joan Dawes, the emergency contact, to return her call.

Sloane idly scrolled down the spreadsheet to find her name, confirming Jason Howard was her emergency contact. Scrolling up, she stopped on Irving Paulson. His emergency contact was Marguerite Paulson, his sister, also a graphic designer. Irving had once sent Sloane a link to a website that featured one of Marguerite's designs. "For inspiration," he had written. "Perhaps we can discuss your Lakeside Motors design over coffee." Sloane was designing a poster for a client of Mark Grier, one of the agency's account managers, to advertise a charity barbeque. As this was a goodwill gesture with no revenue attached, Irving had suggested to Mark that he talk to Sloane. Mark was grateful for Sloane's help, and Sloane appreciated the opportunity but she never followed up Irving's coffee invitation.

Sloane scrolled up some more and found Adele. Her emergency contact was . . . Travis Wright? Why not Lawrence Avery? Maybe Adele had updated her information after listening to his voicemail.

As if summoned, Sloane's desk phone rang, showing Adele Mack. Sloane answered in her agency voice, just in case Joan walked in. "Good morning. Account Services. Sloane Sawyer speaking."

"Sloane?" Adele's voice was gruff.

"Adele? You don't sound like you."

"You don't sound like you, either."

"I had the worst night. You too?"

"Not the worst." Adele's breakup with Travis had likely been the worst. Firsts were always the hardest.

"Did you break up with Lawrence last night?"

"No. I'm ignoring his calls."

"You haven't talked to him since the voicemail?"

"Remember Steve?"

"The guy who lost his license because of his seizures?"

"He got his license back."

"Oh. Does that mean he's a candidate again?"

"Sloane, I'm out of time. My birthday's on Sunday." She paused. "Eva wants to have a party. She doesn't understand that sometimes a birthday isn't the best day of the year."

Sloane suddenly remembered Joan might be in trouble. "Have you seen Joan?"

"No." Adele cleared her throat. "But Gary's on his way over."

"What?"

"Sloane." A different voice. Close. In person.

Sloane stood so fast that her glasses fell off her face. She caught them mid-air, the frames crushing in her hand. "Gary!" She hung up the phone and slid her glasses back on, her gaze erratic. She

97

couldn't remember ever being this close to him. He smelled fresh and clean, like mouthwash.

"Hi," she said, her cheeks heating. She smiled—*Oh God, am I flirting?*—and Gary looked at her strangely. Only in a novel would someone as desirable as Gary Goldman be attracted to someone like Sloane Sawyer. Still, in her head she wrote her own fantasy. As if his freckles were tickling, his nose twitched.

He eyed the flickering light above her desk. "You should submit a work order for that."

"I'm used to it." She yanked on her shirt again, conscious of the stain on her pants. "Everything okay?"

"The presentation file won't open," he said, frowning. "Joan needs you."

The quarterly review presentation! She had been pretending to work on the already-completed PowerPoint for days. Scanning the office floor, she realized the cubicles were empty. *How didn't I notice how quiet it is?* Technically IT support wasn't in her job description, but whenever Joan had a presentation, Sloane would arrive early to set up the laptop and screen. That had been her plan before Stephie had flouted the birthday tradition, before Sloane had woken up in Randy Goff's bed hungover and late. *How could I have forgotten?*

"We'd better hurry," said Gary.

We? She had been waiting five years for Gary to say "we." But he was supposed to be walking her to the President's office and announcing her transfer to Creative Services, not escorting her to the conference room to face her furious boss. Joan seemed able to control anyone and anything, except technology. Sloane imagined her fumbling with the laptop, her mouth tight, as the room sat fearfully silent. She quickened her pace.

"Joan's been trying to get a meeting with Daniel," said Gary, just barely keeping up.

"Brownwood's new CEO?" asked Sloane. Of course Daniel Brownwood; his name had only been brought up around the office a hundred times over the past month.

"Apparently the new marketing manager isn't 'connecting' with Lenore."

Sloane could understand that; she didn't have anything in common with Lenore, either. "Joan can assign a new manager for the account," she said. It was a standard solution to a clash of personalities.

"She has to get a meeting with Brownwood first," said Gary, swinging open the conference room doors, "and rumor has it he might be available for a call this morning."

In the doorway, Sloane hesitated. The dark blue carpet and small sea of employees wearing black clothes and distraught expressions made her think of survivors of a shipwreck. The only color in the room was where Creative Services sat together. She blinked hard and straightened her glasses.

Irving was at the front of the room, fiddling with the laptop. His attempt to help Joan really was an act of valor. Joan's fists were on her hips, her toe tapping impatiently. When the first slide of the presentation suddenly projected onto the screen, the collective exhale in the room sounded like a wave meeting the shoreline. That was when Joan's gaze met Sloane's.

"Sloane," she said loudly.

Sloane turned to escape, but Gary was blocking the exit. "Go on," he said, giving her an encouraging smile.

She turned slowly. *Is she really going to blame me in front of the entire team?*

Joan hurried across the conference room floor. As she approached, every muscle in Sloane's body tensed. Then in the doorway, she pushed past Sloane without a word.

"I'll reschedule the presentation," Sloane told Gary.

He shook his head. "Joan wants you to present it."

"What?" *I didn't even shower this morning!*

Sloane surveyed the room. All eyes were on her.

"You put it together, didn't you?"

She nodded. The last time she had presented anything was in university to a small group of students and a teaching assistant.

Knowing how nervous she got, Jason had slipped into the back of the room. His presence made her feel that everything was going to be okay. But everything wasn't going to be okay today, not if she failed and got fired. Jason would have to pick up more overtime shifts. *Is this my punishment for being late?*

"Go on," Gary encouraged.

Numb, Sloane made her way to the front of the room, where Irving handed her the clicker. She accepted it as if it were a gun, like she didn't know how to use it, like she didn't want to know how to use it, like it went against her morals just to handle it. She longed for Jason. From the back of the room, Gary smiled but it wasn't the same. He didn't have dimples.

The crowd was growing even more restless, shifting in their chairs. Now that Joan was no longer in the room, some of the account managers were on their phones. Inhaling deeply, Sloane held the air in her lungs, which made it feel as if her neck were swelling. Her eyes watered. Finally, she exhaled. She cleared her throat and, with the quickest swipe of her sleeve, absorbed the perspiration from her chin. Reaching for the podium, she squeezed the edge until her fingers turned white. At least it hid the stain on her pants. In her hand, the presentation clicker was so wet she was concerned it would slip out of her grasp.

Then, as if pulled by a string, her chin lifted. *I can do this.* She hummed, testing her voice. Though shaky, it was there. "Thank you," she shouted, causing those in the front row to lean back in their chairs. She glanced at the Creative Services team and was surprised to realize there was a small part of her that hadn't given up. Adrenaline rushed through her veins. "We'll get started," she said.

Chapter Sixteen

SLOANE MET JASON in the student center. He was sitting on their couch in the café—it was "their" couch now—his knees bouncing and his eyes jetting around the large room. Sloane worried she was late.

Roma had phoned just as she was leaving her room. The only reason she had answered her phone was because Stephie still wasn't picking up hers and talking with her mom seemed a better option than pacing her room. She didn't want to arrive early and risk appearing too eager. On the phone, Sloane made the mistake of mentioning that she had spent the day in the library researching video-game development. She eventually revealed her evening plans and then couldn't get off the phone, not without first answering the one hundred questions—literally one hundred questions—Roma had about "this Jason boy."

In the student center, Sloane was trying to be cool, but really she was freaking out. She had barely slept the previous night, unable to stop thinking about Jason. She couldn't decide if tonight was a first date or if the night before had qualified as one. If it was a second date, it didn't make her less nervous. *What if Jason doesn't think either is a date?*

As Sloane entered the café, she began to question her choice of wardrobe. She had settled on jeans, a gray sweater with extra-long cuffs and flat black ankle boots. She kept her hair down to cover her ears and rejected her contacts, which made her eyes itchy, in favor of her glasses, which she hoped made her look smart, but not too smart. Elizabeth approved. She also said that sitting on a couch with a guy for two hours and then being walked home by him definitely qualified as a date. Elizabeth was cool; Sloane wondered why it had been so hard to knock on her door.

When Jason spotted Sloane, he sprang to his feet. He was wearing dark jeans and a black long-sleeved shirt with round blue buttons that looked like candy. The tiny red dots of dried blood on his neck were evidence he had shaved. He had cleaned his sneakers too; they almost looked new. *Definitely a date, right?*

"Hi," he said.

Sloane's eyes dropped. "Hi."

Jason rubbed his knuckles. "Will you walk with me to the Computer Science building?"

Sloane nodded. She would have agreed to anything.

"I've got an assignment to submit," he said. "Does that make it the worst date ever?"

Confirmed: Date.

Sloane's chin lifted. "No," she said, relieved she didn't have to be the one to decide what they would do. "It's fine, really."

The Computer Science building was at the opposite end of campus. Jason walked close; not touching Sloane, but at a distance that would require little effort to take her hand. She liked the possibility and kept swiping her clammy palm down her pant leg, just in case.

During the walk, Jason told Sloane about Game Design—his favorite class this semester—and how his homework was to play video games and write an essay on what makes a game fun. She told him about the essay she was writing for her English Lit course—how the roles of men and women are portrayed in *The Handmaid's Tale*—and the eight other books on the semester's syllabus. Jason said he couldn't imagine getting through a single novel, let alone eight. Sloane replied that she couldn't imagine playing an entire video game. Ever. Or reading a textbook on computer code. Jason laughed.

"But I'm reading a book on typography," she said. "It's amazing how the arrangement of text can affect a design."

"What class is that for?"

"No class. Just interested in it."

"You have the time?"

"I'm really organized." She didn't want to admit that she didn't have any friends on campus to spend her spare time with.

"So you're interested in graphic design?"

Sloane nodded. "I get excited about typefaces." *I'm talking about fonts! On a date!*

"I get it," said Jason. "Yesterday, I got a rush out of creating the texture for a shirt on a character standing in the background of the scene."

He reached for the side of her face. "Sorry," he said. "Your hair was just caught around your ear."

Sloane was sure her face had turned red. "It's okay," she said, looking away. She didn't want to discuss the shape of her ears.

"What kind of things do you like to design?" asked Jason.

"Band posters," said Sloane. It wasn't true—she hadn't designed a single one—but it was what she and Stephie were going to specialize in when they started their business together. "Stephie does the drawings and I do the design. Well, that's what's going to happen. We haven't actually collaborated on anything yet. She's taking a little break from sketching right now, but after she graduates high school, she's going to go to art school. We'll start our business then."

"You've got it all planned out."

"What's your game going to be like?"

"I've just started to map it out. I'm a long way from writing code. There's a lot to consider first."

"Like all the game assets?"

Jason looked impressed. "Yes, exactly."

"There's the characters," she said, "and the tools and the choices they have to make to try to defeat the obstacles, whatever they are, and sound effects and background music and scenery, not to mention the whole purpose of the game, the plot, and if it should be in 2D or 3D. 3D pixels are like digital clay." The concept had made her smile in the library. "Will you use Unity?" She had read that Unity was a popular new game engine.

"You sure you're not secretly minoring in game development?

Maybe when I'm finally ready to build my game, I'll hire you on the team."

"I'm not really into playing video games," said Sloane.

"It's not so different from reading novels, I imagine. You escape in a book, don't you? Games are just a different way of telling stories."

By the time they arrived at the Computer Science building, Sloane wasn't as nervous. Jason led her into an empty lab, where he turned on one of the computers. It felt dangerous to Sloane, for no other reason than she and Jason were alone. It wasn't as if they had broken in; Jason had swiped his student card to unlock the door. He rolled a chair over for Sloane to sit next to him. "I just need a minute," he said.

He double-clicked an icon on the desktop and the screen filled with colored text—letters and numbers and symbols—a language Sloane didn't understand. "What is it?" she asked.

"Source code." He clicked the mouse and the screen changed to an image of a house. "It's just a simple background for a hypothetical game scene, but it took me all week to get it right." He laughed. "What do you think?"

"It's nice," she said.

"Would you live in it?"

Sloane hesitated, and Jason frowned.

"You wouldn't," he said.

"It's not that," she said, quickly. "What about a white picket fence?"

Jason's eyes expanded. "Okay. A white picket fence."

Sloane watched the muscles in his forearms constrict and relax as his hands jigged over the keyboard, his fingers stabbing the keys in a surprisingly even rhythm. Focused on the screen, he was able to keep his eyes open for long periods of time. Sloane counted: he blinked every nine seconds. The range of his thick eyebrows was impressive, able to climb high on his forehead and then drop so low they crowded his nose and forced his eyes to shrink. If Sloane listened carefully, she could hear his throat humming. Squinting, she could see his Adam's apple vibrating or maybe she just thought she could. He stopped typing, but only for a moment, to push up a sleeve that had slid to his wrist. His eyes didn't shift from the screen. He was so focused that Sloane wondered if he had forgotten she was there.

Then suddenly, his chair rolled back. "There," he said. "Would you live there now?"

On the screen was the image of the house, now with a white picket fence. An unsettled feeling entered Sloane, similar to the emotion that struck her when the bus to Tippett Valley passed the town's welcome sign.

She nodded, but her thoughts had been hijacked. Jason spun around in his chair and smiled. As if his dimples were a set of headlights, Sloane looked away.

He placed his hands on the armrests of her chair. If she were an experienced kisser, she would know what was about to happen. But she wasn't, and she was fighting off memories, so she didn't expect him to lean in. She jerked back.

He reacted so quickly that the back of his chair smashed into the one behind it. "Sorry," he said. "I shouldn't have done that."

"No," she said, digging her fingernails into her thighs. Tears threatened to escape her eyes. "You didn't do anything wrong."

"We can go," he said, hurrying to submit his project.

"Wait."

"It's okay," he assured her, standing. "I get it."

She grabbed his arm, wanting him to stop. "You don't," she said firmly. How could he know that she wanted to kiss him? He froze and she let him go. "It's just . . ."

"You don't find me attractive."

"No! I mean, yes. Yes, I find you attractive. Very attractive."

"You have a boyfriend."

"No."

"You like someone else."

"No. There's no one else."

"Should I keep guessing?"

105

With her eyes closed, she shook her head. "You'll never guess right."

He sat and rolled his chair closer, eliminating the space that had so abruptly grown between them. "Why don't you tell me what's going on?" he said gently. "You can trust me."

Can I?

"What is it?"

"Nothing."

"Something." He leaned forward. "Sloane," he whispered. "Please tell me what's going on."

"It's just . . ."

"What?"

"Well . . ."

"Yes?"

"I have lethal lips," she blurted out.

His eyes widened. "Is that code for . . . herpes?"

"No! The last person I kissed—" Like a gate, her throat closed. "The last person I kissed—" She couldn't.

"Turned into a prince."

"No."

"Should I keep guessing?"

"The last person I kissed . . . died."

Jason leaned back. Sloane immediately regretted saying anything. It wasn't something to tell someone on a date. Her attempts to contain her sobs made her sound like a frog. Jason shimmied forward and pressed his kneecaps into hers.

"What happened?" he asked.

Sloane swiped her sleeve under her nose. "I told you, he died."

"Right after you kissed him."

"A few hours after. That night."

"Was he allergic to your lip chap?"

"No. He fell. In a bathtub."

"How did your kiss cause him to fall in a bathtub?"

"If I hadn't kissed him, then I would've been there."

"In the bathtub?"

"In the house. I would've heard him fall."

"So he still would've fallen, even if you hadn't kissed him."

"He wouldn't have drowned."

"He drowned?"

Sloane nodded. "I would've heard him fall in the bathtub, if I was in the house, which I would've been, if we hadn't kissed, then he wouldn't have drowned."

She had never said these things out loud to anyone. She suddenly realized she was holding Jason's hand. When she moved to slip out of his grasp, he gently clamped down on her fingers. His thumb rubbed over her knuckles and she stopped pulling away.

"What happened?" he asked, his voice a whisper.

There was something about the way he was looking at her that made her feel like she could tell him the truth. If she turned out to be wrong, and Jason never wanted to see her again, then at least she had tested the truth on someone who wasn't her best friend. Letting her thoughts have a voice was strangely cathartic, and Jason was inviting her to tell him the truth. To tell him her secret.

So she told him about Tina Johnson's party, about her kiss with Benjamin, how she had driven him home but didn't even get out of the car, and how he passed out and drowned in an inch of water, his hair clogging the drain. She ended with the worst detail of all: "I told him to take a shower. To sober up. So Stephie wouldn't get in trouble. It's my fault he died."

Jason's knees slid to the outside of Sloane's shaking legs. He was silent. Speechless. His hands lifted and his fingers marched up her wrists, raising the hair on her arms. Released, Sloane sank into the chair, trying to pull herself together. Then Jason's hands were on her wet cheeks, gently lifting her chin. He was so close she had nowhere to look but into his eyes.

What are you doing?

"I'm going to kiss you. Is that okay?"

Sloane held Jason's wrists. "After the story I just told you?"

"It's sad. Terrible, really. I'm sorry for what happened and how you feel about it, but it doesn't make me not want to kiss you."

Sloane was sure she looked awful. "Like this?"

"Just like this."

He gently moved her hair away from her face. Sloane tried to turn away, but it was too late. No doubt her ears were visible. Before he could comment, she said, "I don't like my ears."

"I do. May I kiss you?"

It was her first kiss since Benjamin. Against Sloane's dry, chapped mouth, his lips were soft and warm and moist. The kiss was quick, but not rushed.

"You okay?" asked Jason.

Sloane smiled. She couldn't help it. For the first time since the tragedy, she didn't feel like a monster. She knew that wouldn't last forever, but Jason had shown her that it was possible to be wanted. He had listened to her story and kissed her anyway.

"I've never told anyone," she said. "If Stephie ever found out the truth about that night, she would never forgive me. Promise me you won't tell anyone."

"I promise," he said.

Sloane believed him.

"Do you want to go somewhere else?" he asked.

"Where?"

"I've never been to the English building."

"I can take you."

Chapter Seventeen

SLOANE WAS ON the last slide already. She glanced at the clock. *I've been talking for twenty minutes!* She had been so focused on not fainting that time had passed unnoticed. *Did I speed through the revenue numbers too quickly? Did the graphic designers notice the spacing, the choice of color, the font in the graphs? Was Irving the only one paying attention?*

"Are there any questions?" *Please no questions.*

The audience stood all at once, dozens of disembodied heads levitating like helium balloons. Gary swung open the doors and the room emptied.

Sloane's thigh throbbed, punctured twice by the edge of the podium, the only two moments during the presentation she vividly recalled. Both times, the impact had caused the laptop to teeter on the edge of the platform. The second time, the laptop had disconnected from the screen and the presentation went dark. Irving had jumped out of his seat to reattach the cord.

She hurried to the washroom and spent the next fifteen minutes drying in a stall.

When she returned to her desk, Joan was in her office in the dark, typing on her laptop and talking on the phone, while she threaded the toe of her shoe through the handle of a file cabinet. Sloane was impressed. But she was also angry for being punished so severely. It had been six minutes—a cost to the agency of $2.80. What about the times she had been early or had stayed a few minutes late? She had never been asked to build *that* graph. At least she had gotten through the presentation. Not everyone survived Joan's retribution. Sloane wanted Joan's praise, or at least the assurance that her job was secure, but this was the last day she wanted scrutiny. The agency was at risk of losing its top client; Joan had bigger worries. Wordlessly, Sloane sat at her desk.

There was a sticky note attached to her computer: "Lights dead – JD." Sloane immediately submitted a work order to Michael in Maintenance. Years ago, she had designed the invitation for his wife's baby shower and had received priority service ever since. Within thirty minutes, Michael was changing the light bulbs in Joan's office. Sloane wondered if her boss knew how uncommon it was for Maintenance to respond so quickly. She thought of asking him to fix the flickering light above her desk, but she couldn't be bothered.

Surreptitiously, she checked her cell phone, expecting a text from Jason and hoping for one from Stephie. Instead, there were two from Roma.

10,120! How many?

Have you checked in on your dad?

Quickly, Sloane replied. If she ignored her mom, Roma would just keep texting. Or worse, would call in a panic.

5,100 already. Before lunch! Bruins are winning, so Dad's fine.

She closed her drawer and opened her email. Adele was canceling lunch again. Apparently Eva was sick and Travis was stuck at work. Sloane couldn't believe Adele was willing to take a half-day off work and an hour bus ride to bring soup to her ex-boyfriend's girlfriend. Maybe she just wanted a change of scene to take her mind off Lawrence and her birthday. Or maybe she was looking for opportunities to reconnect with Travis. Was Eva a pawn in Adele's game to win Travis back? Was Lawrence always just a back-up plan?

There was another email from Irving. "Check out the long shadow on the text. Amazing." He had attached a link to *Layers* magazine. She replied: "Thanks, I'll check it out. And thanks for this morning in the conference room."

As soon as she hit send, she worried her message could be misinterpreted: "Thanks for this morning in the conference room." *Oh, God.* Before she could send a clarification, he responded: "Great job on the presentation. You were so confident up there!

P.S. Posting closed. Didn't see your resume in the pile. Might want to follow up."

Irving was the only one to mention her presentation. Sloane began to worry that she hadn't survived it as well as she had hoped. She wondered if the account managers were talking about how she had bombed.

Suddenly, Lenore Robinson was hovering over Sloane's cubicle, looking like she might throw up. "I've got nothing in common with her," she said, breathing heavily.

"Who?" Sloane asked, surprised by the attention.

"Brownwood's new marketing manager! She's half my age." Lenore squinted and a gray curtain of hair swept over her forehead. "Like you," she said. "What do you like?"

"Me? Books, I guess."

"Sure. But what do you want? What motivates you millennials?"

The question rattled Sloane. She used to be motivated by the potential of her career, the dream of owning a house and of having a baby with Jason. What motivated her now was a good question.

Lenore huffed and the collar of her blouse fluttered. "The only thing we have in common is that we're women. I need something more than that."

"I saw the campaign," said Sloane. "It's brilliant."

The rebranding of Brownwood Industries had been the agency's top priority for the past month. Because Joan would be making the pitch, Sloane had put the presentation together. The campaign promoted a proposed high-rise condo building: "Stand Tall in Torren Hills." It was Irving's work and he had manipulated the perspective to make it look like a young couple were giants, a metaphor for success. The presentation also included market research, a strategy proposal, budget options and, at Brownwood's insistence, an introduction to the entire Kaye Agency team. The pitch was scheduled for Friday morning; she had finished it last week.

"It'll take more than a great campaign," said Lenore, her panic intensifying. "We need to connect on a personal level." She gripped the top of Sloane's cubical wall. "Brownwood's secretary wouldn't confirm the meeting. What if they've already counted us out?"

"Joan will make sure they show."

"How can you be sure?"

"It's Joan."

Lenore scurried off and Sloane blindly entered numbers into a spreadsheet to look busy, but she couldn't stop replaying the morning's presentation. At lunch, she hurried to the washroom to hide. To disappear.

Chapter Eighteen

AFTER STEPHIE MOVED in with Randy, she started texting Sloane again. Sloane was relieved and continued to return to Tippett Valley, though with less frequency; visits with Stephie weren't the same with Randy always around.

The summer after first year, Sloane stayed in Torren Hills, moving into a one-bedroom apartment and working as a cashier at the university bookstore. Stephie had encouraged it, but didn't insist, which made Sloane feel like their friendship was getting closer to normal. Jason moved back home, to live with his mom and work as a landscaper. Twice he visited Sloane and, on one of the trips, they took the bus to Tippett Valley, so Roma could meet the boy her daughter had been dating. More importantly, so Sloane could introduce him to Stephie.

"Don't forget," she warned Jason on the bus, "don't mention anything about the night Stephie's brother died. Don't mention Benjamin at all. To anyone. Jason, promise."

"Sloane, I promise." He rubbed her thigh. "It's going to be okay."

"My mom's kind of going through this thing. She might be weird."

"Menopause?"

"Jason!"

"My mom tells me everything. I'm used to it, really."

"I don't know, maybe. My whole life she's been my mom and not much of anything else. Now that I've moved away, I guess she's still . . . adjusting."

"Don't worry, I'm familiar with weird. My mom's going through a spandex phase."

"Stephie might be weird, too," said Sloane, caught in a loop of apprehension. "We don't hang out as much as we used to."

"Friendships can be like that. People change. Grow apart."

"Not us," said Sloane, though she knew it had already started to happen. She stared out the window. "I want you to meet her like how she normally is."

Jason took her hand. "What's normal?"

"Cool. Fun. A really great artist. Since Benjamin . . . she's been different."

"I imagine losing her brother changed her. It changed you, didn't it?"

"Benjamin wasn't my brother."

He squeezed her hand. "You're worried."

"I really want this visit to go well."

"You want Stephie to like me."

"She doesn't like anyone. Except Randy for some reason. I want her to like you, too." The bus passed Tippett Valley's welcome sign. Sloane shivered.

"You cold?"

"I'm fine. Can you smell it?"

"What is it?"

"Pollution from the steel plant."

Roma was waiting in the parking lot. She honked her horn and waved. Sloane rolled her eyes. *I see you, Mom.*

"Jason! Jason!" Roma hollered, her head sticking out of the car window.

Jason wove an arm through each strap of his backpack. "That's her?"

"That's her," said Sloane. "She enjoys embarrassing me."

"She's excited to see you."

"She's excited to see *you*."

"Because I'm dating her daughter."

In the car, Roma quizzed Jason as if he were a game show contestant, firing questions about his university classes and his hobbies and his future plans.

"Mom, let him take a breath."

"I don't mind," said Jason, from the backseat. "Really. It's okay."

"He doesn't mind, Sloane," said Roma, driving slowly.

She moved on to questions like, "What do you think about Sloane's apartment across the street from that place?" Then she inquired about his relationship with his family. "Do you make excuses for your mother not to visit like Sloane does?"

"Mom, *please.*"

Jason answered honestly and didn't cringe when Roma's queries turned shamelessly personal.

"Mom!"

"What?" said Roma innocently. "Aren't you curious how men deal with it? It's not as if I can ask your father."

"Why not?"

"He doesn't ride a bicycle."

Passing in front of the Harringtons', Roma lifted her foot off the gas pedal. Sloane wondered if the old picket fence was still stacked in the garage. She suspected it was, as the cars were parked in the driveway. There was a large gray dot on the front door where the paint had chipped off and the corner of the step had crumbled away, crushing the weeds around it. Sloane remembered when the Harringtons' house had been one of the nicest in the valley.

"Is this it?" asked Jason.

"It's where Stephie lived," said Sloane, "when she first moved here. Her parents still live there."

Roma's eyes jumped to the rearview mirror. "Sloane told you about Stephie's brother?"

In the backseat, Jason nodded.

"Sloane used to babysit him."

"Mom, I babysat Benjamin once, for an hour." Sloane was eager to change the subject. "Is Dad home?"

"He bought me all new cookware," said Roma.

"Why?"

"I kept throwing out food, I was so used to cooking for three."

"So?"

"Smaller pots," said Roma, "make less food." She glanced into the rearview mirror. "Do you like lasagna?" she asked Jason.

"Love it."

Finally, Roma pulled into the Sawyers' driveway. She kept the car running, used to the routine. "Don't be late for dinner," she warned Sloane and then smiled at Jason.

"We won't," Sloane promised.

Roma got out of the car to allow Sloane to take over the driver's seat. "Drive safe," she said.

"It's two minutes to Stephie's," said Sloane.

"Say hello from me and your father."

As Sloane backed out of the driveway, Roma ran beside the car. "Honey!"

Sloane slammed on the breaks. "Mom, what?"

Roma reached through the window to adjust the strap on Sloane's seat belt. "It should go over your breast, not under."

"Mom!"

Sloane had to press the doorbell three times before Stephie answered. One of her eyes was her natural green color, the other an artificial aqua blue. Her dyed-black hair was matted and her eyelids half-closed, as if the light were painful. She chewed on the ends of her bangs.

"You're just getting up?" asked Sloane. It was after noon. *God, Stephie, not today.*

"What are you doing here?" Stephie's voice was hoarse and almost hostile.

"I wanted you to meet Jason, remember?"

Stephie's forehead creased.

"My boyfriend," said Sloane, lowering her voice. *You didn't forget?*

Jason stepped forward. "Hi," he said, as if Stephie didn't look like a zombie. "Really nice to finally meet you."

"Look, it's not a good time," said Stephie, glaring at Sloane.

"It's the only time. My mom's making dinner and we're taking the bus back to Torren Hills in the morning."

Stephie's blue eye watered. She removed the contact and

retreated into the house. "Whatever," she mumbled. The place was a disaster. Empty bottles covered every surface, chip crumbs were embedded into the carpet and multiple ashtrays were overflowing with cigarette butts and roaches. Randy's guitar was on the couch and a full drum kit had been set up in the living room. In the kitchen were at least twenty folding chairs—some stacked, some collapsed, some tipped on their sides. A t-shirt hung from a lamp and a pink bra had been draped over the TV.

Sloane wrinkled her nose. "Did you have a party last night?"

Stephie moved the guitar off the couch and plopped down in its place. "Randy's band played."

"In the house?"

"Until the cops shut it down."

"Where did all the chairs come from?"

"Oasis Rentals."

"Randy stole them from work?"

"He borrowed them. He knows where the owner keeps the key to the warehouse."

Sloane glanced at Jason, who looked remarkably calm.

"Where *is* Randy?" asked Sloane.

Digging her fists into her face, Stephie rubbed her eyes with her knuckles. "Passed out in the bathroom." When she dropped her arms, her cheeks were blotchy and her eyes bloodshot, but at least her irises were the same color. "Don't worry," she said sardonically, "he's on the floor and I pulled his hair back."

"Congratulations on graduating high school," Jason cut in. "Sloane tells me you're on your way to art school."

Stephie's eyes closed. "She would tell you that."

"You *are* going to art school," said Sloane. "Right?"

Stephie shoved a chunk of her hair into her mouth. "I got a job," she said.

"You did? Where?"

"The Stairway." She rolled her chin from one shoulder to the other.

"What about art school?"

"I'm not going to art school. I'm staying here."

"In Tippy? With Randy?"

"Yes."

Sloane's temper rose. "But what about art school?"

"There is no art school."

"But that's what you've always wanted."

"I don't want it anymore."

"If you would just come for a visit to Torren Hills, you would see how great it is."

"I want to stay here."

"You love drawing. It's your dream to go to art school. We were going to start a business together!"

"Sloane, not anymore."

Jason probably didn't realize how hard he was squeezing Sloane's hand. Her face tingled as she fought off tears.

"It's Randy," she said. "He's holding you back."

On the couch, Stephie lifted her feet and rolled onto her side. "He's holding me together," she mumbled, slipping a pillow under her head. Then louder, "Look, you don't have to be here."

Sloane shrieked as Randy emerged from the bathroom. Stephie moaned and rolled her face into a pillow. Jason seemed stunned.

Randy's hair was a mess, a large chunk of material was missing from his shirt, and his pants were unbuttoned and hanging below his hips, exposing his boxers. He turned the ring in his lip and swiped his mouth, flashing his sister's name, before stumbling over to the chair in the living room.

"This is Randy," said Sloane, deeply regretting bringing Jason to Tippett Valley at all.

Randy held out his hand. "Jason Howard," he said, surprisingly coherent. "Sloane's boyfriend. The video-gamer."

Jason nodded. "And you're . . . the roommate."

"I've been called worse."

"God, Randy," said Sloane, unable to keep quiet. "Look at her."

On the couch, Stephie had fallen asleep.

"She's okay," he said calmly.

"This is what okay looks like to you?"

Jason squeezed Sloane's hand.

"Maybe you're part of the problem," said Sloane, glaring at Randy. "You make her think this is okay."

Randy wasn't riled. "It's her okay."

Sloane slapped her thigh. "What does that even mean? How is she ever going to move on like this?"

Randy squinted, thoughtfully. "Maybe it's not about moving on."

"If she doesn't move on she'll never recover."

"Maybe it's not about trying to get back something that's been lost."

Jason tugged on Sloane's arm. "How about we go back to your parents', spend the afternoon? It'll make your mom happy."

Sloane inhaled deeply. Arguing with Randy was futile, and she was embarrassing herself in front of her boyfriend. She glanced at Stephie. "She's just tired and hungover from last night. We'll come back after dinner."

Jason nodded. "Sure."

Sloane followed him to the door. "She'll be more herself later." As the door was closing, she turned and saw Randy carrying Stephie to her bedroom.

That afternoon, Jason fixed the Sawyers' computer and showed Roma a sketch of a character prototype for his new game. The evening was spent with Roma too, looking through her scrapbook of anniversary announcements and a dozen family photo albums. Sloane was mortified, but Jason claimed he couldn't think of a better way to spend a night. By the time she was making up the couch, Roma was in love with Sloane's boyfriend.

On the bus ride back to Torren Hills, Sloane learned that her dad had woken up Jason when he came home from the graveyard shift and turned on the TV.

"Did you talk?" asked Sloane.

Jason yawned. "A little. Not much. He wanted to catch up on

sports scores. It was okay, though. Words aren't the only way to communicate. I like your dad."

The sleeve of Jason's shirt was bunched up over his shoulder, revealing a tan line from a summer working outside. Sloane ran a finger over his burnt skin. "Don't you think my parents are the weirdest couple?"

"Why do you say that?"

Sloane shrugged. She didn't really want to talk about her parents.

"I wish you had liked Stephie, too," she said. "She's not always like that. You saw her place; she must have been partying all night."

"She wasn't very nice to you."

"She was hungover."

"She's often hungover when you visit, isn't she?"

"She's not always mean."

"So you agree she was mean to you."

Sloane's voice hardened. "I told you, she's not always like that. People have bad days. It doesn't make them terrible friends."

"You're right," said Jason. "But I still didn't like the way she treated you."

She changed the subject. "I can't believe she's staying in Tippy to work at the Stairway. She could walk to Wilson, it's that close."

He kissed her forehead. "I'm sorry, I know it's hard for you to come back here." The tension between them dissipated as he tucked a strand of hair behind her ear.

"I'm sorry my mom made you sleep on the couch," she said. "She knows we've slept together. Maybe that's why. I'm sure she hasn't slept with my dad since I was conceived. She was probably jealous. Let's never be like my parents, okay?"

Chapter Nineteen

IN HALF AN hour Sloane's workday would be over, then she could finally go home to shower and sleep. Maybe when Jason arrived home at midnight they would make love. *When's the last time we did that?*

To pass the time, Sloane clicked through the proofs on the Creative Services drive. The designs she particularly liked were always Irving's. She sent him an email: "Love the Hummingbird Gallery ad. Is that typeface Romana?"

When she noticed that she wasn't wearing her wedding rings, she stifled a shriek. A few heads popped up over cubicle walls as she sat unmoving, holding her breath, staring at her bare ring finger, debilitated by the symbolism. She was sure she had taken them off in the washroom so soap wouldn't get caught behind them and irritate her skin. *Please still be there. Please, please, please.*

She thought of Tonya Gleeson, a cashier she had worked with at the bookstore. Tonya had been doing her Master's thesis on witchcraft, which was unsurprising considering how she dressed and acted. She had black fingernails and a ring on each finger, including her thumbs. She wore black lipstick and black eye shadow, a dog collar with silver spikes, a thick leather bracelet on each wrist, black skin-tight pants, a black t-shirt and black ankle boots with laces she didn't tie; the strings slapped on the floor when she walked. She waved her fingers over the books like tiny wands and moved her lips as if casting spells.

One day, Sloane had arrived for her shift and found Tonya curled up in the corner, rocking and tugging on her bootlaces.

"Hey," said Sloane, approaching cautiously. "You okay?"

Tonya looked up. Her cheeks were streaked with bleeding black eyeliner, and her smudged lipstick made her chin look bruised. She sniffled. "Me and Arlo broke up."

Sloane exhaled loudly. *No one died.* "Arlo's your boyfriend?"

"My husband," said Tonya.

"You're married?"

"We're getting a divorce."

Sloane had a hard time imagining Tonya married. In addition to looking like a witch and acting like one half the time, she was also a student.

"What happened?"

She rubbed her cheeks, spreading around her makeup. "I lost my wedding ring."

"He broke up with you because you lost your ring?"

She swept the tip of her tongue over her lower lip. Sloane imagined all the toxins in black lipstick.

"I broke up with him."

"Because you lost a ring?"

"Don't you get it?" said Tonya, as if Sloane were a child. "It was a sign. Signs are how Fate speaks to us."

"Maybe you just misplaced it. Have you looked for it?"

"Everywhere. It's gone."

"It doesn't mean your marriage has to be over," said Sloane. "Maybe it has nothing to do with it. Maybe you just lost your ring."

"Everything has to do with everything."

"What if it's a sign for something else? Don't you love him?"

Tonya huffed and looked hard into Sloane's eyes. "More than anyone or anything, which is why I had to end it. Fate *knows.* Avoiding a sign just makes things worse. For Arlo's sake, I had to."

Sloane never did shake Tonya's adamant belief in the language of Fate. A decade later, Sloane reconsidered her skepticism as she rushed to the washroom. She knew something was wrong with her marriage; she had been feeling it, and ignoring it, for months. *Is Fate sending me a sign?*

Stumbling through the washroom door, Sloane nearly cried out when there, on the counter, were her rings. She hadn't lost them. It wasn't a sign. Or if it was, it was a good one. She quickly slipped them onto her finger and texted Jason.

I love you.

She stared at her phone, willing him to respond. It was 4:34 p.m. He should be on his first break, checking his phone. Finally, he replied.

Everything ok?

Sloane's stomach turned. Why didn't he text, 'I love you too'? *Because he doesn't anymore?* After a shower and some sleep, Sloane would talk with him—have a real conversation about real things—but right now, she just had to get through the rest of her workday. She replied with a thumbs-up icon. Then she texted Stephie. She had to be awake by now.

Call me.

Returning to her desk, Sloane cleared hundreds of bogus numbers from a spreadsheet. She imagined Adele on the bus, escaping her cheating boyfriend by running away to her ex-boyfriend's, who had also cheated on her, to take care of his sick girlfriend. Then she thought of her mom in China, traveling with her friend because her husband would rather watch hockey on TV than vacation with his wife. Then she wondered if Randy would be mad at Stephie for sleeping with Nasser on the same day she had slept with him. Maybe she and Jason weren't doing too badly.

Chapter Twenty

IF SLOANE HAD an avatar, she would name her MirandaMin. She had always liked the name Miranda—at sixteen, she had named her hypothetical future daughter Miranda—and she thought of Min after the tragedy, thinking herself clever to use just the last syllable of Benjamin's name as a private tribute. No one would guess MirandaMin was Sloane Sawyer, not even if she came across someone she knew in real life.

But when Jason offered to create MirandaMin for her, she declined. "Video games are your thing," she said.

"Avatars can do more than play video games," he replied.

Still, Sloane wasn't interested. "I'll stick with books."

Jason's basement apartment had flooded so he was spending the weekend at Sloane's on Jarvis Street while she visited Tippett Valley. He had arrived with a tote bin of electronics and had spent the past hour taking over Sloane's tiny living room.

"I didn't think you were supposed to use your real name," said Sloane, looking over his shoulder at his laptop screen.

Jason named his avatar JasonHoward, as if eliminating the space between his first and last name made him incognito.

"Never," he said, smiling.

"But you named your avatar your real name."

"No one would suspect that I'm really Jason Howard."

Sloane went back to her laptop. "It's the first thing I'd suspect."

"That's because you're the only one in the world—in *any* world—who really knows me."

He jumped to his feet and grabbed her hand, pulling her into him. It was these moments, dancing to a silent song, that Sloane was in awe that she had a boyfriend as wonderful as Jason Howard.

He followed her into the bedroom. She liked that he came to

124

bed with her even when he wasn't tired. A pulsing light flashed through the window: *Girls! Girls! Girls!*

Jason squinted. "How do you sleep like this?" He said it each time he slept over.

"I told you," she said, "you get used to it after a while."

Roma had been horrified when Sloane leased the Jarvis Street apartment, convinced the street was populated with "riffraff" seeking to lure her daughter into an unspeakable underworld. She had been right about the block being busy—there was always someone lingering below the window—but Sloane never felt unsafe. Roma was also concerned that some of the "girls" who worked at the club would move into Sloane's building. "A short commute," she said. She was right about that, too. A dancer named Olja lived next door. She was a tall woman with toned arms and calves who could walk in really high heels without wobbling and bend in amazing ways. Yesterday, Sloane had entered the laundry room to find Olja stretched over two running washing machines, an ankle tucked behind her head while her entire body vibrated. "Cheaper than a chiropractor," she said as she jumped off the machines.

"Ouch." Sloane winced as Jason hugged her.

"You okay?"

As if he were a seat belt, she buckled herself in against him. "I'm fine," she said.

"What is it?" he pressed.

"I hurt my back."

"Doing what?"

"Running to class." A lie. After Olja had left the laundry room, Sloane had climbed on top of a washing machine during its spin cycle. She didn't come close to getting her ankle behind her head and injured herself trying. Roma had been right to worry that Sloane's neighbor would be a bad influence.

"I'll be okay," said Sloane.

Jason hugged her more gently. She liked how he kept her body warm, how the crown of her head tucked perfectly beneath his chin, how the soft whiskers on his chest tickled her cheek.

"Some of the Computer Science students are putting together a dodge ball team," he said. "I thought maybe we could join together."

"I don't play sports."

"Is dodge ball a sport?"

"Do I have to run?"

"It's recommended."

"I don't run."

"Didn't you just run to class?"

"And I hurt myself. Also, I turn into a Smurf."

"A Smurf?"

"I hold my breath and my face turns blue." A boy in Grade 9 gym was the first to call Sloane a Smurf. Stephie had kicked a soccer ball at his face, causing his nose to bleed and his eyes to water. Sloane had actually felt kind of sorry for him. "Maybe I can keep score," she suggested to Jason. "We can still do it together."

"I bet you're just as pretty blue," he said.

With his arm, he propped up his head. Sloane looked into his eyes and ran her fingers over his head, his spiky hair soft like the tufts of pussy willows.

"What is it?" she asked. "Are you imagining Smurfette?"

Jason remained serious. "Maybe you should move in with me."

Sloane used her hand to shield his eyes from the flashing letters. "The light doesn't keep me up," she said.

Pressing his lips together, Jason shook his head. Below his cheek, his bicep flexed, the muscle elevating his head. "I mean, maybe you'd like to live with me."

Sloane dropped her hand. "Oh."

"We spend a lot of time together," he said. "It'd be nice to not have to go back to our own places just to pack a bag of fresh clothes, wouldn't it?"

He was right. There weren't many nights they didn't spend together.

"Your apartment just flooded," she said.

"It'll be back to normal after the weekend. Or I could move in here."

"With the light?"

"Like you said, I'd get used to it. We practically live together already. We could make it official. Be officially roommates."

"You really want to live with me?"

"Aren't we already, sort of? We're just renting two different places."

Imagining it, Sloane started to giggle.

"Is that a yes? Can I move in?"

She sat up. "No," she said. "I mean, not here. Or your place. Somewhere else. Somewhere we pick together."

Jason smiled, and Sloane placed her thumb in a dimple.

"Maybe a house," he said, sitting up. "With a white picket fence."

Chapter Twenty-One

SLOANE USUALLY DIDN'T mind being home alone. In a strange way, she felt closer to Jason when he was at the plant. When he was home, he would claim the basement to play video games while she read in their bedroom, engrossed in her own fantasy. At Foodland, picking up coffee on her way home, she reminded herself it didn't have to be like that. Maybe when they were home together they could go for a walk. Like Roma had suggested.

With the house to herself, Sloane used to focus on her portfolio, but she couldn't remember the last time she had done that. She decided that tonight she would take advantage of the empty basement to watch TV.

After a shower and an Advil, Sloane turned on a show about vampires and werewolves. It reminded her of when she had dragged Stephie to the theatre to see *Underworld: Evolution*. Stephie had laughed at all the wrong scenes and nodded off before the ending. Driving home, Sloane had laughed as Stephie tried to guess the ending. Benjamin twisted around in the front seat, asking questions that his sister ignored, while his dad kept telling him to wear his seat belt properly. It wasn't often Sloane thought of a happy Tippett Valley memory and she held onto it as long as possible.

If Stephie were watching with Sloane now, she would likely be laughing. She said she laughed when she was supposed to cry because the wiring was messed up in her brain. Randy said laughing and crying were the same thing, the release of emotion, and it was wrong to attach predetermined meaning to either. Sloane thought the wiring might be messed up in *his* brain.

On the TV, the werewolf bit the star vampire. He was at risk of dying because werewolf venom was fatal, curable only by the rare blood of a vampire/werewolf hybrid, a detail introduced earlier in the episode. He would be saved though, because that was what happened on TV. Sloane wished she could script reality. She never would have kissed Benjamin Harrington. He wouldn't have died. Stephie would have gotten out of Tippett Valley.

Stephie hadn't texted or called since her birthday. What if something had happened? Sloane considered calling Randy, but that was something Jasmine used to do to check in on her daughter; now the two of them didn't communicate at all. Sloane could drive to Tippett Valley. How many times had she showed up at Stephie's doorstep uninvited? *Oh God, am I like my mom?* For a brief moment, Sloane missed her mom's phone calls and drop-in visits. She would probably regret that thought on Friday, when Roma came home. Sloane texted Stephie.

Just want to know you're okay.

On her phone, she searched for Tonya Gleeson on Facebook, curious to know how Fate had treated her. *There she is.* Scrolling through Tonya's Facebook feed, Sloane discovered her wardrobe was still black. And she had a kid. Sloane's hand landed on her belly. She knew it wasn't fair to be jealous, but when was jealousy ever a choice? Was Jason jealous of other dads?

In university, Sloane drank coffee to stay awake when Jason had a night class. He would reciprocate by getting up with her in the morning when he didn't have to. After they moved in together, Sloane stopped drinking coffee at night. Maybe it was because her time with Jason wasn't so precious anymore. Once they lived together, they saw each other all the time, and it was their time apart that she made an extra effort to cherish. But Jason never stopped getting up in the morning with Sloane, not even after a graveyard shift.

Determined to do better, Sloane set up the coffeemaker. As the coffee percolated, she stretched out on the couch in the basement and tried to come up with the right words to say to her husband at midnight.

Chapter Twenty-Two

FOR THIRD-YEAR UNIVERSITY, Jason and Sloane rented the top half of a house on Truman Avenue, just off Main Street and not too far from the university. It was the last of the original homes in the now gentrified area, by far the smallest on the street, and the apartment was not strictly legal. The landlord, Mr. Yin, cautioned Sloane and Jason about telling the neighbors that they were renting. But the rent was affordable, especially after Jason agreed to mow the lawn in the summer and shovel the driveway in the winter.

Mr. Yin also promised that when the tenants below moved out, the entire house could be theirs for a nominal increase in rent. Sloane didn't know why Mr. Yin would think they would want a second apartment, but then she discovered the suite below was really just a basement—one large room with a bathroom, a microwave and a beer fridge. The only legal thing about it was its separate entrance. The tenants, an elderly couple, hardly ever left and rarely made a sound.

Sloane imagined a younger version of Jason and his mom living in the basement. She started taking food down to the Zimmermans' door—leftovers from dinner they could heat up in their microwave.

The neighbors on the street had jobs and kids and dogs, and they asked Sloane questions like, "What do you and your husband do?" and "Got kids?" and "Can I get the contact information for your lawn guy?" Sloane told them that Jason was a video-game developer and that the two of them were trying for a baby and that she would dig up the number for her landscaper. She told them she was employed by the university, which wasn't a lie, since she still worked at the bookstore two evenings a week. When pressed further, she said she worked as a graphic designer, which was only a half-lie, since she had designed the promotional material for the bookstore's end-of-semester sale. Besides, one day she really would be a graphic designer and Jason really would be a video-game developer, and they would be parents. Caught up in the fantasy, Sloane asked a neighbor for the name of the company who had built their fence.

After she and Jason officially moved in together, Sloane was amazed how much she learned about her boyfriend. Jason didn't match up his socks; he put them away in a drawer as loose singles. Glasses in the cupboard had to be arranged in order of height, but it didn't seem to matter if a spoon ended up in the fork slot in the utensil drawer. He was casual with trash, carelessly mixing it in with recycling, and he kept leaving his toothbrush on the bathroom counter where Sloane kept knocking it off. It always seemed to fall right behind the toilet where neither of them could fit their hand to clean so she would have to buy him a new one.

Sloane missed the familiar sound of Olja's voice traveling through the kitchen wall and the flashing sign across the street. For weeks, she couldn't sleep without the TV on, replicating the sounds that used to spew through her window from street level. Jason missed the musty smell and constant darkness of a basement and seemed jealous of the tenants below. He kept the curtains closed and each day Sloane widened the slivers of brightness, slowly introducing natural light.

When she lived alone, Sloane didn't think twice about analyzing her body in front of a mirror or stinking up the bathroom or shaving her legs in the sink. But now that she lived with Jason, she was at constant risk of having her privacy interrupted. Every room, every space, was "theirs." She started to spend more time in the bathroom, the only room where it was possible to close the door and not have it mean something.

Jason's video games were another challenge. He left them in large bins and got frustrated when he couldn't find the one he wanted. In the living room, he set up at least a dozen game consoles and just as many controllers; he spent hours each day playing.

The living room was short on electrical outlets, so cords stretched across the floor. When Sloane tripped over one, she yanked the cord out and abruptly terminated the game Jason was playing. She could tell that he was trying not to be upset, but he was. He stayed up all night getting back to where he had been before the plug was pulled. It was the first time he didn't go to bed when Sloane was tired.

"Maybe you should stop playing video games and start building yours," Sloane teased one night.

"I'm studying," he said, seriously, and then grabbed her waist and pinched her sides. "Aren't you doing the same thing? Looking at designs to be a better graphic designer? Besides, I've started. I've got notes."

"Can I see them?"

"They're just notes."

"Will you show me?"

He handed over a thick blue binder. She was careful opening the cover, but the pages still fell into her lap.

"Don't worry," said Jason, unconcerned. "They're not in any order anyway."

"Can I read them?"

"I can barely read them," he joked.

The next day, while Jason was in class, Sloane organized the blue binder. She sorted all the pages into piles based on a set of keywords she had identified: Features, Interface, Controls, Protagonist, Antagonist, Back Story, Rewards, Challenges, Levels, Design, Sound, Weapons, Power-Ups, Obstacles, Environments. She put aside notes and sketches she couldn't classify. She purchased a three-hole-punch and two sets of dividers with tabs. She presented the completed binder to Jason, who flipped through it in awe.

"Now you can file your pages by category," she said. "And here, I got you this." She handed him the three-hole punch. "Trust me, you need it."

"You didn't have to do this," he said.

"It's better though, right?"

"It's amazing, but it must have been a lot of work. Did you even go to class today?"

"I wanted to do it. For you. You've got some really great ideas, Jason."

"It's barely anything. Just notes."

"I especially like Clara."

"She reminds me of you."

"Clara's a commander!"

Sloane decided she also had to do something about the bins of video games. She sorted the cartridges first by brand, based on their shape, and then alphabetized each title. She purchased a bookshelf off Kijiji, sweated through her clothes getting it home on the bus, and then made letter labels to stick on the shelves. Running out of room, she gave up a row on her own bookshelf for T-Z. When Jason got home from class, he was stunned.

"Name a game," said Sloane. "Any one you have."

"Grand Theft Auto: San Andreas," he said, and within moments Sloane had pulled it off the shelf. "Say another one."

"Super Mario Galaxy."

She crouched and found it immediately. "What else you got?"

"Resident Evil."

Sloane searched the Rs. "Which one? One, two, three or four?"

"You're amazing," he said.

It took about five months for Sloane to accept that socks could live in a drawer single and spoons and forks could cohabitate. She got used to picking out recycling from the trash and buying toothbrushes in bulk, and she learned how to read books and practice graphic design without being distracted by Jason's "studying."

It was harder to believe that he had just as easily adjusted to the unflattering aspects of her life. She wasn't even certain what things about her he was working to accept. He always seemed so content, which meant she had to guess what was bothering him.

They shared the household chores equally, but in reality, Sloane did them all the time while Jason did his half. If it was his turn to clean the bathroom, Sloane would clean it first, to ensure a clump of her hair or a bodily fluid hadn't stuck to any surface. If Jason went grocery shopping, she made a special trip out for tampons so she didn't have to add them to the shopping list. On his weeks to do laundry, she kept a secret stash of worn underwear in the back of her closet to wash when he was out.

In fourth year, Sloane asked Stephie if she felt the same way about living with Randy, even though they were just friends.

"You're having sex. You don't think that's sticky and personal? Picking up tampons and washing each other's underwear, that's next level, Sloane. Before you know it, he'll be proposing."

Sloane couldn't be sure if Stephie was teasing or being supportive. At least she had answered her phone.

"I'm going to be meeting Jason's mom," she said. "I've only ever talked to her on the phone." On the line, she heard a voice in the background. "Is that Randy?"

"Yeah. I gotta go."

"Why?"

"Going out."

"Where?"

"The Stairway."

"You're working?"

"No."

"Are you going with Randy?"

"I've got a mom, Sloane. I don't need another."

"Sorry, it's just—"

"See you later."

"On Friday?"

Silence.

"Stephie?"

"I'll text you."

Jason rented a car to visit his mom a couple of times a year, usually on holidays when Sloane was in Tippett Valley. The one time they had planned to visit Roseanne together, Sloane had canceled at the last minute because Randy was leaving on a road trip with his band and Stephie was going to be alone. "Stephie needs me," said Sloane. "It's just that it's Benjamin's birthday. Or it would've been. Last year Stephie didn't do too well." She had picked open the scar on the back of her ankle. Jason nodded, like he understood. When he returned home, Sloane was too embarrassed to tell him that when she arrived in Tippett Valley Stephie wasn't there. She had gone with Randy on the tour.

Jason used the money he earned grading papers to bring his mom to Torren Hills. Roseanne was arriving on Wednesday and leaving on Friday, which meant both Sloane and Jason would be in class half the time. But it wasn't the weekend, so Sloane wouldn't feel compelled to get on a bus to Tippett Valley if Stephie texted. She was nervous to meet Roseanne, even though their telephone conversations had been pleasant. She was afraid Jason's mom would be disappointed.

Roseanne Howard was quirky and wonderful, and Sloane liked her instantly. She had curly brown hair and big glasses and the same smile Sloane saw every day—matching dimples on mother and son. She wasn't much over five feet tall and wore spandex and leg warmers and long sweaters that reached her knees. Unlike Roma, Roseanne didn't put up a fuss about sleeping on the couch, declaring it more comfortable than her bed at home.

She repeatedly complimented Sloane, telling her she had a lovely jawline, that her hair was the perfect blend of blond shades and that portrait artists would pay hundreds to draw her cheekbones. She said the changing color of Sloane's eyes made her smile, and more than once she expressed how happy she was that her son had found such an attractive and smart woman.

"I hate my hips," said Sloane.

Roseanne bellowed, "You're shaped like a timepiece for a goddess!"

Sloane wished Jason's mom would stay longer. It was amazing the effect Roseanne's approval had. After Roseanne left, Sloane added tampons to the shopping list.

Jason texted her from the grocery store.

    Right?

On her cell phone, up popped a photograph of a box of tampons. She texted a thumbs-up icon, and then hurried to the bathroom to splash water on her flushed cheeks. Jason was taking pictures of tampon boxes in the grocery store. When he returned home, he placed the box on the counter like it wasn't a big deal. Maybe it wasn't.

A week later, Sloane opened her top dresser drawer and found it full of clean underwear. Checking the back of her closet, she confirmed the week's secret pile was gone. "Jason!"

He was in the living room, so focused on the TV screen that he hadn't heard his name being called. He didn't even seem to notice that Sloane had entered the room.

"Jason!" she shouted again.

Alarmed, he looked up. The sound of defeat spewed from the speakers.

"Sorry," she said.

Jason breathed heavily, catching his breath. "I was losing anyway. What's wrong?"

Sloane's voice dropped. "You did my laundry."

"It was my turn."

"But you did my other laundry."

"Wasn't a big deal."

"It's my underwear."

He stood. "You wash my boxers."

"Yes, but . . ."

"What?"

"It's just . . ."

"What?" Approaching, he plopped his hands on her shoulders. "Are you really upset that I did your other laundry?"

"It's just that it's my underwear," she said. "It's private." Her underwear was bigger than his. Well, maybe technically a smaller size, but not by much.

His thumb stroked her collarbone. "You don't hide your bras from me."

Sloane's eyes rolled. "That's different." She considered her breasts the highlight of her body. She wanted Jason to wash her bras.

"I also like the parts of you that your underwear covers," he said.

Reaching around her waist, he squeezed her butt cheek. At first, Sloane squirmed, but then he moaned and she realized he was turned on. He tugged her closer.

"Relax," he cooed, his breath tickling her ear. He led her into the bedroom and gently guided her onto the bed.

Moving in together had been an adjustment, even in the bedroom. When they had lived apart, Sloane could choose not to go to Jason's, or tell him not to come over. But now that they lived together, she shared a bed with him every night. It took some learning to navigate the expectation of sex, to be okay with not having it. Before her bed had become theirs, Sloane didn't understand that it was more than a platform for pleasure. It was also a stage for argument and conversation and sleep. It was the place she felt her most vulnerable—because of Jason—and yet, the safest—because of him.

Sloane started to relax, to let go. Rolling on top of him, she kissed his forehead and then his nose and mouth. She slipped off her glasses and lowered her body on top of his.

With the sound of splitting wood, one side of the bed dropped. Sloane shrieked as she slid out of Jason's arms and down the sloped mattress. She landed on the floor with a thud, bringing him down on top of her.

She grabbed her arm. "Ouch."

"You okay?"

He helped her to her feet, but she had to stick her naked butt up into the air. *Have I gained weight?* Unable to look at Jason, she quickly put on her glasses and robe, eager to escape.

"Well," he said, standing over the broken bed, "it wasn't made for two people in love."

Sloane stopped in the doorway. "What?"

"I said it wasn't made for two people in love."

She twisted a strand of hair around her ear. "You love me?"

"You didn't know?"

"You've never said it."

"My mom taught me to say it only when I really meant it."

"Do you want to take it back?"

"No. Do you want me to?"

"I just broke the bed and mooned you and probably gave you permanent ear damage from my scream."

"I still don't want to take it back," he said. "Is that okay?"

"Really?"

"Really."

"I love you, too," she said.

"Do you mean it?"

"Yes."

Jason smiled widely, his dimples deep indents on each cheek. He took her hand and pulled her down the hallway. "Come on."

"Where are we going?"

"To the living room," he said. "The couch is made in Italy. Italians know about love."

Chapter Twenty-Three

A FLASH OF light through the basement window woke Sloane. Something was against her neck. Panicked, she discovered it was only her phone. It had slid from her chest to her throat. She glanced at the clock on the cable box: 11:57 p.m. *Jason.*

She must have fallen asleep while the coffee was brewing. Another failure. Weighed down by fatigue and self-loathing, she made her way to the bedroom, where she pulled the sheets over her chest. She rotated onto her stomach and buried her face in a pillow.

"Sloane?" There was a faint whistle to Jason's breathing. "You awake?"

If his voice had a physical texture, it would be velvet. The softness of his tone was her undoing. Struggling to control her tears, she didn't trust herself to answer.

"Sloane?"

She flinched when Jason leaned in.

"You're wearing your glasses," he said, removing the frames from her face.

When he got into bed, Sloane rolled over. He shifted closer and pressed the front of his body into the back of hers.

"How was work?" he asked softly.

It was as if her voice were a separate entity, out of her control; like she was listening to someone else speak. "I almost lost my job for being late," she said.

"I doubt that. Joan needs you."

"Anyone can do what I do."

"Not as well."

"I did a presentation. In front of the whole department. The graphic designers were there, too."

"I bet you impressed them."

139

"I had a stain on my pants. From last night at the bar."

"You went out?"

"The Stairway."

"Changing tradition."

"I didn't know we were going out, so I only brought one pair of pants. Stephie slept with Randy."

"Is she dating him now?"

"No. They're just roommates. She slept with Nasser, too. On the same day, I'm pretty sure."

"Who's Nasser?"

"A guy Stephie met outside the bar." Sloane unclenched her hands. "She hasn't texted or called."

"That's not unlike her." Jason squeezed Sloane's shoulder. "I'm sorry. I know that's tough." He managed to slip his arm under hers. "You have other friends. How's Adele?"

"Next week she turns thirty and she just broke up with her boyfriend."

"Lawrence."

"Right. She left the agency early today to take care of her ex-boyfriend's girlfriend."

"Eva."

"Yes. I think she regrets breaking up with him."

"Lawrence or Travis?"

"Travis. She spends so much time with Eva, like maybe it makes her feel like *she's* still the girlfriend. Like maybe she's friends with Eva only to stay in Travis' life. I shouldn't worry so much. We're just colleagues."

"A colleague can be a friend, too."

She removed his hand from her hip. "I slept in Randy's room last night. Nasser was with Stephie in her room, so it was either that or the couch, and I think the couch would've been worse. Randy wasn't home. It was the only good thing about the night."

Jason's hand slithered to the front of her thigh. "I like you like this."

"Like what?" *Manic?*

"Talking. To me."

"We talk all the time."

"We speak."

"Same thing."

"Speaking is reminding me to take out the garbage. Talking is telling me about your day and how you feel about things."

Then we're not talking now either. If Sloane were "talking" she would have told him how demoralizing it was to be a secretary for a boss who barely acknowledged her existence, or how depressing it was to have to beg her best friend to spend time with her, or how her heart ached knowing she had failed him by not getting pregnant with his baby. If Jason were "talking" he would have told her how much he wanted to be a dad, or how he resented working at the steel plant, or how the world of video games was more satisfying than a wife who had disappointed him in every way.

She shimmied to the edge of the bed. "Goodnight," she said, blinking away tears.

"Sloane? Sloane, look at me." Jason gently tugged her shoulder. "What just happened?"

"Nothing."

"Something."

"I've got work in the morning. I can't be late again. Goodnight."

"Sloane?"

After a long moment, Jason's hand lifted from her shoulder. "Your dad says, 'Hi,' by the way."

His voice was no longer velvet. More like Velcro.

In the morning, Sloane slipped on the fitness tracker and read the manual over coffee. She hadn't planned on ever wearing it, but the box was on the counter and it was better to appear busy than to make small talk with Jason. She convinced herself that she wasn't avoiding fixing her marital problems; she was just starting with her weight.

"I'm sorry," he said. "About last night."

At the door, Sloane tiredly slipped on her shoes and swung her purse over her shoulder. Around her wrist, the fitness tracker knocked against her chin. "It's okay. I'm sorry, too," she said.

"Sloane, we need to talk."

"I'm going to be late," she said, rummaging in her purse for her keys.

She turned and Jason was suddenly close, as if he had cut and pasted himself in front of her. "Jason, I have work."

"Last night, you started to talk to me," he said. "What made you stop? You just shut down."

"I have to go."

His hand gently landed on her arm. "That was the version of you I miss." He tugged her forward. "I love you, you know."

Sloane was surprised that those words made her angry. She used to know that Jason loved her, but she didn't anymore. When they got married, he had loved her with the promise that they would build a successful and happy home together. It wasn't that she had changed; she hadn't changed enough.

"I'll see you after work," she said, opening the door. Like a Band-Aid, Jason's fingers ripped off her arm. She hurried to the car. He didn't follow her.

In the driver's seat, Sloane rotated the fitness tracker around her wrist, absently tapping the screen twice like the manual instructed. Twenty-seven steps already and all she had done was drink a cup of coffee and walk out on her husband.

Turning the ignition, she considered that maybe she had reacted all wrong. Last night, she had complained about her crappy job and her inconsiderate friend and her peculiar colleague, and Jason had said that he liked it. Maybe it didn't matter that her days were shitty. Maybe what he missed was her sharing it with him. What if hiding her disappointments was not as kind as she intended? What if it made him so light that he felt hollow?

Shaking her head, she glanced at the car's digital clock. *I can't be late.*

Chapter Twenty-Four

IN HER LAST semester of university, Sloane was having both her hair and eyebrows done, when the stylist said, "Should I get this one here?" and brought her tweezers close to Sloane's chin. Sloane jolted back, causing the chair to rattle. If she angled her head up and to the side, she could see the coarse dark hair on the chin of her reflection in the mirror.

Turned out, it was relentless, like a blade of grass growing through a crack in the pavement. Every morning it was back, after being plucked just the morning before. Sloane worried one day she would forget to pull it and Jason would notice. How long would it grow if she let it?

"I need you to promise me something," she told Stephie over the phone.

"What."

"It's stupid." Only it wasn't. To Sloane it was serious.

Stephie didn't respond.

"Okay, so if I ever end up in a coma, I need you to promise me that every day you'll visit me in the hospital. And bring tweezers."

Silence.

"Stephie, are you listening?"

"If you're in a coma, go to the hospital with tweezers." She sounded distant, uninterested.

"Right. Every day. That's important."

"Okay."

"You're not going to ask why?"

Silence.

"To pluck this one hair on my chin," said Sloane. "If I'm ever in a coma."

"Okay."

"Seriously, you can't miss a day. It grows that fast."

"Okay."

"You'd really do that for me?"

Stephie finished a yawn. "If you're in a coma, you won't know, will you?"

"I will when I wake up! Stephie, I'm serious."

"Calm down. I promise."

"Thank you." Sloane felt ridiculous, but better, even though Stephie didn't have a reputation for keeping commitments. "What do you want me to do for you if you're ever in a coma?"

"Pull the plug."

Sloane didn't have a response to that. "How're your parents?" she asked.

"The same."

"My mom said she saw them at the movies. Said your mom was smiling."

"Probably just had something stuck in her teeth."

"Maybe she was laughing."

"Doubt it."

"It was a comedy."

"Still doubt it."

"My mom said it was funny." Sloane heard talking in the background. "Is someone there?"

"Just Randy."

"What are you two doing?"

"Nothing."

"What do you guys do when you're doing nothing?"

"Nothing."

"What's he saying?"

"That if I'm in a coma at the same time as you, he'll pull the plug for me and pluck the hair on your chin for you."

Sloane gasped. "Stephie, you have me on speaker!"

"It's just Randy. Look, I've got to go."

"Why? You said you weren't doing anything."

"Right. With Randy."

"Will you call me back, after you're finished doing nothing with Randy?"

Sloane spent the evening finishing her paper for RomCom Lit—why Shakespeare's *Romeo and Juliet* is the ultimate romantic tragicomedy—and worrying what would happen if she and Stephie were in a coma at the same time. She knew it was unlikely. But so was drowning in an inch of water. She needed a backup plan and no way was it going to be Randy Goff. She texted Stephie.

> Tell Randy not to bother with the hospital visits.
> Jason won't let you down.

Stephie was right about Jason, but Sloane couldn't imagine waking up and discovering he had been the one to pluck the mutant hair from her chin.

When she arrived at the townhouse, Stephie was in the shower. It had been over a month since Sloane's last visit to Tippett Valley. It wasn't all because of Stephie; Sloane liked spending her weekends in Torren Hills with Jason. After a month though, the guilt started to set in.

Sloane waited in the living room where Randy was eating a burger while replacing the strings on his guitar. Ketchup had gotten trapped in his mustache. He looked ridiculous.

"I don't know if Stephie told you," she said, "but I changed my mind. If we're in a coma at the same time, I want you to pull my plug, too."

Randy inserted a wire through a small hole on the front of the guitar. "I'm not going to do that," he said, taking the last bite of his burger.

"Why not? It's my decision."

"Not whether I'm the one to pull the plug."

Sloane huffed. "I figured you'd do anything for Stephie." She hated how loyal Randy usually was. It made it difficult for her to be better.

He scratched at his sister's name on his forearm, reminding

Sloane he would always understand Stephie more than she ever could.

"It's not what she wants," he said, calmly.

"It's exactly what she wants," said Sloane. "If she's ever in a coma, she said to pull the plug. If I'm in a coma at the same time and can't do it, she wants you to. She said that."

"Right."

"So you'll pull the plug?"

"For her. Not you."

Sloane was angrier than she should be about a hypothetical scenario. "Why do you care?" she mumbled.

Randy bit the end of a string, holding it in his mouth. "Because Stephie cares," he said, his words garbled.

Stephie walked into the living room, wearing ripped jeans and a t-shirt so faded that only Sloane could identify it. No way would Randy know it was a Violent Downfall t-shirt. The band wasn't even together anymore. For a moment, she savored her secret knowledge and then felt even more inferior.

The shoulders of Stephie's t-shirt were damp from her wet hair and her eyes were bloodshot. Maybe she had gotten shampoo in them. More likely, she had slept with her contacts in. Or maybe she was high. She yanked on a thread hanging from a tear in her jeans and dropped it over Randy's head. He smiled, and Sloane brooded.

"Remember in Grade 9 the time Ashley Simpson emptied Greg Radford's sunblock and replaced it with hand lotion?" said Sloane, wanting to prove to Randy that she had something he couldn't touch: history. She also liked reminding Stephie of who she was before the tragedy. "You saw her do it, and switched the bottles so *she* was the one who got sunburned on Track and Field Day, remember?"

On the couch, Stephie sat beside Randy. A thigh sunk in between two cushions. Around her palm, she wound a loose guitar string.

"Her skin was as red as her hair, remember?"

"I was a terrible teenager," said Stephie.

"No you weren't. You were sticking up for Greg."

"I should've stuck up for Benji."

It had been so long since Stephie had spoken of her brother that it threw Sloane off. Randy didn't seem to be affected, like maybe Stephie often talked about her brother. Maybe it was only with Sloane she had stopped.

"You did," she said, remembering the black arc on the bathroom wall.

For no apparent reason, other than Randy did weird things, Stephie allowed him to push the end of a guitar string through a hole in the knee of her jeans. Sloane kept waiting for Stephie to yelp out, but Randy was careful. There was trust between them.

Sloane glared. "I was with her when she bought that shirt," she said.

She imagined Randy's response: *So what? I was with her through years of recovery after her brother died. After you left Tippy.* He didn't say it though, and Sloane was grateful. She knew she was acting like a child. "Sorry," she whispered, embarrassed.

Randy carefully fished out the guitar string from Stephie's pants. "See you later," he said, standing. At the front door he slipped on a jacket and shoes, and then left the house.

"Where's he going?" asked Sloane.

"Work."

"Still with Oasis Rentals?"

Stephie nodded.

Sloane figured he would have been fired by now. She moved onto the couch. "You ever think about getting married?" It was hard to talk about things like this over text, and on the phone Sloane was rarely able to keep Stephie's attention for longer than a few minutes.

Stephie picked at the tear in the knee of her jeans. "No."

"Really?"

"Really."

"What about having kids?"

"No."

"You used to," said Sloane. "We talked about it, remember? You were going to name your kids Hansel and Gretel. They were going to play with Miranda."

Stephie shrugged.

"Jason and I are starting to talk about it. What do you think?"

"Does it matter what I think?"

"You're my best friend."

Stephie closed her eyes.

"You know, it's not too late for art school," said Sloane.

Stephie stood. "It's too late for a lot of things."

"You don't have to go to art school. We can start our business now. You're good enough already!"

Stephie moved to the front entrance.

"I'm designing a poster for the bookstore," said Sloane, following. "I know it's not a band poster, but you could draw something for it. I could incorporate it into the design."

Stephie slipped on her shoes.

"Where are you going?"

"Movie theatre."

"But you never stay awake and we can't talk there."

"You don't have to come."

"No, I want to," said Sloane, quickly putting on her shoes. "What's playing?"

"It doesn't matter."

Chapter Twenty-Five

JOAN IGNORED SLOANE all morning. Everything was normal.

By lunchtime Sloane was as addicted to the fitness tracker as Roma had predicted she would be. She loved watching the numbers increase; each tiny effort, every single step, measured, recorded, accumulated.

Sloane walked over to Human Resources, watching the steps on her fitness tracker add up. Adele wasn't in her office, but Gary Goldman was. Lined up across his desk were a dozen supplement bottles and three different models of handgrips. A mirror beside his computer screen was angled low, apparently so he could monitor his pectorals. He met Sloane outside his office.

"I was looking for Adele," she explained. "To confirm the numbers for Account Services' new chairs." She had already verified it twice.

Gary scratched his nose; none of his freckles came off. "Eva's sick again," he said.

"Oh." Sloane was surprised Adele had told her boss about Eva.

"We got the same one," he said, shaking his wrist. He and Sloane had the same fitness tracker.

"Oh." She turned, worried she was blushing. She had a sudden vision of them meeting for the first time, their hands touching as they reached for the same fitness tracker.

"Do you do supplements, too?"

Sloane snapped out of her perfect-man-falls-for-awkward-girl fantasy. "Vitamin C," she said.

He smiled. "You saved Joan's butt yesterday. Adele was right to suggest you."

"Suggest me?"

"To do the presentation, so Joan could try to reach Daniel Brownwood."

Adele did that?

Grace from Finance entered the department.

"Got something for me?" said Gary, reaching for the file folder in her hand.

"Hi, Grace," Sloane said.

During Sloane's first year at the agency, Adele had introduced her to Grace, who was looking for a designer to do the branding for her daughter's flower shop. She couldn't afford anyone with experience, but Sloane was so thrilled that she agreed to be paid in flowers. Five years later, the logo was still on the first page of Sloane's portfolio, and she had yet to collect her payment.

"Was Joan able to get a meeting with Brownwood?" asked Grace.

Sloane didn't know. "Joan's been really busy," she said, "we haven't had a chance to connect on it yet."

"Let's hope she works her usual magic," said Gary, scanning the papers in the folder. "The numbers don't look good if we lose Brownwood."

"I heard she's considering moving the account to Sara," said Grace.

At thirty-three, Sara Cooper was one of the younger account managers. If Lenore was right, and it would take more than a great campaign pitch to keep Brownwood's business, then maybe Sara, by age alone, had a better chance of making a personal connection with Brownwood's new marketing manager.

Gary slipped the folder under his arm. "Let's hope these renovations turn out to be a good investment." Both he and Grace smiled uneasily.

"I should get back to my desk," said Sloane.

"Of course," said Gary. "You must be busy."

Sloane spent her lunch hour walking laps around the parking lot. If she weren't so worried about returning to her desk looking like Smurfette she could have amassed more steps. Even walking slowly, she still required time to dry out in a stall. Her fitness tracker read just over three thousand steps. It seemed like a lot before she realized it was seven thousand short of the daily goal. She wasn't even close.

A magazine had been left on her chair, a sticky note attached to the cover: "Check out page 58. Stellar. - Irving." Sloane agreed, the ad popped off the page. She might have chosen an even hotter shade of pink for the border. She squinted, trying to imagine it, and then emailed Irving for his opinion: "More magenta for the border? Looks like around 45%. I would have tried 50%+. You?"

Catching her eye was the headline of the article printed on the opposite page: "Tips to Help You Keep Your Customers." According to someone named Greg Ciotti, content marketing manager at Help Scout, "the quickest way to get customers to ignore you is to not stand for anything." The article referenced a study that found that almost two-thirds of consumers polled believed "shared values" was the primary reason they supported a company. "It's pivotal to connect in a real way," she read. "Get personal." The article's final challenge was, "So what do YOU stand for?" Sloane quickly closed the magazine as Joan returned to her office.

Determined to reach ten thousand steps, she spent her afternoon break walking around the food court below the agency's office. Then she made up excuses to walk through the departments, racking up steps. She paced at her desk while she confirmed tomorrow's after-hours removal of Account Services' chairs and the delivery of their ergonomic replacements. Everything was set.

Her phone rang.

"Good morning. Account Services. Sloane Sawyer speaking."

"This is Barbara Cummings from Brownwood Industries." The voice on the line was firm, with little intonation. "Confirming Daniel Brownwood will see Joan Dawes tomorrow morning at nine."

Joan got a meeting with Daniel!

"Thank you," said Sloane calmly. "I'll let her know. She'll meet Mr. Brownwood at his office?"

"Mr. Brownwood prefers to meet at the agency. He looks forward to being introduced to the team."

But tomorrow's Regina Kaye Day! On the birthday of the agency's founder, each department ran a fundraiser in support of a non-profit group chosen by Regina. The department that raised the most money won bragging rights for the year. The agency also provided a two-week marketing campaign, *pro bono*, that ran in various media spots across Torren Hills. Streamers and balloons festooned cubicles and employees were encouraged to dress down. Regina Kaye Day was not the day for Mr. Brownwood to visit the agency's office.

Thinking quickly, Sloane responded, "Unfortunately, the Account Services team will be attending a seminar all day. Joan would be happy to meet Mr. Brownwood at the Juniper instead. I can arrange for a meeting room."

Barbara hesitated. "Very well."

Sloane immediately called the Juniper, the grandest hotel in Torren Hills. *Please, please, please.* She was either going to be a hero or a goat, depending on whether or not she succeeded in booking one of the first-class meeting rooms. With some coaxing, and the agreement to pay a premium, Sloane managed to convince the hotel manager to accommodate the last-minute request. She sent Joan an email with the details and hoped she wouldn't get fired for approving an exorbitant expense.

Chapter Twenty-Six

SLOANE KEPT HER job at the bookstore after earning her bachelor's degree and enrolled in a two-year online graphic design program, taking out more student loans. Jason took a job at a small landscaping company while he applied for work more suitable to his degree. He eventually landed a job at Ace Solutions, a developer of business apps that helped companies be more efficient and collaborative. He would have preferred to be developing a video game—building and coding an arsenal of weapons rather than icons for file depositories—but those jobs weren't in Torren Hills. Sloane was grateful he didn't suggest a move to the city.

After completing her online program, Sloane resigned from the bookstore and took an eighteen-month secretarial contract at Jones and MacAvoy Law. When she started, the office was a disaster, but a month in, she had everything in its proper place. The senior partner, Mr. Jones, said he wished he had a permanent position to offer her. She was flattered but not disappointed—the job was always supposed to be temporary and she planned to have a graphic designer job lined up before her contract ended. Then it would be Jason's turn to focus on his career.

The Zimmermans moved out of the house on Truman Avenue; Mr. Zimmerman had a fall and Mrs. Zimmerman wasn't able to provide adequate care. For just two hundred dollars more, Sloane and Jason could have the entire house, doubling their living space. It meant Jason could move his video games downstairs and Sloane could stop worrying about tripping over the cords stretched across the living room floor. They would also gain a second bathroom.

An extra two hundred dollars a month was a lot of money. Sloane had just invested the last of her student loan on a new laptop with updated design software, a down payment on a used car and a pair of trendy red glasses. Repayments would soon be added to their monthly expenses.

Jason sat beside Sloane on the couch and waited for her to finish a poster for the bookstore. Even though she didn't work there anymore, she had volunteered to continue designing their promotional material to help build up her portfolio.

"Raj quit," said Jason, when Sloane closed her laptop. Raj was Jason's co-worker at Ace Solutions. "Alana offered me extra hours, if I'd come in on Saturdays."

"You work on your video game on Saturdays."

"It would cover the increase in rent."

"But your video game."

"We need the extra space, Sloane. Maybe one day we'll really need it, and if we don't take it now, Mr. Yin's going to rent it to someone else."

"One day?"

Jason's eyes scanned the apartment. "Where would a baby sleep?"

Miranda. Sloane smiled. Almost twenty-four, she and Jason had started talking more seriously about marriage and kids and careers and the house they were going to own one day. If Jason's video games moved into the basement, a crib could fit in the living room—*one day*. When their second child was born, they would buy a house that was bigger. They had already started saving. An empty yogurt container labeled House Fund sat on the counter by the door. Jason dropped change, sometimes even bills, into it each week. Sloane rarely added to it and borrowed from it when she was short, but planned to make a lump-sum contribution as soon as she became a graphic designer.

"You already pay a greater share of our rent," said Sloane, imagining what it would be like to have more space. "It would be nice though, to have a whole house."

"Agreed."

"I almost have a full portfolio. I'm working on an application for the Kaye Agency. For a graphic designer, they're one of the top employers in Torren Hills. When I get the job, you can go back to working on your video game on Saturdays. Maybe I'll win an award and get promoted and be given a raise, and then maybe you'll only need to work part-time, or not at all, and then you can work on your video game as much as you want."

Jason leaned in, his dimples zooming in on Sloane.

"I'm serious," she said. "You believe me, don't you?"

"I believe you can do anything you put your mind to. Now start putting your mind on me." He smiled and tugged on her arms, pulling her on top of him.

"Don't tell my mom, okay?" said Sloane, looking down at Jason. "About the basement. I don't want her to think she can visit now that there's space." On the couch, she rolled onto her back, repositioning Jason on top of her. "We'll tell your mom, though," she said. "Roseanne can visit whenever she wants."

He lowered his head, his eyes closing. Just as his lips were about to meet Sloane's, she pressed on his chest. His eyes opened. "What is it?"

Struck with a thought, Sloane lit up. "Maybe Stephie will visit now."

Chapter Twenty-Seven

WHEN SLOANE ARRIVED home, Jason had dinner searing on the stove. Steam from the rice cooker beaded on his upper lip. Tonight was the start of his regular rotation at the plant: day one of three graveyard shifts.

Sloane kicked off her shoes. "What's that?" she asked.

"Stir-fry."

"No, I mean, *that.*"

Around Jason's wrist was the fitness tracker Roma had given him on Sloane's birthday. "Noticed you started wearing yours," he said. "Thought maybe we could do it together."

"Do what?"

"You know, get fit."

So he had noticed she had gained weight. Yesterday, walking together seemed like a good idea, but today it felt like criticism.

"We work opposite schedules," she said.

"Not always."

"A lot of the time."

"Which isn't always. We could make it work." He turned off the stove and the sizzling sound faded. "What's wrong?"

"Nothing." *Everything.*

"Something."

"Can sometimes nothing be wrong? Nothing is ever wrong with you and that seems to be okay."

Jason disengaged and Sloane felt terrible. She remembered when he first started working at the plant, they often made love in the short period of time their schedules overlapped. He would often rush out the door with a flushed face and his hair all disheveled, looking like he just had sex. She liked that, and even more, the fact that she was the reason for it, but that was before her future of possibility had turned into a present of disappointment.

Jason scooped stir-fry onto two plates. With his bicep, he wiped his upper lip, and then carried dinner to the table.

"I'm sorry," said Sloane. She was the problem, not him. The frustration was in not knowing what to do about it.

Jason smiled, but his dimples didn't surface. Before sitting at the table, he removed the fitness tracker from his wrist.

Over dinner, they barely spoke. Finally Jason broke the silence. "How was work?"

"Fine." Work was surprisingly fine today. She had managed her way out of the would-be disaster of having Daniel Brownwood visit the office on Regina Kaye Day and it felt good. *Unless I get fired tomorrow for booking the Juniper.*

"Joe called me."

Sloane dropped her fork and looked up. "About the fence?" The Harringtons' fence hadn't come up since her birthday.

He nodded. "Said he got my number from Roma a while back. Took this long to actually call it."

"What did he want?"

"Help clearing out his garage. Said since I've got the truck and drive to Tippy for work, maybe I wouldn't mind."

"Are they putting up a new fence?"

"Didn't ask him about that. Said he bought a new car and wants to park it in the garage over the winter."

Sloane suddenly wasn't hungry anymore. She started to clear the table.

"Sloane?"

"You can relax," she said, not making eye contact. "It's my turn to do the dishes. Besides, you've got to leave for work soon."

Jason seemed to hesitate, but then eventually went down to the basement.

At the sink, Sloane raised her arm so her fitness tracker emptied from the dish glove and slid up to her elbow. Her step count filled the screen: 9,712. Still 288 steps to go to reach the daily goal. *Am I really going to fail at walking?*

She marched on the spot, emphasizing the swinging of her arm. Her knees banged against a cupboard door and water splashed on the counter. As she warmed up, she pulled up her shirt and unzipped her pants. If she could just get to ten thousand steps she was sure she would feel thinner. Maybe Jason would notice.

One hundred and fifty steps to go. The anticipation of success got her running on the spot. Her heartbeat raced as her pores released sweat. *Just a little bit more. Almost there.* One hundred. Fifty. Forty. Thirty. Twenty. Ten. Five. Two.

The device vibrated and she buckled over. On the screen, pixilated fireworks shot off. She had done it. 10,002 steps. For the first time, she would text her mom and it wouldn't be a lie. Catching her breath, she smiled widely. Then she reared up, her hip ramming into the counter and rattling the dishes in the drying rack. "Jason!" She hadn't heard him come up.

He stood at the top of the stairs, looking into the kitchen. "I didn't mean to—"

"Sorry," she said, urgently wiping the sweat from her neck. She turned to hide her face, which had likely turned blue.

"I heard banging," he said.

Sloane sucked in her belly and yanked the zipper of her pants.

"You don't have to be embarrassed," said Jason.

She turned to face him. "You're the one who looks sunburnt."

He grinned and rubbed his knuckles. "It's not every day I come upstairs to find my wife . . ."

"Your wife what?" *Marching around like a fool, looking like a Smurf?*

"Masturbating in the kitchen," he finished.

Sloane's face flamed. She couldn't believe he thought that. "I'm going to take a shower," she said, making her escape as he moved toward her.

When she got out of the shower, Jason had already gone back down to the basement. She stood at the top of the stairs, not sure whether she should call him or just go downstairs—she was clean now and ready to be touched.

On the counter, her cell phone vibrated. It was Randy. *Why are you calling me?* Something must have happened with Stephie.

Sloane answered. "Randy?"

"Hey, Sloane."

She heard what sounded like a match being struck. She imagined a cloud of smoke releasing from his mouth, the vapor distorted by the piercing in his lip. "Is everything okay?" she asked. "With Stephie, I mean."

"Saw the note you left her," he said.

On the line, she heard him order a meal. He was probably at the food truck up the street. "Is everything okay with Stephie?"

"Depends on your definition of okay."

"Based on your definition." She didn't trust it. He thought it was okay to smoke pot and miss bill payments and skip therapy sessions and sleep with a roommate on occasion. "Never mind. Did something happen? Is Stephie in trouble?"

"Bee almost died."

Sloane's throat closed. "He did?"

"Forgot to move him back after making dinner."

Stephie didn't want her pet goldfish exposed to electromagnetic radiation, so Bee was to be moved into the living room before using the microwave.

"I left him by the window in the sun," said Randy.

Sloane imagined an overcome Stephie pattering her fingers against Bee's bowl, hugging him a thousand times. She must be furious with Randy.

"She's definitely not okay," said Sloane. "You know how important Bee is to her." As her hand formed a fist, her fingernails burrowed into her palm. "How could you let her down like that? Is she there? Can I talk to her?"

"No."

"No she's not there or no I can't talk to her?"

"She's not here."

"Where is she? The Stairway?"

"Maybe."

"What does 'maybe' mean?"

"I'm not at the Stairway, so I can't be sure."

Sloane inhaled deeply, struggling for calm. "Is that where she said she was going when she left the house?"

"Uh huh."

"So she's probably there."

"Probably."

"She left Bee with you, after you almost killed him?"

Randy didn't respond.

"Will you tell her I called?"

"No."

"Why not?"

"Because you didn't."

Randy was so . . . frustrating! Sloane pressed her knuckles hard into her hip. "I really need to talk to her. Will you tell her that?"

"Uh huh."

Sloane heard a door close. She moved to the front window to see Jason getting into his truck. He hadn't said goodbye. Maybe he had tried to, but she hadn't noticed. *Damn it, Randy.* She was supposed to be reveling in the accomplishment of reaching ten thousand steps, not feeling guilty and irritated.

"Will you tell her to call me?" she said, to Randy on the phone. "Never mind, I know you won't." She hung up before she could say anything she would regret.

It was so hard to be nice to Randy.

Chapter Twenty-Eight

"I'M APPLYING FOR a job at the steel plant," Jason announced.

Sloane dropped her spoon into her cereal, splashing milk onto the back of her hand. "No," she said emphatically, licking her knuckle.

"We need the money."

"Not that much."

But they did need the money that much. Jason had been laid off from Ace Solutions and had been doing odd landscaping jobs since. Sloane still had nine months left in her contract with Jones and MacAvoy Law, but she had already started to worry about what she would do in October. She hadn't received a single call from any of the graphic design positions she had applied for. The only response was an email from the Kaye Agency suggesting she apply for an administrative position: "A role more suited to your experience." Jason had already asked Mr. Yin for an extension on the month's rent.

"Your dad said there was an opening for a crane operator."

"You talked to my dad?"

"It's a lot like playing a video game, operating a crane. It's a joystick control, did you know that?"

"How do *you* know that?"

Jason fidgeted with the cuff of his sweater. "Edward took me to the plant."

"You went to the plant with my dad?"

He nodded. "Yesterday. I passed the aptitude test."

Sloane slapped a palm on the table. Her spoon tinged off the side of her bowl. "Jason, you can't." He wanted to develop a video game, not move coils around in a steel plant. At least the job at Ace Solutions had been relevant. How was operating a crane forty hours a week going to make him a better video-game developer? And the shift work. *I don't want us to be like my parents.*

"We'll figure something else out," she said adamantly.

Jason reached across the table. "It's the right thing to do."

"It's not the right thing for you."

"It's the right thing for us."

She loved how he thought in terms of "us." But for "us" he had already worked six days a week for the past six months.

"You can't ride your bike to the plant," she said. "Not on any shift. At least one way will be dark."

"We'll get a second car. Maybe a truck."

"We can barely afford the car we have. And you'd be an Out-of-Towner. People in Tippy don't like it when people from Torren Hills take their jobs."

Holding her hand, he walked around the table. "I don't care what anyone thinks except you." Standing beside Sloane, he pulled her to her feet. "Come here."

"When I'm a graphic designer, you'll quit? Get a normal job? Then one day, maybe you can work on your video game all the time. Maybe I'll make enough money to support the two of us."

"Or the three of us. When we're ready."

Sloane smiled and swiped the milk from her lips. She could tell by the way his eyebrows were pushing down, forcing his eyes to narrow, that he was about to say something serious. She picked off the Cheerio that had stuck to her sweater. He wrapped his arms around her ribs, and whispered, "I love you, Sloane Sawyer." He had said it a hundred times before.

"I love you, too." She lifted her chin so that he could plant a kiss on her mouth. Instead, he dropped slowly, as if sinking in quicksand. She pulled on his arms to lift him, but then let go. "Oh," she breathed.

On one knee, Jason reached into his back pocket and pulled out a silver ring with a single diamond. "Sloane," he said. "Will you marry me?"

"Jason, I—" It wasn't hesitation. Her throat had involuntarily closed.

Of course it was a yes. Neither doubted that their futures would be together. Still, the moment was overwhelming. Their future would start today.

Jason smiled, his dimples deeper than Sloane had ever seen them. "Is that a yes?"

"Yes," she said, nodding.

The ring slid smoothly onto Sloane's finger. It was perfect. She threw her arms around his neck—around her fiancé's neck. She didn't want to let go; she never wanted to let go.

"Sloane, you're choking me."

She eased up, and Jason stood.

"We can't afford this," she said, holding out her hand, admiring her ring. And then, "Does your mom know?"

"You should call yours."

"The plant," she said, "it's just temporary. Until I get a graphic designer job. Then we'll have our kids and buy a house with a—"

"White picket fence."

Sloane smiled, and Jason hugged her.

"You know how I know everything's going to be okay?" he said.

"How?" asked Sloane.

"Because we love each other."

She tipped forward and stuck her forehead to Jason's chin. "Let's always be okay, okay?"

"Okay."

Sloane broke away.

"Where are you going?"

"To call Stephie!"

Chapter Twenty-Nine

SLOANE WOKE UP early and alone. Jason hadn't yet arrived home from the steel plant. Fumbling for her phone, she noticed her fitness tracker had reset to zero. Today would take just as much effort to reach the goal. So would the day after that. Maybe it wasn't about hitting ten thousand steps every day; maybe it was about trying to hit ten thousand steps every day. If achievements could be erased so easily, so could disappointments. Determined, she decided to go for a walk before work.

Outside, every fifteen or so steps, she checked her fitness tracker, to ensure it was working properly, recording her success. After the fourth lap around the block, she started to worry the neighbors were watching. What if someone thought she was a criminal, scoping a burglary? She imagined being stopped by an officer who asked, "Which house is yours?" Sloane would have to admit that she rented from Mr. Yin and then the neighbors would find out that she and Jason didn't belong.

When she arrived home, Jason's truck was in the driveway. She hurried to the bathroom to clean up.

"Oh!"

Jason was standing at the counter, shirtless and with a towel wrapped around his waist. Sloane backed away.

"Come in," he said. "I'm almost done."

"It's okay."

"Sloane," he said, seriously. "Wait."

She stopped.

"I'm sorry about yesterday," he said.

"Me too."

She turned and he lunged forward. His hand grabbed her butt cheek, something he hadn't done in months. He squeezed and Sloane swore it was like he was wringing a sponge; sweat

164

dripped down the inside of her leg. He gently pulled on her arm, encouraging her to look at him. She imagined slipping on her own perspiration.

"I'm all sweaty."

"I don't care," he said, brushing his knuckles up and down her arm. He tugged on her hand. "Let's make up."

"I'll be late for work. It's already quarter after."

"You won't. Look at me," he whispered.

His fingers skidded over her skin. She wasn't smooth; she was clammy. "I've got to get ready," she said.

"You can get ready after."

She pulled away. "Tonight, okay? When I get home from work." She would shower again, shave her legs, moisturize, suck in her belly, think thin thoughts. She would light a candle and turn off all the lights.

Jason's arms dangled like empty sleeves. He turned and stared into the fogged mirror.

"Did you hear me?" asked Sloane.

He dabbed his chest and shoulders with a towel. "Tonight," he repeated softly.

"For sure tonight, okay?" She meant it. Dodging disappointment wasn't making either of them happy. Actual rejection couldn't be any worse than her imagination. At least it would add a layer of honesty to their relationship. Why couldn't her imagination embrace Jason like it did Gary? In a fantasy, if she had walked in on Gary with only a towel around his waist, she would have made love to him. Real life was so much more complicated.

"Jason."

The cell phone in her pocket vibrated. She twitched, but didn't shift her eyes away from her husband. *I'm not getting it.*

"It could be Stephie," he said.

"I don't care." *You're more important.*

"Just answer it." He walked past her into the bedroom.

She checked her phone: Unknown caller. "Hello? Hello?"

"Gloria?"

Sloane slumped. "Wrong number."

"You sure?" asked the voice playfully.

"Am I sure I'm not Gloria?"

"It's Nasser."

"Nasser? How did you get this number?"

"You gave it to me."

Sloane felt like crying. *Stephie gave him my number.*

"Please don't call again."

Holding back tears, she hung up. Jason had already dressed and gone downstairs.

In the kitchen, she stood over the air vent, holding her breath, faintly hearing the soundtrack of a video game. Jason was just ten feet below, but he might as well have been in China.

Her fitness tracker vibrated, reminding her to move, to keep trying. Maybe it was about trying with Jason, too.

Chapter Thirty

ROSEANNE WAS ONE of those moms who passively lobbied to be a grandmother. As an only child Jason bore sole responsibility and it really was the only thing she asked of her son. It was an easy wish to accommodate since both Jason and Sloane wanted to be parents.

Roseanne's campaign for a grandchild started at Sloane and Jason's wedding at Tippett Valley's town hall, just three months after Jason's proposal. Nine guests attended: Roma and Edward Sawyer, Roseanne Howard and her brother Jim, Jasmine and Joe Harrington, Jason's friend, Raj Patel, and Stephie Harrington and Randy Goff—Randy only because Stephie threatened to not show up if he wasn't invited. During the mother-of-the-groom speech, Roseanne presented her new daughter-in-law with a set of tiny knitted booties.

After the wedding, Jason told his mom that he and Sloane had decided to wait before becoming parents. They wanted to first pay off a portion of their debt, establish their careers and save for a house. Roseanne took it like a champ, but frequently inquired if the time was right. Though she could barely pay her own rent, she started to give Jason and Sloane financial gifts to advance the timeline. She cloaked her determination in sweetness, and Sloane adored her for it.

Then Roseanne got sick. Really sick. Sloane watched her steady decline—the weight loss, the pale skin, the shaking hands and finally the cancer diagnosis. If she and Jason waited any longer, Roseanne might not live to see a grandchild. Jason had to be thinking it, too.

"Let's start trying," she said one night in bed.

"But we're not ready," said Jason.

"You want to be a dad, right?"

"Yes."

"I want to be a mom. So, aren't we ready?"

"What about everything else?"

"We're just changing up the order of things. This is more important."

The muscles in his cheeks and forehead pulsated. He groaned a little when she rubbed his knuckles.

"Let's do this for your mom," she whispered.

His face lit up. "Okay," he said. "Let's make a baby. But for us."

At first, Sloane loved that Roseanne doted on her, hoping her grandchild inherited Sloane's eyes, her smarts and her punctuality. Sloane much preferred her hypothetical child to take after Jason. His dark brown eyes were more serene than eyes that couldn't make up their mind what color they were, and while he didn't read novels, he was really smart about a lot of other things, especially technical stuff. Perhaps most impressively, he could be casually late without getting stressed, something Sloane had yet to master. There was no argument that Miranda was to get Jason's dimples.

Sloane quit a month early from Jones and MacAvoy Law to start a new permanent position with the Kaye Agency—not the graphic designer position she had hoped for, but as Executive Manager for Account Services. It sounded promising, and she was certain she would prove herself as a hard worker and talented graphic designer and be rewarded with a transfer to Creative Services before her pregnancy became obvious. Everything was set.

Month after month Jason's mom got worse, and Sloane got her period—a twenty-eight-day reminder of her failure to conceive. Roseanne was just as good at staying positive as Jason, but to Sloane their optimism was starting to feel sarcastic. All Roseanne wanted was to die a grandmother, and Sloane was standing in her way. Talking to Jason's mom made her feel even more guilty, so Sloane started to let Roseanne's calls go to voicemail.

Sloane was afraid to suggest fertility testing. What if there was something wrong with her and she could never have a baby? There was no one she could talk to. Stephie had her own troubles. Roma would ask a million questions and bombard her with advice. She hadn't even told her mom that she and Jason had started trying for a baby. At the agency, Sloane had lunch once a week with Adele, but she didn't want to tell anyone at work. And if Jason wanted to talk about it, he would have brought it up.

Then the call came. Roseanne Howard had passed. Sloane decided then that when she finally had a girl, she would name her Miranda Roseanne. It was a consolation prize, but still a prize.

Driving home from the funeral, Jason asked Sloane, "You okay?"

No. She was responsible for his mom's passing without having held a grandchild.

"I'm sorry if the service brought up memories of Benjamin," he said.

She hadn't connected the inevitability of Roseanne's death with Benjamin's tragedy. "I didn't go to his funeral," she said. "Stephie couldn't face it, so I stayed home with her." Thinking of Roseanne again, Sloane wept into her hands. "I'm so sorry." All Jason wanted was for his mom to pass in peace. But she didn't. *Because of me.*

That night, Jason set up the Atari 2600. The obsolete game console was older than he was, but Sloane knew it reminded him of Roseanne. His copy of Pac-Man was dented in a corner and the sticker worn, and he had to blow into the cartridge to get it working. The joystick creaked as Pac-Man escaped pursuing ghosts.

In the coming days, Jason didn't speak of his mom. Then weeks and months passed and still Roseanne didn't come up. Then Jason brought home a dozen boxes of tampons from the grocery store.

"What's this?" asked Sloane, as she watched him stack the boxes on the kitchen counter.

"They were on sale," he said.

169

Sloane held back tears, remembering what he had said after meeting her dad for the first time: "Words aren't the only way to communicate."

He was giving up on her.

Chapter Thirty-One

REGINA KAYE BELIEVED in using her success as a businesswoman to help give important messages a loud voice, and she wanted no recognition for it. For this year's charity, Regina had chosen the Crawford Foundation, a group advocating for women's and girls' rights. Media space had been secured and a billboard on Main Street had been plastered with the creative: "The length of my skirt is not a measure of my consent." Accompanying the slogan was an image of a young woman with big eyes that seemed to exhibit both strength and innocence.

On Regina Kaye Day, Account Services transformed from a factory of robots to a carnival. Blinded by so much color in the glare of the flickering light above her desk, Sloane squinted. It was a welcome distraction; she hated how the morning at home with Jason had played out. She sank into her chair with relief. Her body ached from all the recent walking.

Joan wasn't in her office, which was expected. She was at the Juniper, meeting with Daniel Brownwood.

Sloane drafted an email to Account Services reminding the department's employees that at the end of the day their desks had to be tidied and all balloons and streamers taken down. Not only were their chairs being replaced overnight, but the Brownwood pitch was scheduled for the morning, assuming Joan's meeting with Brownwood was going well and that the pitch wouldn't be canceled. Sloane cc'd the other Executive Managers, making sure that all departments were ready for the all-important visitors. She confirmed the catering order for the boardroom.

Sloane then called the cleaning service to ensure the later-than-usual start time had been communicated to the cleaners, so vacuuming of the office would happen after the delivery of the new chairs. Finally she called Security—*again*—to verify that both Tanner Delivery and Manning Office Supply were on their list, and that one of the guards would be available to supervise the workers tonight.

That done, she considered sketching out a poster for the Christmas party, but it was three months away and it was hard to be creative without the proper software. She organized her desk drawer, pausing to twist the cap off a bottle of Wite-Out. The smell triggered memories of her and Stephie giving each other French manicures in high school. All the while, she paced the length of her desk, feeding steps to her fitness tracker.

At lunch, she bought a raffle ticket and a cupcake, and then settled into a booth in the lunchroom. From her purse, she removed a black notebook and leafed through its pages.

"What are you doing?"

Sloane slapped her hand over her notebook. Wearing a bright red faux-fur sweater that clung to her like Saran wrap, Adele slid into the booth.

"You're back," said Sloane.

"What are you doing?"

"What do you mean?"

"That doesn't look like one of your usual novels."

"Oh. I'm tracking my steps." Sloane held up her arm to show off her fitness tracker.

"Secretly?" said Adele.

"No. Privately."

She launched a mini carrot into her mouth. "You know," said Adele, "there's an app for that."

Sloane shrugged. "How's Eva?"

"Better." With her front teeth, Adele scraped off the orange shrapnel that speckled her lips.

"I know what you did," said Sloane. "Suggesting I present the quarterly review."

"I heard it went well."

"From Gary?"

She catapulted another mini carrot into her mouth. "Uh huh."

"Did you hear how Joan's meeting went with—"

"Daniel Brownwood?" finished Adele. "She's briefing the executives now."

"She is?"

"Gary said she convinced Brownwood to show up for the pitch tomorrow. You didn't know?"

Sloane picked at the corners of her notebook. "Joan and I haven't had a chance to connect yet." She changed the subject. "Have you talked to Lawrence?"

"No."

"Still? Why not?"

"I'm in the 'I'm never going to talk to you again' stage."

"You've been through this before. With Travis."

"From the other side, yes."

"The other side?"

"The side that needed forgiving."

Sloane leaned forward. "*You* cheated on him?"

Adele nodded.

"But, you said—"

"What?"

"Nothing. I guess I just got confused." Sloane tugged on a strand of hair.

"Is that Wite-out?" A brushstroke of correction fluid had dried on Sloane's knuckle. "I used it on my teeth once. It was before whitening toothpaste came out. What were you really writing in your notebook?"

"I told you, I'm tracking my steps."

"Isn't that what the device does?"

"Are you never going to talk to Lawrence again?"

"What's there to say? You heard the voicemail."

"I don't know. You thought you were going to marry him. It's just going to end, just like that?"

"I think you've got a secret."

Sloane could feel the weight of her blood draining from her face. *Benjamin.*

With her index finger, Adele tapped Sloane's notebook. "Come on, what secret you got in there?"

Relief passed through Sloane. Before she could stop herself, she said, "I was tracking . . ." she lowered her voice, "intercourse."

"Sex?"

"Ssshhhhhh."

Adele leaned forward. "You're trying for a baby."

"No. Not really. It's complicated," she mumbled.

It occurred to Sloane that she and Adele hadn't talked about having kids, only that Adele's hypothetical fiancé had to want one. They never talked about much of anything except office gossip, Adele's desire to be married before she turned thirty, the multiple candidates she had dated over the past five years, and the details of her wedding, which she had already planned. Half the time Sloane zoned out. Maybe now that Adele was giving up on marriage, it would open the door to new topics of conversation. Sloane wasn't sure she wanted to start by admitting she couldn't remember the last time she and Jason had made love.

"How often do you and Lawrence, you know, sleep together?" she asked, easing into the topic.

Adele frowned. "You mean, did."

"Right. Sorry. I—"

"What metric?"

"Oh. Let's say, in an average week, over the past month."

Adele's lips moved in numerical shapes. "I told you he's got a roommate."

"Noted."

"You know my feeling on living together before a proposal."

"No living with a boyfriend, only a fiancé."

"Six or seven days every month I'm on my period, so that brings down the average."

"Of course."

174

"Last month Lawrence's car needed a new transmission, so it was off the road for a few days."

"What does that have to do with sex?"

"He couldn't drive to the agency on his lunch break."

"Right. Just an average."

Adele's hand formed a fist. She began releasing fingers one by one. "Wait," she said. "Average number of days or average number of times?"

"What?"

"Does having sex twice in a day count as one or two?"

"Two, I guess."

"What if I orgasmed twice, but in the same session, how do you want me to count that?"

Sloane sunk into the bench. "Never mind," she said. "I get it. You have lots of sex."

"Had."

Sloane winced. "Sorry."

"That's some sweater he's wearing," said Adele, her gaze directing Sloane's attention to Irving, who was standing beside Gary in the kitchen.

Irving's sweater was brown with tiny white pill-sized knitted balls sticking to the chest like lint. In contrast, Gary's shirt was white with thin pink stripes. He looked sharp, professional and put together, but in Sloane's opinion, boring, especially on Regina Kaye's birthday. "At least Irving's unique," she said, returning to Adele.

"You think Irving's still a virgin?"

"What?"

Sloane twisted around again. Since starting with the agency, Irving had gained weight. Not like Sloane, more like filled out. His acne had almost cleared and he looked his age: twenty-eight. "He got kind of cute," she said. She hadn't meant to say that. Not exactly that. Certainly not out loud.

Adele's eyes popped. "Are you crushing on Irving Paulson?"

"No!" Sloane looked around to make sure no one else had heard. "I'm married. Geez, Adele."

"That's not a reason why you're not crushing."

"I would never do that to Jason."

"Do what? Think another man is attractive? It's an observation, Sloane. That's not doing anything." ⸣

Adele should have been the last person to be accusing Sloane of having a crush. *What do you call Travis?* "I just meant Irving has changed a lot since we all started here."

"You said cute."

"I meant different. He's a really good graphic designer," said Sloane. "That's what I meant." It really was what she meant. She admired Irving for his successful career, and for the efforts he made to include her in Creative Services. "I don't find him attractive," she went on; he would never be a main character in a Harlequin novel. "Like, I don't want to kiss him or anything. It's not as if he's Gary." *Shut up.*

Adele smirked, but she let it go. "How often do you and Jason have sex?" she asked.

Sloane squirmed. "It's different when you're married."

"That's not an average. Why do you think it's different?"

"I don't know, it just is."

"That's not an answer." Adele leaned forward. "Don't look."

Sloane looked and Adele threw herself back against the bench. Irving was approaching.

"Hi," he said, unable to make eye contact for longer than a millisecond.

"Hi," said Sloane, barely audible, as if it were safer to say quietly. She worried what Adele would think if she invited him to sit.

Irving lingered.

"We're kind of having a private conversation," said Adele firmly, but not unkindly.

Sloane imagined Irving blushing, but she didn't look up to confirm it. His body rocked from side to side.

"The team's all read the latest *Creative Review*," he said. "I'll drop it off at your desk this afternoon."

Sloane nodded, and Irving moved on. She wished she had

invited him to join them. She could have asked him how he was feeling about the Brownwood pitch tomorrow.

"What's so wrong with him?" she asked.

Adele frowned. "Have you seen him working on his computer? His posture is atrocious. Look at him now. Even walking, he's slouching."

"If Irving's posture was better, you wouldn't be so mean to him?"

"I'm not mean. I'm honest. Anyone can see he slouches. And we were having a private conversation, weren't we? Or did you want to share with him what you're tracking in your notebook?"

Sloane's chin dropped.

"No one ever said honesty was kind," said Adele. "And it wasn't as if you were nice."

"I wasn't mean," said Sloane.

"You weren't anything. Sometimes that's worse."

Adele's cell phone vibrated. The Caller ID displayed "Travis Wright." She shimmied out of the booth. "I've got to go," she said. "You going to eat that?"

Sloane shook her head and Adele took the cupcake.

Sloane dropped her notebook into her purse and slid out of the booth. Her phone vibrated. She fumbled to read the screen, expecting a text from Jason. After a graveyard shift, he would sleep in the morning and then message Sloane when he got up. But instead, Roma had texted.

> 10,211 steps!
> How many?

Sloane didn't have to be back at her desk for another fifteen minutes, so she walked to her car to accumulate steps, slowly though, so as not to break a sweat. She would text Roma her step count when she returned to her desk. It would be a higher number then. The covered parking lot smelled like garbage, but it was still nice to be out of the office. As she walked, her pants rubbed against her waist, a pink line marking the circumference of her body. She thought of a Russian nesting doll that could be opened to reveal a smaller version. If only she could jump out of her body like that. Walking, she texted Jason. It wasn't like him to not have made contact by this time of the day.

Playing video games?

By the time she reached her car in the lot, she had a reply.

Yep.

A single word? She worried Jason hadn't texted earlier on purpose. Was he that mad? Sloane decided she would make a stop on her way home to pick up his favorite bottle of wine—the one that was too expensive to have all the time, but perfect for special occasions. Tonight wasn't a special occasion, which would make it even more special. She would wear her lingerie and maybe Jason would look at her the way he did on their wedding night, when she had last worn it. When she got home there would be time for them to make love, before he had to leave for the steel plant. Tonight she would have something to write in her black notebook.

See you after work. Maybe we can . . . you know.
Before you have to leave.

Maybe.

Sloane slapped the hood of her car. Her palm stung from the impact. *Can't you see I'm trying?* He didn't believe her and, to be fair, she couldn't blame him. By the time she got home, she was usually tired, didn't feel like a glass of wine or trying to squeeze her body into lingerie she had purchased fifteen pounds ago. She would apologize and he would understand and accept her promise about next time. But Jason had stopped co-operating. Good intentions weren't enough anymore.

Sloane had three minutes to be back at her desk. She was suddenly determined to make it in time—to make the effort, even if she didn't want to, even if she was the only one who noticed. She took off running, narrowly missing a few pedestrians. She slipped on the escalator and skidded on something that had been spilled on the floor in the food court, barely staying on her feet. Arriving in Account Services, she was panting and sweating and her cheeks were probably blue, but she had made it in time. If only Jason had been there, he would have seen how hard she had tried. *I never run.* She texted Roma.

3,945 and it's only lunch.

At Sloane's desk, Lenore was waiting. "Sloane!" She must have just arrived, she was still catching her breath. "Joan finished her meeting with Brownwood. We need to add examples to the pitch," she said, talking fast. "Images from some of our biggest campaigns. Their new marketing manager needs to see that we can handle their rebrand just as well or better than any city agency. I just spoke to Irving. He's adding creatives to the Brownwood folder. Joan wants the revised presentation in her inbox by end of day."

"I'll get it done," said Sloane, sitting.

Lenore nodded, but she didn't seem reassured. "You've arranged for catering?"

"Of course."

She took a bite out of an apple. It sounded like a bone cracking. "The office looks like a playground," she moaned.

"I've already sent out an email," said Sloane, "and I cc'd the other Executive Managers. It won't look like this tomorrow. It's going to be fine."

Lenore dropped her apple and it rolled away. She chased it down the hallway.

On her computer, Sloane accessed the Creative Services drive and opened the folder titled "Brownwood." Inside were folders named for each campaign, including one titled "Rebrand." Inside that folder were two more folders, one labeled "Pitch" and a new folder labeled "Kendra Jamieson." Sloane leaned back. *Kendra Jamieson?* It took her a moment to realize why the name was familiar. Inside the folder were the files to impress Brownwood's new marketing manager, images from campaigns executed for Torren Hills Toyota and Cullen Foods. Was this the same Kendra Jamieson who had once been Stephie's friend?

Refocusing, Sloane added a new section to the presentation.

179

She uploaded the images, and then saved the revised PowerPoint. With that finished, she googled Brownwood Industries. Since Daniel had become CEO, the company's website had been updated with a contemporary design. She clicked on the Meet Our Team tab and scrolled down the list.

Kendra Jamieson, Marketing Manager, had straight, brown hair and short bangs and her smile seemed not quite full, like maybe she had relaxed before the camera clicked. Her bio highlighted her beginnings in New Carlton and then her recent move to Torren Hills.

To be absolutely sure, Sloane logged into her Facebook account and searched for Stephie Harrington. Even though Stephie had abandoned her Facebook page after Benjamin's death, it was still searchable. Sloane clicked on Stephie's Friends tab and entered "Kendra." In a matter of seconds, the photograph from the Brownwood Industries' website popped up. It was the same woman.

Sloane viewed Kendra's Facebook page. Her relationship status was "single." Her last post was a month ago when she had updated her profile picture and announced her move to Torren Hills for a job opportunity. Before that, she had posted a picture of herself in a #MeToo t-shirt waving a flag in a crowd. Not wanting to be seen on Facebook at work, Sloane logged out of her account.

She emailed Joan and Lenore the revised presentation. That was when she noticed her ring finger was bare. For the second day in a row, she had forgotten her wedding rings in the washroom. Fate was yelling at her.

Chapter Thirty-Two

OVER DINNER, SLOANE'S mind wandered, unable to shake the hope that it had finally happened. A baby. Pregnant at twenty-eight.

When Jason reached for her hand, she pulled away as if she had been bitten.

"Sorry," she said, returning her hand to the table. "You scared me."

"My touch scares you?"

She leaned so far forward that her ribs crushed against the table. She forced her hand on top of his. "You surprised me. I was remembering the day we took over the entire house." Four years ago. She rubbed her belly. Was it finally going to be worth it? She rubbed his knuckles. *Miranda Roseanne*. If she were pregnant she would have a reason to bring up his mom. It had been two years since her passing and he hadn't once talked about her.

She wouldn't tell him she was late. She would wait until she was sure she was pregnant. In the beginning, he had been with her for each pregnancy test. Recently though, she had started taking them alone. It spared her his response: "Next time," he would say and then smile and hug her and tell her, "Everything's going to be okay." It was easier to bear the disappointment alone.

"You done?" he asked, his hand slipping out from under hers.

"Done what?"

"Dinner," he said.

"Oh. Yeah. Thanks."

He cleared the table and Sloane leaned back in her chair, watching him wash dishes. She considered stealing in behind him, wrapping her arms around his chest and blowing hot breath against his neck, like he sometimes did to her. She could whisper, "I'm late," and he would know what it meant. But she had said it so many times before.

Jason moved toward the basement door. As Sloane stood, the legs of her chair screeched across the floor. "You're going downstairs?"

He paused. "You don't want me to?"

No. Let's go upstairs. Me and you. Together. Let's make love. Let's celebrate! But until she was sure, she couldn't say it. They could still make love though, for no other reason than because they were in love.

"Come upstairs," she said.

He didn't hesitate. He led the way and she followed.

During sex, she had started to notice how her body responded to gravity. On top of Jason her breasts sagged like water balloons and her belly bowed as if it were reaching for his. She rolled onto her back and gravity flattened her figure, making her appear thinner, but her breasts flopped off to the sides. If she were pregnant, her body would have to expand and change. Childless, there was no excuse.

With Jason on top, she looked at the books about pregnancy and fertility stacked on her bedside table. As he held his weight, his arms shook. He groaned and lowered onto his elbows, careful not to crush her. His face sunk into a pillow on his side of the bed. Catching his breath, he lifted himself off, rolling onto his back.

Sloane sat up and noted the date in the black notebook she kept on her bedside table. It wasn't a prime night in her fertility cycle, but her research recommended that sex occur even on statistically non-fertile nights. *You never know.* Since Roseanne's passing, Sloane had been tracking her cycle and the dates when she and Jason had sex. Tonight was their three hundred and twelfth attempt, and that was just since she had started recording. If she added the number of tries before she purchased the black notebook it had to be over four hundred. She had failed four hundred times, at least. After sex, Jason used to say things like, "I think we did it this time," or rub her belly and whisper into her ribs, "You in there?" Now he just smiled.

Sloane got out of bed.

"Where are you going?"

"To pee," she said, slipping on her robe. She had read that urinating after sex lowered the possibility of conception, but it wouldn't matter if she were already pregnant.

In the bathroom, she dropped her robe to allow the moisture on her skin to evaporate more quickly. She pulled back her hair, exposing the ironic shape of her ears, and then drank water from the tap, slurping from her palm. With a damp washcloth, she wiped the inside of her thighs, and then turned in the mirror and pushed out her belly. Was there finally a baby inside her?

She shrieked when Jason appeared in the doorway. Her stomach deflated and the washcloth dropped to the floor with a splat. She scrambled to put on her robe. Jason smiled. He was in his boxers, still erect, his chest sparkling with sweat.

"Did you . . ."

"Did I what?" asked Sloane, flustered.

"You know . . ." He reached for her robe. "If you didn't, we can keep going."

She pulled the belt out of his grasp. "I'm good."

"I want you to be great," he said.

"I am. Really." It wasn't true. She couldn't remember the last time she had orgasmed. Sex hadn't been about that for a while— not since they had started trying for a baby.

Jason took her hands and placed them on his face, guiding her fingers up and down his stubbled cheeks. He moved her thumbs into the crevices of his dimples. "I love you," he said. He planted his lips on hers, his hands landing on her waist, his fingers slipping through the opening of her robe.

Sloane pulled away, not wanting him to see her naked under bright lights.

He touched his cheek, as if he had been punched. Then he turned away without a word.

"Where are you going?" asked Sloane.

He was heading downstairs.

"I love you, too," she said to his retreating back.

Sloane called Stephie, anxious to share her news.

"Hi, Sloane," Stephie answered. "This isn't a good time."

"What are you doing?"

"Going out."

"To the Stairway?"

"Pet store."

"Why?"

"Randy's buying me a goldfish."

"Really?"

"Yeah."

She could barely take care of herself. A goldfish would be dead by the end of the week. *What's he thinking?*

"I gotta go," said Stephie.

"Wait."

"What?"

"Nothing."

Alone in her bedroom, Sloane picked up *Snow Crash*. Science fiction wasn't a usual choice, but the story had elements of computer science and reading it made her feel closer to Jason.

When she got up to use the bathroom, she discovered she wasn't pregnant after all. Sobbing quietly, she opened a box of tampons. If she held her breath, she could hear the faint soundtrack of a video game being played in the basement.

Chapter Thirty-Three

SLOANE PICKED UP the wine on her way home. When she arrived, Jason's truck wasn't in the driveway.

"Jason?" she called, entering the house.

Silence.

Opening the basement door, she listened for the sound of a video game soundtrack or the clacking of a keyboard. Nothing.

"Jason?"

She checked her phone. No new messages. She ran upstairs to see if he was having a nap before his graveyard shift, and then went downstairs to check the basement. He wasn't in the house.

It wasn't like him not to be home before his shift. Maybe he had run out to get milk or something. Sloane's fitness tracker knocked against her hip, reminding her of her new commitment to actually achieving her goals. She started marching back and forth across the basement, pumping her arms to ensure each step counted, careful not to trip over a cord. All the while she listened for the click of the front door. When Jason arrived home, she would present the bottle of wine, and then shower and put on lingerie and they would make love. They would lose track of time and he would have to scramble to make it to the steel plant for eleven. In the crane, he would think of Sloane.

She shrieked when the fitness tracker flew off her wrist. It pinged off a monitor and landed on the keyboard, waking the computer on Jason's desk. Three screens lit up in sequence, windows into the virtual worlds where Jason spent so much of his time. The feeling that she had done something wrong was quickly overwritten by curiosity. Her gaze jumped from one screen to the next.

On the left screen was a dark world with dragons and elves and what looked like a Sasquatch stretched across a rock with a dagger in its heart and blood dripping from its mouth. Sloane couldn't decide if the Sasquatch was JasonHoward or if Jason's avatar had been the one to kill it. The middle screen was a much brighter and more realistic world, with men and women dressed in combat fatigues and carrying heavy artillery. The characters' muscles burst through their tight clothing and their expressions were rigid, ready to kill. Was one of them JasonHoward or were these villains out to kill him? Or did he create them?

The right screen was some kind of chat room with speaking bubbles stacked one on top of the other, a conversation between two avatars: JasonHoward and HarperKennedy. JasonHoward had brown spiky hair, super-white teeth and dimples. Just like Jason. HarperKennedy had curly blond hair, pink lipstick and the same super-white teeth.

Sloane had never been in a chat room before, but guessed it was where participants in multi-player games coordinated strategies. Or maybe Jason used them to discuss source code with other developers. Or maybe this was an example of what he had meant when he said avatars could do more than play video games.

As she slipped the fitness tracker back onto her wrist, she read the bubbles of text. It didn't take long for her to realize that JasonHoward and HarperKennedy weren't plotting or strategizing or negotiating or discussing computer language. They were conversing. Sloane's breathing quickened. *What is this?* Sinking into Jason's chair, she read on.

Favorite book?

The Fountainhead. It'll blow your mind. Yours?

Art of Game Design. It'll turn your blown mind into ash.

Gotta go. Work. Tmr?

Until then.

Sloane rubbed her hands, her knuckles cracking like fireworks. *Who the hell is HarperKennedy?* She slipped her hands beneath her thighs.

HarperKennedy could be anyone, from anywhere in the world.

The anonymity of the internet produced an immeasurable number of possibilities. HarperKennedy wasn't even necessarily a woman. It was a harmless platonic conversation about books between two adults. It wasn't as if Sloane had heard a voicemail with Jason groaning and calling out Harper's name.

She knew she should get up and walk away. Instead, she reached for the mouse. Scrolling up, more chat bubbles loaded on the screen. The conversation went back months.

Shaking, she shifted to the front of the chair and started reading from the beginning. It started with HarperKennedy.

> Hi.
>
>> Hi.
>
> You're not a psycho, r u?
>
>> No. Are you?
>
> No. Can't sleep.
>
>> Me neither.

JasonHoward and HarperKennedy had talked about all kinds of things—*real* things: books, movies, work, pets, preferences. JasonHoward described what it was like to spend forty hours a week alone in the cab of a crane: "Like sitting in an empty movie theatre playing Tetris on the big screen." HarperKennedy explained what it was like to be a travel agent: "Think of it like preparing a meal and not being invited to the table." Both agreed that bike lanes should be mandatory on all streets, that peanut butter should be kept in the refrigerator, that *Thor* was the best Marvel movie, and that spoiling a ballot *was* a vote. HarperKennedy preferred Coke to Pepsi, and JasonHoward replied, "Our first disagreement, lol." HarperKennedy talked about her dog and asked JasonHoward if he liked animals. He replied, "I wouldn't mind having a cat." Jason had never mentioned a cat to Sloane.

Her hand separated from the mouse. Leaning forward, she read the four lines again.

> u got someone?
>
>> ???

Girlfriend? Wife? Husband?

No.

Sloane clawed at the inside of an elbow as her eczema flared up. Why had he typed that? He had a wife. *Me!* In her mind, HarperKennedy transformed from a cartoon avatar to a real-life Harper Kennedy—a skinny, sexy woman, with clear skin and narrow hips, who wasn't drowning in student debt, hadn't failed to get her dream job, and who had a uterus suitable for a baby.

Sloane's teeth chattered and her breath stuttered out of her mouth. She had no idea that Jason was doing this in the basement. What if there was an entirely other layer to his virtual relationship with Harper? Did they meet for coffee or go to the movies or . . . *Is Jason having an affair?* Sloane's hands started to shake. Was this how Adele felt when she discovered Lawrence had cheated on her?

Sloane was barely able to use her phone. She called Stephie but got her voicemail. *What do I do now?* It was as if the basement were filling with water—like she was drowning. She hurried upstairs.

"Hey."

Sloane shrieked. "Jason!"

He was at the front door, taking off his shoes. "What's going on?" he asked.

"What do you mean?" Her heart raced.

"You're out of breath."

"Oh. I was exercising."

"In the basement?"

"It's the biggest room." Flustered and frenzied, she moved to the counter. "Where were you?"

"I should've texted. I thought I'd be back before you got home. You got wine?"

She pointed to the plastic bag on the floor beside his foot. "What's that?"

"A book," he said, picking up the bag.

"A book?"

"Yes."

"Which one?"

"*The Fountainhead.*" He said it like it didn't mean anything. Like he hadn't bought it because it was Harper Kennedy's favorite book. "You've read it?" he asked.

Sloane's bottom lip quivered. "Where'd you get it?" Her tone was harder, laced with accusation and the effort to keep it together.

"A bookstore. Where else?"

He didn't know she knew. *He thinks he's still fooling me.*

"You never buy books," she said, her voice cracking.

"I bought dozens in university."

"Textbooks. Not novels."

"I decided to give this one a go." He set the bag beside the wine on the counter. "What's wrong?"

"Nothing."

"Something."

"It's just that it's a big book for someone who doesn't read novels."

"It comes recommended," he said. "Did something happen at the agency?"

"From who? Who recommended it?"

"Someone at work."

Sloane reached for the counter. "At the plant?" *Harper works at the plant?* "A woman?"

He seemed to hesitate. "Yes."

"What's her name?"

She braced herself for his answer.

"Heather."

"Heather?"

Heather could be an alias for Harper. Or maybe Harper was an alias for Heather.

"What does Heather do at the plant?"

"Works in the office. Puts orders together."

"When are you ever in the office?"

"To pick up the orders for my shift."

"You go into the office?"

"To get the orders."

"Every day?"

"Sloane, why are you all of a sudden curious about my job?"

"I just didn't know you went into the office."

"Well, I do."

"I thought you were in this . . . box, all by yourself, wearing earplugs and never interacting with anyone." *Like sitting in an empty movie theatre playing Tetris on the big screen.*

"Pretty much. After I get the orders from Heather."

"What's she like?"

"Heather? Nice, I guess."

Sloane turned, her back to Jason. Any moment, she might cry, and she didn't want him to see how upset she was. He would hug her and tell her everything was okay, when it wasn't. She feared she would believe him, and then things would go back to the way they were, but nothing was good about that. The way they were, Jason was having a relationship with another woman.

"Sloane?" He moved in behind her.

She didn't turn around. She couldn't. To keep the tears in her eyes, she needed all her concentration. *Ask him about Harper.* She had already gotten this far; it would be too difficult to get back to this point. *Ask him.*

A click and then a creaking sound alerted her. She spun around to discover Jason had the basement door open. "You're going downstairs to play video games?"

He paused, confused.

"Is that all you do down there?" she asked.

He blushed, which scared her. She realized she wasn't ready to talk to him about Harper and what it meant for their marriage. She had to go. She dipped her hand into the House Fund and pulled out a handful of bills. "I'll pay it back," she said, gathering her jacket and purse.

"Where are you going?"

"Tippy," she said, slipping her phone into her pocket. "Stephie needs me."

She'd said it so many times before, but now Sloane needed her.

She was in no shape to drive. On shaking legs, she walked toward the corner of Truman Avenue and Main Street. She hoped she had taken enough money to cover cab fare to Tippett Valley.

The driver of the cab kept glancing in the rearview mirror. In the backseat, Sloane was trying not to sob and the effort was creating all kinds of frog-like sounds. She played with the seat belt, the window buttons, the zipper of her purse and her fitness tracker. None of it helped to distract her from what she had read on Jason's computer. On her phone, she searched for Harper Kennedy on Facebook. Each profile picture was of a woman prettier than Sloane. There were too many to guess which one was *her*.

"You on drugs?" asked the driver. In the rearview mirror, the reflection of his eyes narrowed.

Sloane made an effort to stop fidgeting. "No," she said.

In the mirror, he eyed the dozen tissues she had piled beside her on the seat. "You take those with you," he said.

She nodded and started to gather the waste. She had been careless with a few; snot and saliva streaked the middle seat. As she leaned to drag the back of her forearm across the leather, the driver sped up so abruptly that Sloane's head hit the cushioned backseat. Then the car halted, and she was pitched forward. The seat belt dug painfully into her waist; her fitness tracker slid over her knuckles.

Grabbing onto the door handle, she pulled herself upright. She was in the middle of an intersection; the driver had misjudged the traffic light. If the steel plant had been on a shift change, there would have been traffic crossing. *I could've died.*

"Please keep your eyes on the road," she warned, shaken. If she had wanted a life-threatening commute, she would have driven herself. She slid the fitness tracker back to her wrist, and then gathered her purse, which had catapulted to the floor, along with many of the tissues.

She reached for her phone and froze with her hand inside her pocket. Would Jason even care? He was probably thinking about Harper, not Sloane. He had probably been thinking about Harper for months.

Sloane considered asking the driver to turn around, to take her back to Torren Hills, to Truman Avenue, to Jason. *Give me a second chance. I'll do better. I promise.* She could lose weight. Work harder on her portfolio. Apply for graphic designer jobs outside of the agency. Start contributing to the House Fund. Talk about IVF or adoption—there were alternative ways to become parents.

At home, she would lead Jason to their bedroom, where she would pull his body over top of hers and guide his hips between her legs. She would make love to him in the lingerie she had planned to wear, to remind him that he loved her. *What's wrong with me?* He was having a secret relationship and she was thinking about making love to him?

Part of her wished she had smashed Jason's computers before leaving the house. Would he be more upset that his computers got trashed or that his wife had discovered his secret? She hiccupped and coughed and croaked. It was such a strange combination of emotion, to love someone and to feel betrayed by that very same person.

Out the window, the Tippett Valley welcome sign passed. She wished her mom were home and not somewhere in China. If Roma were, would Sloane tell her about Jason and Harper? Sloane had believed she and Jason were better than her parents, but they weren't. *Dad would never tell anyone Mom didn't exist.*

Finally, the cab pulled over in front of Randy and Stephie's townhouse. Sloane paid the fare in small bills and change, and then gathered the scattered tissues. With her hands full, she shouldered the door open, and then managed to get out of the car. She kicked closed the door and the driver sped away.

With her elbow she stabbed the doorbell. It took her a couple of attempts, but she finally succeeded in ringing it.

Wearing boxers and a long white tank top with coffee stains down the front, Randy answered the door. A half-smoked cigarette stuck out from behind his ear, and the hair on the one side of his head was tousled, as if he had just woken up. The skin around his lip piercing was infected, swollen and red. Or maybe it was just ketchup. On his wrist was an elastic band he pulled as far as it would stretch, and then let go. The loud slap of the rubber against his skin caused Sloane to grimace. His expression didn't waver. He did it again.

"Stop it," said Sloane. "Why are you doing that?"

"Doing what?" He snapped the band again.

"That!"

"Oh," he said, as if he hadn't noticed. "It's an experiment."

"For what? That has to hurt." She cringed.

"Have you ever asked yourself if pain is a choice?"

"Are you high?"

He snapped the band again, and Sloane looked away. "Is that what you're doing," she asked, "training to be an emotionless human being?"

"A painless one."

"Because you think happiness is the absence of pain?"

"I don't know." He snapped the band again. "That's the experiment."

Sloane suddenly felt weak. Like she was sinking. Like she might collapse. She transferred most of the tissues into one arm to free a hand. Her purse slid off her shoulder and she grabbed Randy's wrist for balance, her baby finger grazing his sister's name tattooed onto his forearm. The elastic band snapped against her fingers. "Damn it, Randy!" she cried out, shaking her wrist. The pain caused her stomach to turn.

"Choose not to feel it," he said.

Sloane's eyes watered. "It's not a switch, Randy!"

"What if it is?"

193

She opened and closed her hand, encouraging feeling to return to her fingers. "I need to talk to Stephie," she said, barging into the house.

She kicked off her shoes. "Stephie!" She hurried into the bathroom, where the trashcan was overflowing. As an alternative, she dropped the dozen tissues all at once into the toilet, wrenched on the lever and then watched the paper struggle to be sucked away. "Stephie!"

Catching her reflection in the mirror, it wasn't just her flushed skin or the swelling around her eyes that she didn't recognize, but the intensity of her gaze. It was as if her eyes had been swapped out for new ones. *Who am I?* She splashed water on her face, ignoring the globs of toothpaste shaped like white chocolate chips on the taps and the dark hair streaking the basin. *Have I lost Jason?* She reached for a towel—the green one she hoped was Stephie's—and patted her cheeks sparingly, just in case it was Randy's.

"Stephie!" She peeked into Stephie's bedroom and then met Randy in the kitchen. "Where's Stephie?" she demanded.

Bee's fishbowl wasn't in its usual spot and, for a brief moment, Sloane worried he had died. Then she spotted him in his bowl on the living room coffee table.

"Randy! Is she in your room?"

"No," he said, removing a steaming bowl of something from the microwave. He didn't wait for his food to cool. Instead, he chewed like he was gnawing on glass, his mouth open, his jaw clenching uncertainly. He breathed heavily from his throat, as if fogging a mirror, holding the bowl close to his chin and using his fork like a shovel. He closed his eyes and started to chew normally, likely choosing not to feel pain.

"Randy!"

His eyes shot open.

"Is Stephie at the Stairway? Is she working tonight?"

He swallowed dramatically and then pounded on his chest. Seemingly unable to speak, he nodded. Maybe his vocal cords had melted. He snapped the elastic band around his wrist and Sloane flinched. She couldn't take another minute. She would find Stephie at the Stairway.

Chapter Thirty-Four

SLOANE FIGURED SHE could make it to the Stairway in forty-five minutes if she speed-walked and didn't care about looking like a Smurf. She had sworn she would never walk the route again, but tonight she was desperate. She checked her phone. Three messages, all from Jason.

> You took the bus? A cab?
>
> I could've driven you.
>
> You okay?

Such a loaded question disguised in two simple words: You, Okay.

She considered ignoring the texts. She wanted Jason to wonder if something tragic had happened to his wife on her way to Tippett Valley. She wanted him to feel the same shock she had felt when she discovered the messages between JasonHoward and HarperKennedy. But what if he didn't care? If something happened to Sloane, then he and Harper wouldn't have to be a secret anymore. They could buy a house together, have a couple of babies, work their dream jobs. Jason wouldn't have to end his marriage with Sloane. He would be admired for moving on, for finding love again. He would still be the hero in the story and he would be happy. Wasn't that what Sloane wanted? Maybe he deserved a successful, beautiful woman. Replying, her thumbs jabbed her phone.

> Cab. Ok. Have a good shift tonight.

It took her forty-eight minutes to arrive at the Stairway. Her fitness tracker was at 9,324 steps. Before entering the bar, she checked her appearance in her phone's camera app. She had cried the entire way, which had got her breathing, so at least her face hadn't turned blue. She wiped her soggy cheeks with the collar of her shirt and took heaping breaths to encourage the rosy color of her skin to fade. Not that anyone would notice inside.

Her phone showed six missed calls, all from an unknown caller. Nasser? Another of Stephie's one-night-stands? It didn't matter; she just needed to find Stephie.

It was eight o'clock on a Thursday night and the Stairway was packed. It reminded Sloane of a sports field, where customers competed for the attention of the bartender, for space on the dance floor, for their favorite song to be played by the DJ. Servers competed for tips and bouncers refereed, ensuring a clean game. Then there were spectators like Sloane. Only tonight, she would have to play. Harper Kennedy could be there.

Sloane spotted Stephie leaning against the bar, circling an ankle behind her. A drunk teenager kept trying to pet her arm. Stephie threw the girl's hands off her and seemed to growl, as if she didn't know she did the same when she was drunk. Stephie climbed on a stool and waved to get the attention of the bouncers chatting at the opposite end of the bar. The one with a child's face and a cross-fit challenger's body weaved through the crowd, moving people out of the way like pawns in a chess game. His nipples showed through his skin-tight translucent shirt, marking two dark bull's-eyes on his chest. Stephie had likely slept with him.

She slid a tray of drinks onto her flattened palm. The drunk teenager followed her into the crowd until the bouncer intercepted and politely directed her back to her table of friends. She petted him too, but he didn't seem to mind.

Sloane refocused. "Stephie!" She barely heard her own voice above the noise. Securing her purse, she crossed her arms to protect her chest and pushed her way forward. Every few seconds, she apologized for nearly bulldozing someone over. It was impressive how Stephie managed to keep the drinks on her tray.

Stephie stopped at a table of five women, each with a pink feather in her hair and one with a twisted white sash running across her body. She removed drinks from her tray, and the women cheered as if she had performed a magic trick. Sloane powered forward, arriving as Stephie moved on.

The woman with the white sash squealed, "I'm getting

married!" Sloane pressed her palm against her ear, the noise like a punch. How many shrieks of hers had Jason endured over the years?

She stood on her tiptoes and searched the nearby tables. *Where'd you go?* One of the women shook a small paper bag. "Advice for the bride!" she shouted, misting Sloane's cheek with saliva. She had long, jet-black hair that was tangled in her belt loops, and perfectly shaped breasts that jiggled just the right amount. Her nose was slightly flat, like a puppy's. Sloane wondered if Jason would think she was pretty. Was she Harper Kennedy?

Sloane shook her head and waved off the bag, but the woman wasn't accepting no for an answer. Into one of Sloane's hands, she shoved a pen; into the other, a blank strip of paper. "Advice for the bride!"

Around Sloane, a human cage formed, all five women circling. She imagined snatching the bag, popping the air out of it, and then kicking the pieces of paper as each one floated to the floor. She would stomp all over the advice, like the mass murder of an ant colony. But it was only a thought. "Advice for the bride! Advice for the bride!"

"Fine!" Sloane snapped. She leaned over the table, pen in hand—and froze. What advice could she give? *I've failed at everything, especially marriage.* Breathing heavily, she was concerned she was having a panic attack. At least there was a paper bag to breathe into if she needed it. She dropped the pen and gripped the tabletop.

The bachelorette party finally lost patience and the wall of women came down around Sloane. She spotted Stephie heading to the back of the bar and pushed her way through the crowd, hurrying to catch up.

She burst into the women's washroom with so much force she nearly knocked over the three women standing tightly together like bowling pins, waiting for a vacant stall. She raised her hands. "Sorry," she said to all three.

An Out-of-Order sign was stuck to the door of two out of the four stalls. A set of feet was pacing beneath the door of one of the useable stalls, as a woman whispered, presumably on a phone. One of the waiting women banged on the door with no effect. A woman wearing red heels and clocking possibly the longest pee in the Stairway's history occupied the second useable stall. The three women in line looked both impressed and irritated.

"Stephie!" shrieked Sloane.

She was standing in front of the mirror with her eyes closed and her hands flat on the counter. Her eyes opened. "What are you doing here?"

"I need to talk to you," said Sloane.

Stephie lowered her head into the sink. She turned on the tap and drank, water gushing down the side of her face. She swiped her hand across her mouth, spreading lipstick across her chin. She looked like a vampire after a meal. Leaning into the mirror, she scrubbed her chin and then reapplied crimson red to her lips. The droplets of water clinging to her cheek could have passed for tears.

Now that she was here, Sloane didn't know how to begin. *Start with Bee.*

"I heard about Bee," she said.

With her middle finger, Stephie dabbed at the corners of her mouth. "Randy called you, didn't he?"

"He told me he left Bee in the sun."

Stephie smirked, and then glared. "I left Bee in the sun."

"No. Randy said—"

"That's Randy being Randy. Don't you know that about him already?"

A cramp gripped Sloane's side. "Oh." Why had Randy said he was responsible? "He's okay though. Bee, I mean."

Stephie shoved her lipstick into her pocket. "Look, I know what you're going to say. It wasn't my fault, right? Look, I'm fine, really." She smiled—the same smile she used when serving drinks.

"But—"

199

"Don't. Really, Sloane. It doesn't change anything."

Sloane couldn't help herself. "But it wasn't your fault," she said.

"Saying it doesn't make it so."

"It was an accident."

"Negligence isn't an accident."

The three women standing in line were openly eavesdropping.

"I treated him just like I treated Benji," said Stephie, gripping the edge of the counter.

"You didn't forget to do anything with Benjamin," said Sloane. How easily the conversation had turned to Stephie's brother.

"I was supposed to be his sister."

"You were," said Sloane.

"Not a good one."

"You weren't even there when he died. How could you be responsible?"

"Maybe that's exactly why I am responsible." She rotated her ankle and Sloane noticed that blood had seeped through her sock. Had she picked open that old scar again?

The sound of a toilet flushing broke the tension as the woman in the red heels exited the stall. Harper Kennedy? Like Sloane, she had wide hips and acne speckling her chin. She wore glasses, too, and her hair was frizzy—crimped, almost—and tied back in an off-centered ponytail. "Don't let me stop you," she said, stepping up to the sink. She rubbed her hands so fast it was as if she were trying to start a fire. Water sloshed all over the counter.

Sloane refocused. "I didn't come here to talk about Benjamin," she said. "Or Bee."

Stephie didn't respond and Sloane lost courage. "Kendra Jamieson is in Torren Hills," she said instead.

Stephie's hand slipped off the counter. She blinked slowly. "So?"

"She was your best friend."

"Was. I don't know her anymore."

Red Heels yanked on the paper towel dangling from the

dispenser, made a performance of drying her hands and then stuffed the paper into the overflowing trashcan. *Just go already.* She finally walked out, trailing a streamer of toilet paper stuck to her heel.

As she left, the bachelorette party entered, the annoying woman with the paper bag shaking it like a cheerleader's pom-pom. She spread her legs and stretched her arms wide as if holding everyone hostage. "Advice for the bride!" she shouted, flipping her long black hair over her shoulder.

The women swarmed Stephie, demanding her participation. Sloane was surprised when she accepted a pen. As she watched Stephie give strangers her attention, the floor seemed to disappear beneath her. She leaned into the reassuring solidity of the wall. *I'm losing my mind.* She had to tell someone about Harper, and if not Stephie, then who? Not her mom traveling in China or Adele who she didn't have a number for. Obviously not Jason. There was no one else in Sloane's life to tell.

The bride-to-be's face zoomed in on Sloane. "Just write something," she said, her nose scrunching into a tiny set of stairs.

Sloane's jaw clenched. The bride-to-be was no doubt in love, the kind of love that was unquestionably safe and naively unbreakable, where even the possibility of infidelity didn't exist. That had been Sloane's mistake—she never believed it to be a risk, so she never put effort into preventing it.

Accepting the pen, she scratched her advice onto a piece of paper: "Be on guard." It wasn't meant to be a threat, but rather a genuine warning that the love between two people required protecting. She should have written it like that instead. It was too late; she had already dropped the piece of paper into the bag.

She had the urge to grab hold of Stephie to ensure she didn't disappear on her again. "Stephie, I need to tell you something."

She didn't even look at Sloane.

"I think Jason is having an affair," Sloane blurted out.

The washroom suddenly went quiet. The bride-to-be's eyebrows crowded together and her mouth pouted with anger or disapproval, Sloane couldn't be sure. Behind her, the bachelorette party stood like statues, each woman frozen in place. She scratched at the inside of an elbow, while Stephie leaned into the mirror and stared at her reflection. *He's having an affair.* The realization sunk deeper into Sloane's consciousness.

A hand landed on her shoulder. It belonged to one of the women who had been waiting in line. "How'd you find out?" she asked.

Sloane looked to Stephie, as if she had been the one to inquire. "I knocked something on his desk," she said. "His computer woke up. On one of the screens, I saw messages between them."

Butting in was a member of the bachelorette party wearing a jean jacket and hoop earrings. "Intentionally?" she asked, far less empathetic.

Sloane spun her head around. "What do you mean?"

"Did you intentionally knock something on his desk, so his computer would turn on?"

"No!" Sloane focused back on Stephie, who was squinting at her reflection as if she weren't certain it was hers. "Her name's Harper Kennedy." Sloane scanned the faces of the women; no one reacted as if it were familiar. "At least that was the name of her avatar."

"Cool name," someone said.

Sloane ignored that. "She asked him if he had someone, like a wife, and he told her no."

Jean Jacket stepped forward. "What did he say?"

"I told you, he answered no."

"I mean when you confronted him about it, what did he say?"

"I haven't. Not yet. Stephie, what if he says it's all true? What if he loves her? What if they've . . . "

Jean Jacket tugged on her hoop earrings, stretching her earlobes. "Had sex?"

Sloane reached for the wall. *No. He wouldn't. Would he? Did he?*

"That's the point of asking," said Jean Jacket, "to find out for sure."

Advice Bag weighed in. "There could be a perfectly good explanation." She pulled on a strand of long hair, releasing it from a belt loop. "Maybe this Harper woman is only attracted to married men, and because her husband"—she threw her chin at Sloane—"isn't interested in having an affair, because he's perfectly happy with his wife, he told Harper he wasn't married, so she wouldn't be interested."

"That's stupid," said the bride-to-be.

"But possibly true."

"They've been talking for months," said Sloane, "after he told her he wasn't married."

"See?" snapped the bride-to-be. "He told her he wasn't married so she *would* be interested." She turned toward Sloane. "He's never mentioned her?"

"No."

The bride-to-be huffed. "If they're just friends, why would he keep it a secret?"

Jean Jacket leaned into Sloane. "Have you ever asked?"

A woman with lips stained blue by the Stairway's Blue Lagoon special, bellowed from behind Sloane, "If he's having an affair? Are you saying it's *her* fault?"

"Of course not."

"To suggest he was justified in not telling his wife about Harper because *she*"—with her index finger, Blue Lips stabbed the air in front of Sloane—"didn't specifically ask about her is victim-blaming."

"That's not what I'm saying."

"What are you saying?"

"Only that she should talk to her husband."

"Or she could talk to the woman," another suggested. "Impersonate her husband online. Get all the answers from Harper."

Blue Lips shouted: "Harper's not the one having an affair! Not on her." Her finger almost made contact with Sloane. "Harper doesn't even know this guy has a wife! And even if she did, it was his choice to get into it. Let's not forget he could have chosen not to. Her issue is with her husband."

Sloane pushed away the woman's arm.

"He could lie," warned Jean Jacket, "when she confronts him about it."

"So could the other woman. At least she knows her husband."

"Not that well, apparently."

Sloane could barely breathe. She worried she would start crying again. She turned to Stephie, who was still staring hard at her reflection. "Stephie, what if he doesn't love me anymore? What if he loves her?" He had bought a novel because of her. He had never done that for Sloane.

Stephie blew past everyone.

"Stephie, wait!"

Back in the bar, it seemed louder and busier than before. Music filled Sloane's belly as if sound were a solid, making her feel full. Someone bumped into her hard, and she spun, losing sight of Stephie. Everyone on the dance floor was jumping, causing the floor to shake. She had to get out of there.

She stumbled onto the street and walked through a cloud of cigarette smoke before making it to an open area where the cooler air cleared her lungs and dried her tears. *Adele would understand.* But even if Sloane had a way to contact Adele, she didn't have a right to expect sympathy. Not after she had practically abandoned Adele on the day she discovered Lawrence's affair.

Sloane didn't know what to do next. She couldn't just wander the streets of Wilson. Maybe after a couple of hours, Stephie would be friendlier. But waiting at the Stairway with so many people and loud music and the rumbling floor would only fuel her anxiety. She could go back to Randy and Stephie's in Tippett Valley, wait for Stephie there, but the thought of Randy and his elastic band turned her stomach. Calling her dad or showing up at her parents' would lead to all sorts of questions she wasn't ready to answer. Jason would be leaving for work soon. She didn't want to be alone with his computer, but home was the best option.

She wasn't certain she had enough to cover a cab fare to Torren Hills. When she arrived home, she could always dip into the House Fund again or charge the fare to her joint credit card. Jason would discover the payment when he checked the statement. Would he wonder why? Wiping her face, she looked left and then right; there were no cabs in sight.

Hopelessness covered her like a blanket. She couldn't stop thinking about the hundreds of JasonHoward and HarperKennedy chat bubbles. What if it wasn't only a relationship between two avatars, but a connection that extended outside Jason's computer, as Jason Howard and Harper Kennedy? If Harper lived close by or worked at the steel plant, it would be easy for Jason to meet her in person. Instead of working an overtime shift, maybe he spent the time with Harper; his work schedule simplified managing an affair. The two of them could have gone to the movies, and then afterward to a quiet café, and then to a hotel. If Sloane looked at the credit card statement, would she see unexplained charges?

All the times she had practically sent Jason to the basement, thinking he preferred playing video games to spending time with his wife, she was actually sending him to Harper. *Is it my fault?*

If Sloane were to guess the day Jason had told Harper he didn't have anyone, it would be the day she had taken her last pregnancy test. For what seemed like the hundredth time the result was negative. Or maybe it was before then, when she had emptied the House Fund to buy another outfit to try to impress the graphic designers at the agency. How much more of their money was she going to invest in a career that was going nowhere? Or maybe it was when he had caught a glimpse of the cracked skin on the inside of her elbows, or the flab of skin hanging over the waist of her jeans, or when he had really looked at the shape of her ears. He had so many reasons to have an affair.

Did he want a divorce? Sloane tried to imagine what life would be like without Jason in it. Quickly, she guided her thoughts to a more bearable possibility: she had jumped to an absurd conclusion based on a conversation she had read between two computer icons. Maybe that was why she hadn't noticed the signs of Jason's affair, because it wasn't Jason Howard having an affair, it was JasonHoward having a conversation with another avatar. JasonHoward the avatar wasn't Jason Howard her husband. As two different entities, the two could have a completely different set of morals, opinions and desires. JasonHoward wouldn't mind a cat, but that didn't mean Jason Howard felt the same way.

Sloane shook her head. She was reaching and she knew it. JasonHoward was Jason Howard's alter ego, his marionette, his puppet, his avatar. Without Jason Howard, JasonHoward would be static pixels. Everything that JasonHoward did, everything that he said, was because Jason Howard allowed it, motivated it, controlled it. JasonHoward wouldn't mind a cat because Jason Howard chose to have JasonHoward not mind a cat. JasonHoward didn't have a wife because Jason Howard chose to have JasonHoward not have a wife.

Sloane imagined her husband explaining that HarperKennedy was the avatar of a sixty-year-old man living in a city on the other side of the world. When Jason was asked if he had someone—*Girlfriend? Wife? Husband?*—and he replied *No*, it was actually in reply to a previous question; the order of the messages had just gotten messed up. It was all a big misunderstanding. It could be true.

She imagined being at home. In bed, she would wrap her elbows in the bedsheets to disguise the unsightly effects of her scratching, and roll onto her back and press the side of her arms into her ribs to prevent her breasts from flattening. In the morning, she would stay in bed and when Jason returned home from the steel plant after the graveyard shift, she would pretend to awaken as soon as he walked into the room. Better yet, she would show him that she was awake, waiting. She imagined listening for his footsteps. She could hear him lingering in the kitchen. *I'm awake! Come upstairs!* Then from a floor below: the sound of a door opening. Was he going down to the basement? Footsteps. Descending.

On the street, her breaths skipped in tiny coughs. Her heart pumped frantically. In the dream, Jason was going downstairs to wake his computer because HarperKennedy wasn't the avatar of a sixty-year-old man living halfway around the world; HarperKennedy was the avatar of a woman who Jason had told that he didn't have a wife, and who he had just chosen to spend Sloane's fantasy with.

Dazed, she stumbled off the curb. Someone caught her arm and pulled her off the street.

"Damn it, Sloane. What the hell?"

Sloane turned. It was Stephie.

"What are you doing out here?" asked Sloane, regaining her balance.

"Saving you apparently."

"Really?" *You left work early for me?*

"Come on." Stephie opened the door to the backseat of a cab that seemed to have magically appeared. "Get in," she said, impatiently.

Sloane quickly got into the cab.

"You again."

Reflected in the rear-view mirror was a set of familiar eyes; it was the same driver who had driven Sloane to Tippett Valley.

"65 Ranger Street," said Stephie.

The car rolled forward.

"Thanks," Sloane whispered.

Stephie stared out the window, ignoring Sloane.

Sloane raised her arm to swipe at her tears. The fitness tracker on her wrist vibrated and pixilated balloons popped on the screen. 10,001 steps.

Chapter Thirty-Five

SLOANE REMAINED SILENT in the cab, afraid she would say the wrong thing, and then Stephie would regret leaving the Stairway early for her.

When the cab pulled up to 65 Ranger Street, Sloane was grateful when Stephie paid the fare. Near the front step, like an ornament, a tissue remained trapped in the branches of a bush. She hoped Randy had left the house.

He was still there. Stuck to his bottom lip was a cigarette and strapped to his back was a guitar. He smelled of marijuana. Thankfully, the elastic band was gone, and he had put on a proper shirt. Sloane waved, scattering smoke. He nodded, as if to a beat only he could hear. Like crumbs, ashes from his cigarette dropped down his chest. Stephie hurried toward Bee in the living room. Sloane followed.

"Sloane!"

Stunned, she froze. "Adele?"

On the couch, Adele looked like she had just gotten off a roller-coaster, her hair blown around. "You didn't answer your phone," she said, catapulting to her feet.

Sloane suddenly remembered the unknown caller. "How did you find me?"

"I looked you up in the agency's files," she explained. "Gary called your phone, but you didn't answer." The unknown caller had been Gary Goldman. "I took a cab to your address. Then Jason gave me a ride here."

"He drove you to Tippy?" Sloane checked her phone; Jason had texted twice.

"Said he was going this way anyway to meet someone. Something about assessing a job before work, a pile of wood or something."

"Joe."

"Maybe." Adele took Sloane's phone away from her and set it on the coffee table. "Sloane, I've got something to tell you."

"It's not a good time."

"I'm getting married!"

Adele's arms wrapped around Sloane. She squeezed hard enough to crack a rib. Sloane lifted her arms, forcing Adele to let go. "To who?" she asked.

"Lawrence!"

"Avery?"

"Yes, Lawrence Avery."

"You said you were in the 'I'm never going to talk to you' stage with him."

"He showed up at the agency just as I was leaving."

"To apologize?"

"To check the Lost and Found. He thought he might have dropped his sunglasses in the parking lot. That was his excuse anyway. Really, he was worried that he hadn't heard from me in a couple of days."

"And?"

"I went off for like thirty minutes about how he pocket-dialed me when he was with Trish. I said a whole bunch of really mean things, I was really awful. Then he said 'Not Trish, Trix.'"

"Trix?"

"As in Beatrix, his sister. Of course I didn't believe him at first, but then he explained he was helping her move into a new apartment without an elevator, so they had to lug a big couch up two flights of stairs." She grabbed Sloane's arm. "He was out of breath because he was trying to get a couch up a flight of stairs with his sister! Isn't that great?"

Sloane wished Jason would have a similar explanation; one they could laugh off before resuming their faithful lives together. *Things'll be different. I promise.*

"After all that, he proposed?"

"Get this," said Adele. "I took your advice. I asked him. It's the

209

twenty-first century, right? That's what you said. My birthday's on Sunday and Lawrence has great posture, so."

"What about Travis?"

Adele looked confused. "What about Travis?" She grabbed Sloane's hand and smiled excitedly. "It's happening, Sloane! Lawrence is on his way to tell his parents now."

Sloane suddenly realized she was standing in Stephie and Randy's living room. Stephie was lying on the couch; her pet goldfish on her belly, her hands securely around the fishbowl. With each of her breaths, Bee slowly ascended and descended, riding the placid wave of her breathing. Randy was standing by the window, struggling to light another cigarette with a match barely sparking. Neither seemed curious about the stranger in their home. Sloane turned her attention back to Adele.

"I guess you've met Randy," she said. "This is Stephie. My best friend."

"Hi," said Adele.

Stephie didn't respond. Instead, she cooed at Bee.

"What's with the fish?"

"Randy left him in the sun," Sloane was quick to reply, even though she knew that was a lie. She wanted to spare Stephie the judgment of almost killing something she loved. It occurred to her that maybe Randy had done the same.

"It really isn't a good time," she said again.

Adele scratched at the birthmark on her chest. "There's something else," she said.

"Can we talk about it tomorrow at work?"

Adele ignored her. "Gary called me tonight because Joan had called him, looking for you."

"Why?" *Because of the Juniper booking?*

"Joan got a call from Manning Office Supply. The delivery truck with Account Services' new chairs broke down. They won't arrive tonight."

"There won't be chairs in the boardroom either," said Sloane, her mind spinning. "They're being replaced, too."

Adele grabbed Sloane's arm. "How are we going to impress Brownwood Industries with no chairs?"

"We can contact Tanner Delivery. Ask them to return the old ones."

Adele shook her head. "Gary already tried. The chairs have already been dropped off for donation."

It was too late to reschedule the pitch or move it to an offsite location. "We can move the chairs from the other departments into Account Services and the boardroom."

"Sure, but what are we supposed to tell those employees? We can't have them stand all day. We'd have to send them home. Think of the cost. And what if he decides he wants to tour all the departments?"

Thinking quickly, Sloane turned toward Randy. "Have you been fired from Oasis Rentals yet?"

He inhaled from his cigarette. As he slowly exhaled the smoke, his eyes closed.

"Randy, can you steal the warehouse key again?"

"He doesn't need to break in," said Stephie. "He's a manager now. He has a key."

Sloane squinted at Randy. "You're a manager?"

Randy nodded and she refocused.

"The Kaye Agency needs to borrow twenty-six folding chairs," she explained. "Not borrow. Rent. The Kaye Agency will pay double. Triple, even. We just need to get the chairs to the office tonight." It pained her to have to ask Randy for help, but her job was on the line. "Will you help me?"

Randy glanced at Stephie.

"I don't have my car," Sloane continued. "Adele doesn't drive. We'll have to take your truck."

He moved to the kitchen, and Sloane followed.

"Randy, will you help me, please?"

"Stephie shouldn't be left alone tonight," he said, his voice low.

"Why not? Because Bee almost died?"

"And because it's Benjamin's birthday."

The realization temporarily paralyzed Sloane. How could she have forgotten? Benjamin Harrington would have been twenty-eight today. That was the real reason Randy had called yesterday. Flashing in Sloane's mind was the image of Stephie's blood-stained sock.

"You're right," said Sloane. "We can't leave her alone. She has to come with us. Then you'll help?"

Randy nodded and Sloane returned to the living room. "He'll help us," she said to Adele, "if Stephie comes, too."

The two of them looked at Stephie.

"Will you come with us?" asked Sloane.

"What about Bee?"

"You're worried about a fish?" said Adele.

"He's important to her," said Sloane, looking desperately at her best friend.

"I don't want to leave him alone tonight," said Stephie.

"What if we put him in some Tupperware?" Adele suggested. "Have him ride on your lap."

"He'll die."

"Tupperware with water."

"Fish don't like change."

"Your lap looks the same in the car as it does on the couch. Your fish won't even notice."

Randy leaned his guitar against the wall, and then sat beside Stephie on the couch. "It's the water," he explained. "Variations in temperature could kill him."

"So could leaving him in the sun," said Adele, "but look, he survived."

Sloane wondered if she was the only one in the room who understood Adele was trying to help.

"Stephie, please," said Sloane.

Randy dropped his hand onto Stephie's arm. "I'll bring the thermometer," he said.

Stephie hesitated. "Fine, I'll go," she finally said.

Sloane let go of the breath she had been holding.

"Thanks," said Sloane. "Really, Stephie. Thank you."

She gently picked up the fishbowl and carried Bee into the kitchen, where Randy was securing the edges of a cardboard box with duct tape.

"I'll call Gary to let him know what's going on," said Adele, nudging Sloane's arm. "I knew you would save the day."

But there was so much more to be saved. *What if I can't save it all?*

Chapter Thirty-Six

BEFORE ADELE GOT into Randy's truck, Sloane stopped her.

"Listen, about Stephie," she said, looking back at the house where Randy and Stephie were still inside. "Her brother died when we were seventeen." She paused, shocked by how easily she had said it. "It was tragic. He died in a bathtub. It kind of screwed her up. We were supposed to get out of Tippy together, but she stayed. She gave up art school for a job at the Stairway, a bar in Wilson. She's a really great artist. She read all the police reports about her brother's death and made drawings of the tragedy. That's how I found out how it happened. I don't think she's drawn anything since. Are you listening?" Putting words to her chaotic thoughts and emotions was a strange, therapeutic exercise.

Adele was texting on her phone. Like popping corn, her thumbs exploded off the tiny screen. "Yes," she said.

"Stephie and Randy just live together," Sloane continued, talking quickly. "They're not a couple. They slept together once—more than once, actually—but that was just Stephie being Stephie and Randy being Randy." Randy and Stephie exited the house. "Stephie's got this weird connection with her goldfish," Sloane went on, talking even quicker. "He's really old. I'm telling you this because I don't want you to think she's weird or anything. There's a reason for it."

"We should go," said Adele. In some ways, Sloane was relieved to have her rambling cut off; in other ways, it was disappointing. She wasn't finished—there were more acts. Like the one where she discovers her husband is having an affair.

No way was she going to let Randy drive high. The truck was a crew cab, like Jason's, and Sloane slid into the driver's seat. She hoped Stephie would sit up front, but she opted for Randy, again.

He took the extra legroom behind Adele, which meant Stephie was barely visible in Sloane's rear-view mirror. Even in the most innocent ways, Randy was irritating.

In her lap, Stephie had Bee's fishbowl in a cardboard box, meant to help keep him steady. She cooed at the goldfish while Randy periodically tested the water temperature with a meat thermometer. Depending on the reading, he told Sloane which way to adjust the air conditioning.

Adele called Lawrence, her phone so loud Sloane could hear him. He sounded genuinely excited, like he actually wanted to marry Adele, like he hadn't been coerced into it by an arbitrary deadline. He was driving with his sister, on his way to his parents'. Beatrix got on the line to express how thrilled she was, and the three of them laughed about the couch getting stuck in the stairway. As soon as Adele hung up, Travis called to congratulate her on her engagement. She insisted he attend the wedding with Eva. *Wouldn't that be weird?*

It took half the drive to Torren Hills before everyone settled. Bee's water was maintaining a consistent temperature, and Adele was quiet, texting on her phone. Sloane's fitness tracker vibrated, reminding her to move. She was already at 10,619 steps, but it was still asking for more. *Will I never be enough?*

Her mind returned to Jason. What if he doesn't come home after his shift? What if he has already left her?

"Sloane, relax," said Adele.

Sloane eased her grip on the steering wheel. She hadn't noticed the terrible rubbing sound her palms were making against the leather. She glanced in the rear-view mirror. Randy's arm was outstretched. Was he holding Stephie's hand? Jason used to hold Sloane's hand, and then suddenly he stopped reaching for it. Maybe not so suddenly. Maybe it had happened gradually, like one day realizing your parents were old or that the paint on the walls of your house had faded.

Stephie had her forehead resting on Randy's shoulder. The two of them were sharing a set of earbuds, listening to the same track

215

on Randy's iPod. He kept sweeping at his chin, tickled by Stephie's staticky hair. *Will Jason and I ever sit that close together again?*

"Tell me about the wedding," said Sloane. If she could focus on something other than imagining a life without Jason, then maybe she could prevent a total breakdown.

Adele's expression lit up. She had it all planned. She started to talk about napkin colors and tablecloths and flowers. She didn't seem to mind that no one in the truck cared. She rambled on: "Blah, blah, blah . . . Lawrence . . . blah, blah, blah . . . Eva, blah, blah, blah . . . Travis." Sloane nodded, but her attention was elsewhere. *Will Jason still be my emergency contact? Will Harper move into the house and take my place? Where will I live? Not with my parents!*

Adele waved her hand. "Earth to Sloane."

Sloane's body melted into her seat. *Should I tell her?* "Eva's feeling better?" she asked instead.

"Yes." Adele squinted. "Haven't you been listening?"

"Sorry." Sloane dug a set of knuckles into her thigh. "When you found out about Trish," she said cautiously. "You know, before you learned it was actually Beatrix. Did you suddenly want to give Lawrence a hug?"

"No. I wanted to kill him."

"Did you also kind of want to be held by him, too?"

Adele frowned.

"I just mean, did it make you realize how much you loved him, and that maybe you didn't express that enough before you found out about Trish? But now it's too late. I mean, you can't undo an affair. Not that Lawrence actually had an affair."

"You can forgive one," said Adele. "Complicated, though. Takes time, but possible."

"I read once that an affair actually brought two people closer."

"It's the actions after an affair that either bring two people closer or tear them further apart."

"We should stop," said Stephie, interrupting.

"Aren't we almost there?" said Adele.

"Bee's looking lethargic. He might be getting carsick. He needs to get out of this box. Swim around in his bowl on solid ground."

"But we're almost there," said Adele. "We're in Torren Hills."

"Sloane, stop."

"Watch out," said Randy, calmly.

Sloane swerved as some kind of small animal ran across the road.

Adele knocked her head against the window. "Owwww!" she moaned. Sloane regained control of the truck, her grip on the steering wheel intensified.

"Think he's okay?" said Stephie. In the rear-view mirror, Randy leaned over Bee's bowl.

"What about me?" said Adele. She pushed down the sun visor to examine her forehead in the mirror.

"Sloane, pull over," said Stephie.

Shaken up by the near-accident, Sloane looked at Adele. "We need gas anyway," she said and veered into a station.

Adele sighed and flipped up the sun visor. She crawled her fingers over her forehead, likely feeling for a bump. She handed Sloane a company credit card to pay for the gas and said she was going to call Lawrence again. She glared at Stephie and Randy in the backseat. "Some privacy please."

Stephie looked as if she was going to rip out Adele's hair, but then Randy handed her the meat thermometer and said he was going inside for cigarettes. "You're right," he added, "some fresh air would probably do Bee some good."

Stephie set Bee's bowl on the hood of the truck. "There," she said, muttering softly. "Now you can see where you are." She pressed her palm against the bowl and dipped the tip of the thermometer into the water.

Sloane desperately wanted to hear her husband's voice or at least read his typed words, but when she searched her purse and pockets, she couldn't find her phone. She knew exactly where she had left it: at Randy and Stephie's house, on the coffee table. She didn't have Jason's number memorized—she never had to actually dial it before.

As the truck filled with gas, she thought of all the terrible things she would text Harper if she had her number—the awful names, the accusations. It was so much easier to be angry with a woman she had never met than to be angry with the man she loved. If Sloane had known about Harper, she would have acted differently. She would have tried harder with Jason.

With everyone back in the truck, Adele hung up her phone. Stephie put Bee's bowl back into the cardboard box and urged Sloane to start the ignition. Apparently the water temperature in Bee's bowl had increased by a degree.

"Sloane, the air," she said.

Sloane poked Adele's shoulder. "Hey. Everything okay?"

Adele scratched at the coin-sized birthmark on her chest. She flipped her hair and slapped the dash. "Lawrence's grandmother wants me to wear her sapphire earrings at the wedding."

"So?"

Adele sighed, loudly. "She's divorced. Twice. And it turns out Lawrence's mom's favorite color is green. Green, Sloane. She has green napkins with a tree printed on them leftover from Christmas and she's telling Lawrence how perfect they'd be for the wedding. And get this: Beatrix wants to invite her high school boyfriend, but Lawrence's dad says if he steps foot in the hall, he'll shoot him with the hunting rifle. I guess the old boyfriend abandoned Beatrix on a backpacking trip across the country."

"Sloane," said Stephie. "The air!"

"Enough with the goldfish!" Adele shouted. "It's a fish. A *fish!* It's not your dead brother."

Sloane's eyes popped. "Adele!" She twisted around.

In the backseat, Stephie stared vacantly. Randy took her hand, but she didn't seem to notice. Sloane awkwardly reached over the seat, wanting to comfort her best friend, like Randy was trying to do, but it wasn't physically possible. Her hand dangled over the headrest.

"Why would you say that?" she said, glaring at Adele.

"You think she named her pet goldfish Bee because he looks like a bumblebee?"

He's black and yellow.

"You think she'd treat a goldfish the way she does if she didn't associate it with something else, someone else?"

You don't know anything.

Stephie started to laugh. To get a better view of the backseat, Sloane shimmied onto her hip. The sad eyes that accompanied Stephie's laugh were haunting, creating an uneasy feeling inside Sloane. "It isn't B for Benjamin, is it?" she said.

Stephie stopped laughing. In a grave, even tone, she said, "Turn on the air, Sloane."

Sloane made eye contact with Randy, whose expression held no surprise. He knew. A suffocating silence filled the truck. Sloane glanced at Adele. Within an hour, she had figured it out. Sloane had known Stephie seventeen years. *How didn't I see it?*

A car pulled in behind Sloane. She started the truck, and air blasted from the vents. Stepping on the gas, she pulled forward.

Not Bee like a bumblebee. B for Benjamin.

Chapter Thirty-Seven

OASIS RENTALS WAS located just two blocks from the Kaye Agency. Randy directed Sloane to park in front of the warehouse, painted orange to match the company's logo. He used his key to unlock a garage-style door that creaked open and disappeared into the ceiling. The space inside was packed with folded chairs, collapsed tables and portable heaters, umbrellas and tents, and boxes labeled "linens" and "dishware." He wheeled over a large cart and started to stack folding chairs onto it.

Sloane and Adele helped, while Stephie set B on the hood of the truck. Like a fortune-teller with a magic ball, she placed her hands gently around the bowl.

Maybe it wasn't such a bad thing that Sloane didn't have her phone. If she discovered Jason hadn't texted, everything would just hurt more. She focused on her fitness tracker and tried to revel in 11,009 steps. If she had her phone, she would have snapped a picture and sent the image to her mom. Roma was coming home tomorrow. What would Sloane tell her? Your prize son-in-law doesn't love your daughter anymore. *Oh, and can I move back in with you and Dad?*

"Travis' forehead does that."

Sloane followed Adele's gaze to Randy, who lifted four folded chairs at once and stacked them into the cab of the truck. His eyebrows moved up and down, like skipping ropes in a game of double-dutch. If Jason left Sloane like Travis had left Adele, was this how it was going to be years from now? Would any man with dimples trigger a memory of Sloane's ex-husband?

"It happens to Eva, too," said Adele, "when she's thinking real hard."

Maybe it wouldn't if she hadn't spent years watching Travis' forehead. Would Sloane stop rubbing her knuckles if she no longer watched Jason rub his?

Randy managed to get all twenty-six folding chairs into the back of the truck. Sloane was grateful the mission would only require a single trip.

"Let's go," ordered Adele. "Everyone in the truck."

At the agency, Sloane spoke to Security, informing the guards on duty of the change in plan. When she returned to the truck, Randy and Adele already had all the chairs in the elevator.

In the office she and Adele began rolling chairs from other departments into Account Services and the boardroom while Randy set up rental chairs at the desks, dressing each one with a linen cover. Spread out across the office, the folding chairs blended in; at least that was the intention. It was Randy's idea, the chair covers, and Sloane was having trouble admitting it was a good one.

"I'll send out an email about the chairs," said Adele, heading to Human Resources.

Sloane rolled a chair up to her own desk. The flickering light above seemed brighter and the buzzing louder, or maybe it was just that she was paying attention now. How long had she ignored it? How long had she ignored the problems in her marriage? Were they just as obvious? She thought of Jason. She still loved him, maybe more since the discovery of Harper Kennedy, which didn't make sense. Maybe not more in volume of love, but more in the conscious acknowledgment of it. The threat of its loss had forced her to pay attention.

She suddenly remembered that Jason's number was in the agency's emergency contact file. Reaching for the power button on her computer, she reeled her arm back in, struck with panic. She wasn't ready to talk to him about Harper Kennedy. Besides, the longer she waited to bring it up, the longer the possibility that it wasn't true remained a valid hope. She already felt like she might crumble.

As she hesitated, she saw Stephie cradling B and walking into the lunchroom. Sloane was struck by how odd it was to see her at the agency. Thinking of Stephie made her think of Kendra Jamieson and what had happened to her as a girl. Then an idea came to her. Regina Kaye was a supporter of the #MeToo movement, anonymously helping to give a louder voice to groups advocating for women's and girls' rights. Instead of trying to impress Kendra with images from some of the agency's biggest campaigns, what if Joan presented what Regina Kaye stood for?

Acting quickly, Sloane turned on her computer and opened the PowerPoint presentation for the Brownwood pitch. She created a new section "What We Stand For" and added slides from the "Regina Kaye Day Campaigns" folder. Then she clipped the "Tips to Help You Keep Your Customers" article from the magazine on her desk and placed it on Joan's keyboard. Finally, she emailed Lenore and Joan the revised presentation: "Lenore, you asked me what millennials want. I think we want to stand for something, and we want your support (Joan, see article I left on your keyboard). I have added a section to the end of the presentation, for your consideration to include in the pitch. See attached. I think this could be the personal connection we need." She hit send before she could change her mind, and then fled to the washroom, heart pounding.

At the sink, Sloane unsuccessfully avoided her likeness in the mirror. Her reflection was tired and scared, and because she had skipped dinner, it was hungry, too. It was hard to look at. Washing her hands, she didn't dare give Fate a voice by taking off her wedding rings. She thought of Jason again. He never told her he was unhappy. She pressed her lips tightly together to prevent tears. Breathing heavily through her nose, she let out little snorting sounds. *He never gave me a chance to be better.*

The electric dryer wouldn't turn on, so she dried her hands on her thighs. Would Jason invite her to his wedding, like Adele had invited Travis to hers? Her knees weakened. To disguise the gasps and gulps and ribbits, she entered a stall and flushed the toilet three times.

"Sloane?"

She shut off her whimpering. She wished it were Stephie instead of Adele.

"Lawrence talked to his mom about the napkins," she said, sounding pleased.

Sloane rolled her eyes and dabbed her wet cheeks with toilet paper. Her life was falling apart, but at least Adele wouldn't have green napkins at her wedding. "That's great," she said, hiding her sarcasm.

"What are you doing in there?"

"Peeing."

"You're not even standing the right way." Adele's face was close to where the door latched; Sloane could see her peeking through the narrow opening. "You're crying," she said.

"I'm fine."

"Your aura is all off. I felt it in Tippy, before all this. You're having marriage troubles?"

Just tell her. Sloane blurted it out: "I think Jason is having an affair and I'm worried if I ask him about it, his answer won't be anything like Lawrence's had been."

"I'm sorry."

"I don't want to talk about it." She exited the stall. "How'd you know Stephie's goldfish was named after Benjamin?"

"She treats that fish more like a brother than a slimy pet."

"It's nothing like how she treated Benjamin. If anything, she treated him like a slimy pet."

Adele joined Sloane at the sink. "Maybe she treats her goldfish the way she wished she'd treated her brother. Maybe she thinks if she had, the tragedy would never have happened."

"It wasn't her fault," said Sloane.

"Try convincing her of that."

"I've told her a thousand times."

In the mirror, Adele pinched her cheekbones. "And?"

"She still thinks she's to blame."

Adele nodded.

"You agree?"

"She's your best friend. You see it, don't you?"

"We haven't been best friends for a long time." The fact had spilled out of Sloane so easily, and yet so unexpectedly. It was the first time she had acknowledged it out loud. "We stopped being best friends after Benjamin died. I'll never know what it's like to lose a sibling. That's why Randy's her best friend now. His sister died."

With the side of her index finger, Adele scrubbed her front teeth. "That's not the reason," she said. "You don't let Stephie have feelings."

"Yes I do."

"Not the ones she has."

"What do you mean?"

"Stephie feels sad and guilty and lonely, right?"

Sloane nodded.

"You said you've told her a thousand times she shouldn't have those feelings."

"Because it wasn't her fault what happened."

"It doesn't matter."

"She's blaming herself for something she wasn't responsible for."

"And yet, she feels the way she feels. Randy gives her permission."

"But it wasn't her fault!" Sloane hadn't meant to shout.

"Invalidating her feelings doesn't make them go away," said Adele, unaffected by Sloane's outburst. She ran her fingers through her hair.

"Validating them doesn't make them go away either," said Sloane.

Leveling her breasts, Adele held one up in the mirror. "Giving her permission to feel guilty says nothing about your opinion. Worse than feeling guilt is having someone say that you have no right to it. Feelings usually aren't choices, Sloane."

Sloane was speechless. No wonder Stephie had gone looking for a new best friend and Jason a new wife. *I rejected them both.*

"Look," said Adele, dropping her arms. "It took years of therapy for me to start to understand. Give yourself a break, okay?"

"What if it's too late?"

"Too late for what?"

"To fix it."

"Maybe it's not something to be fixed."

Numbed, Sloane tugged on the flesh around her waist. Adele grabbed her wrist. "It starts with you, you know," she said.

"Easy for you to say, you don't have my hips."

"I wish I did. I wouldn't have to wear a belt all the time, it's so annoying. And I've got these." She pointed to her lopsided breasts. "Humans are imperfect, Sloane, inside and out. We don't always need fixing. Sometimes we just need accepting."

Maybe Adele was right. Maybe there wasn't anything wrong with Sloane's body. Sloane worried that if she let Adele continue, she would start crying and wouldn't be able to stop. She needed to change the subject. "You sure it's the right thing to do? Marry Lawrence, I mean. You were just saying how you wanted to kill him."

With the cuff of her shirt, Adele cleaned her phone screen. "I was angry," she said. "Everybody says things they don't really mean when they're angry. That's what's so terrible about anger."

"What do you even like about him? Besides his posture. I'm pretty sure sitting up straight doesn't guarantee a happy marriage."

"Nothing guarantees that."

Jason and Sloane would have been happy, if they lived in a house they owned and had two kids running around and Sloane had a job as a graphic designer and Jason spent his days developing his video game.

"I love Lawrence," said Adele, adamantly.

"Have you talked to him about kids?"

"He wants to be a dad."

Sloane's heart muscles clenched. "Sometimes what you want doesn't matter."

"What?"

"Nothing."

"You better get back to your friends, then," said Adele. "You know the policy: non-employees aren't to be left unsupervised."

Sloane entered the lunchroom, where Randy was showing Stephie how close he could hold the lit end of a lighter to his palm without flinching. Sloane smothered the urge to scold him and focused on how best to express to Stephie how sorry she was for not realizing what her goldfish meant to her. Even though what happened to her brother wasn't her fault, Stephie had every right to feel guilty about his death, if that was how she felt. As her best friend, Sloane wouldn't judge her for it. At least not anymore.

"Come on, Stephie," Sloane urged. "Let's go."

Stephie stood and scooped up B's fishbowl.

"Will you wait for Adele?" Sloane asked Randy. "We'll meet you at the truck, okay?"

Catching up to Stephie, Sloane led the way to the parking lot. Finally, they would have a moment alone.

Stephie set B's bowl on the hood of the truck. From her pocket, she pulled a bag of fish food and added two pinches of flakes to B's water.

"You really do love that goldfish like a brother," she said.

Stephie laughed.

Sloane remained serious. "I know you loved Benjamin."

Kicking at the cigarette butts on the ground, Stephie released dirt from the pavement; a cloud of dust formed around her ankles, disguising the bloodstain on her sock. "He didn't know it," she said. "I never told him."

"Some things you don't have to say," said Sloane. "It's just obvious."

Stephie laughed again. "I definitely didn't obviously love Benji. I didn't even go to his funeral."

Sloane remembered. That morning, Stephie's aunt had dragged Stephie halfway across the room before Stephie managed to take her arm back. Her aunt went flying into the wall, where she hit her head and sunk to the floor. After that, she gave up trying to get her niece out of the house and left without her.

Sloane hadn't wanted to go to Benjamin's funeral either. If she weren't there, it might make his death a little less real. Maybe Stephie had thought the same thing. They never talked about it. Should Sloane have tried harder—or tried at all—to get Stephie to her brother's funeral?

Adele and Randy approached the truck. Sloane wished it had taken them longer.

"I'll drive you back to Tippy," she said, still not sure Randy was sober enough to drive.

"Can you drop me off on the way?" asked Adele. "Lawrence's parents live in Wilson. They're waiting up for me."

Before Sloane could suggest a change in seating, Adele settled into the front passenger seat. There was no use fighting it. It wasn't as if Stephie or Randy objected. B's cardboard box was in Stephie's lap and she and Randy were each holding on to a side. Stephie placed her cheek on Randy's shoulder, and he dropped his head on top of hers, their faces stacked like bricks. He kept an eye on the thermometer while Stephie closed her eyes. In the front, Adele texted on her phone. Sloane started the ignition.

Driving to Wilson, she imagined Jason's smile—his dimples especially, and how her thumbs slid into them whenever she touched his face. Would she ever do that again? Looping in her mind was a conversation she imagined having with him in the morning. She tried to think of all the possible outcomes, so that whatever happened, it wouldn't be a shock. She never again wanted to experience a surprise like discovering Harper Kennedy.

An unexpected thought slowly seeped into her mind. She had been wrong about Stephie—what if she was also wrong about Jason? Love was about weathering storms and building dreams; it was about picking each other up in failure and holding each other high in success; it was about growing and surviving together. Had she given up on that? Jason was constantly touching her, kissing her, wanting to make love to her—even in a rented house, even after a shift at the plant, even after she didn't get the graphic designer position, even after a negative pregnancy test, and even after she had gained weight. Did she only assume that her failures made her unlovable? What if she was actually projecting onto him how she felt about herself? What if he never stopped loving her?

"Randy!"

Sloane jolted, suddenly alert to her surroundings. There had been terror in Stephie's voice. Sloane's eyes shot to the rear-view mirror. In the backseat, Randy removed his earbuds and hovered over B's fishbowl, his forehead almost touching Stephie's.

"What is it?" asked Sloane, her focus jumping from the road to the mirror. "Is it B? Is he okay?"

Stephie dropped the thermometer—kerplunk. Her hands landed on her face, where she pulled on the flesh over her cheekbones. Sloane looked for a safe place to pull over.

Parked at the side of the road, she torqued her body fully around. Randy had taken the fishbowl out of the cardboard box. At the bottom of the bowl was the meat thermometer; on the surface of the water B was floating.

"We should've stayed home," said Stephie, chewing on the ends of her bangs.

Randy gently pulled her hair away from her mouth. "If we had, he probably would've died on the counter, even if you never left his side." He squeezed her hand. "I bet no other goldfish gets to brag in heaven that they passed away in the lap of the human who loved them."

"You're an atheist," said Sloane, remembering a past conversation.

"Stephie's not," he said.

For some reason, this surprised her.

Stephie gently poked at the corpse. In the water, B bobbed up and down, his body limp and buoyant. Stephie laughed, and

Randy squeezed her hand harder. "I know you're sad," he said, "but this time, it's not a tragedy."

"We should celebrate," said Sloane, which didn't come out right. "I just mean B lived a really long life for a goldfish. His death isn't something to be sad about."

"Even things that make sense can be sad," said Randy.

Sloane cringed. She was doing it again, telling Stephie it was wrong to have a feeling.

"Of course," she said. "Of course."

Adele leaned into the backseat. "His eyes are still open."

"Fish don't close their eyes," said Randy. "They don't have eyelids."

Sloane stared at B. *God, Randy. Of all possible pets to have gotten Stephie, you picked a goldfish.* A short life expectancy and lived in a miniature bathtub. *What were you thinking?*

Adele dropped her hand onto Stephie's knee. "I'm sorry for your loss," she said, sounding genuine.

"Me too," said Sloane, quickly. She should have said it first. *What's wrong with me?*

Stephie stopped laughing.

"We can bury him," said Adele. "Right here."

"What about getting you to Lawrence's parents?" Sloane pinched her thigh; she was saying all the wrong things.

"It won't take long to bury a goldfish," said Adele. "He's two inches long and probably weighs less than my finger."

"Of course," said Sloane. "We'll have a funeral."

She looked to Stephie, who was looking at Randy.

"What do you think?" he said. "You can be there this time."

Stephie nodded.

Sloane could be there this time, too.

Adele used her phone to shine a light. With the heel of her shoe, Stephie dug a cavity into the ground beyond the ditch. Over the hole, Randy poured out the water from B's fishbowl. B dropped with a splash into the tiny pool, the gravel and miniature plant following. Randy caught the thermometer in mid-air. The earth quickly absorbed the water around B. If only the water in the Harringtons' bathtub had drained as quickly. Sloane braced for the flood of emotion she sensed was coming but was powerless to prevent. *I can't keep it a secret any longer. I have to tell her.*

Stephie crouched. With her hands, she moved dirt over B. To mark his grave, she placed a stone pebble. Sloane swore she heard Stephie whisper Benjamin's name. It occurred to her then that maybe this moment was the reason Randy had gifted Stephie a pet goldfish. So she could love him like she regretted not loving her brother. So she could say goodbye to him like she had been too scared to say goodbye to Benjamin.

The shining light from Adele's phone lifted. "Come on," she said, leading the way back to the truck. With their shoulders touching, Stephie and Randy followed.

Tears streamed down Sloane's cheeks. Her emotion couldn't escape fast enough, building in her throat, smothering her airways. "It's my fault," she said loudly.

Stephie turned and let out a sharp laugh. "It's never my fault, but now it's yours?"

"I drove him home that night. It was me."

Stephie stopped laughing.

"Benjamin. I drove him home. From the party."

Stephie returned to B's grave, where Sloane was quivering.

"He was drunk and, I don't know, probably high," she went on. "You were fighting with him about something, from earlier in the day. He took something from your room. I told him to go inside and take a shower." Sobbing, she grabbed hold of Stephie's elbow. "I didn't think he would drown!"

Sloane let go and Stephie's arms folded in front of her chest.

"We kissed," she said. "At the party, I kissed your brother. That's why I didn't take him inside the house when I dropped him off. I was worried we might kiss again. I just wanted to get back to you. I didn't want you to find out about it from anyone else."

She dropped to her knees and the stone pebble shifted. She frantically worked to repair B's grave. Dirt packed beneath her fingernails and her fitness tracker slid to her knuckles. "I'm sorry. I'm so sorry." Her tears were blinding. "Say something, Stephie. Please."

A weight landed on her shoulder. A hand. Sloane looked up. Like a leaking faucet, tears dripped from her chin.

Stephie squeezed Sloane's shoulder. "You kissed Benji?"

"I should've told you, right after it happened. The rest of the night could've been different. I would've made sure Benjamin was okay before leaving him alone."

She braced herself for impact. She deserved to be kicked, tackled, slapped. But the grip on her shoulder released.

Sloane turned. "I should never have kept it a secret."

"We should go," said Adele, shining the light in Sloane's eyes.

Randy stuck out his elbow and Stephie linked her arm through his as if it were the most natural thing to do. She dropped her head on his shoulder and Randy circled his chin over her forehead. "All this time," he said, "Sloane's been carrying a similar pain. You just didn't know it."

Sloane met Stephie's eyes. *I do understand.* Not what it was like to lose a sibling, but what it was like to feel guilty. *I worried if I told you I would lose you, but keeping it from you was how I lost you.*

Adele nudged Sloane forward, guiding her into the driver's seat of the truck. "Get in," she said. "It's time to go home."

Chapter Thirty-Eight

IN THE TRUCK, Adele slapped Randy's knee sticking up through the space between the two front seats. "That's it," she shrieked, shifting her gaze from the map on her phone to the actual street. "Sloane, pull over!"

Before Sloane shifted the truck into park, Adele had the passenger door open. She sprinted for the house. On the front step, she was embraced by a woman who was likely Lawrence's mother, judging by her age and the handful of green napkins in her hand. Lawrence came outside and lifted Adele off her feet, kissing his fiancé without having to slouch. As if competing for who could reveal the most teeth, Adele and Lawrence didn't stop smiling. Sloane remembered how she and Jason used to smile like that. *I want us to be like that again.*

Both Randy and Stephie slept through Adele's departure. Sloane considered waking Stephie, to have her move into the front seat—now that Adele wasn't occupying it, and now that Stephie no longer had a goldfish to comfort—but instead, she pulled away in silence.

Strangely, alone in the front, she didn't mind the quiet. Something had changed inside her. Maybe it was because she was no longer harboring a secret. She thought about Jason. The pain of discovering his relationship with Harper had highlighted her love for him. Their relationship had faded into the background of her life, becoming a character with few lines. Now that there was an obvious villain, and the threat of losing him, Sloane had to give her love more dialogue or risk the villain becoming the main character. Adele had been right: the affair wouldn't break them up. What happened after the affair would determine whether their marriage survived or perished. She thought of the wedding rings she had twice left in the agency's washroom. She knew she couldn't continue to treat her rings, or Jason, so carelessly.

Sloane hadn't noticed the Tippett Valley welcome sign, so it seemed sudden when she pulled onto Ranger Street.

"We're here," she said, shaking Randy's knee.

In the backseat, both Randy and Stephie shifted, but only Randy awakened.

"I left my phone inside," said Sloane. "Can you bring it out to me? I'll call a cab."

"Take my truck," he said. "A cab could be a while."

"How will I get it back to you?"

"I'll have two of my guys from the warehouse pick it up from your house tomorrow. We've got an early morning delivery in Tippy. They can drop it off to me on their way there. Truman Avenue, right?"

"Number 31."

"Just leave the key in your mailbox."

"Thanks," she said, grateful. "And for helping me with the chairs. Really, I don't know what I would've done if it wasn't for you."

Randy unfastened his seat belt.

"You're a good friend to Stephie," said Sloane. "I've never told you that."

"So are you," he said, placing B's empty fishbowl into the cardboard box.

Sloane shook her head. "I didn't do anything right."

"You cared and did what you thought was right."

"It doesn't make me right."

"It makes you human."

He smiled, and Sloane caught herself smiling back. "Thanks," she mumbled, eyeing the pink lines around Randy's wrist. "You stopped the pain experiment. Why?"

He shook his head. "Just changed up the approach."

"To what?"

"Choosing to feel it."

"You want to feel pain now?"

"Maybe it's not about want, but need. Maybe pain isn't an inferior emotion to happiness. Maybe one needs to exist for the other to exist."

"We have heroes only because we have villains, right?" Her tone was more sarcastic than she had intended.

Randy nodded, thoughtfully. "How will I know happiness if there's no contrast to it? If I embrace my pain, will I better understand my happiness?"

Happiness was volatile and fleeting; if not nurtured, it could so easily slip away.

Sloane remembered something he had said years ago. "I think I might agree with you," she said. "Maybe healing isn't about moving on. I think it's about moving forward. But why does it have to be such a bumpy road?"

"Forward is a direction," he said, "not a texture. Success is measured in the movement."

As she watched him gently shake Stephie awake, she thought about what he said.

"We're home," he said.

Sloane got out of the truck, so Randy and Stephie could get out more easily. On the front lawn, Randy hugged Sloane, which was unexpected and awkward, but surprisingly not unwelcome. He yanked on Stephie's arm and slipped her in between his and Sloane's body. For a brief moment, Sloane felt a part of them.

Then, as quickly as they had come together, their bodies separated. With the cardboard box tucked under his arm, Randy led a groggy Stephie inside the house.

Sloane got back into Randy's truck and drove off. On her way out of Tippett Valley, she passed the Harringtons' house and thought of the picket fence still stacked in their garage. Scolding herself, she squeezed the steering wheel. She was naïve to believe that things could go back to the way they were before the tragedy. Healing was about moving forward.

Chapter Thirty-Nine

WHEN SLOANE ARRIVED at the house on Truman Avenue, the digital clock in the truck's dash showed midnight. Her fitness tracker had reset to zero. It was a new day.

Jason's truck was in the driveway. He was supposed to be at the plant. Sloane's heart hammered. She dropped Randy's keys in the mailbox and entered the house with trepidation.

Jason was sitting at the kitchen table with his cell phone. When he looked up, his expression was difficult to read: angry, relieved, disappointed?

"You're home," said Sloane cautiously.

"I called in." His voice was strangely low.

There was no suitcase at the front door to suggest that he was leaving her tonight, nor anything like a purse or jacket or unknown footwear to indicate that Harper was also inside the house. Sloane kicked off her shoes, swiped the tears from her cheeks, and then folded her arms and squeezed her elbows to give her hands something to do.

"If you were trying to punish me," he said, "it worked."

Sloane met his tired eyes. *You're angry?* It was such a contrast to his usual composed demeanor. He waved his phone in the air. "I've been texting you. Calling. I even drove to Tippy."

"I didn't have my phone most the night," she said, attempting poise. "I wanted to call, but I don't know your number off by heart. I guess that says a lot, not even knowing my husband's cell phone number."

He slid his chair back, the wood legs scraping along the floor. "You're not a failure for not memorizing a seven-digit number." Frustrated, he stood. Opening a cupboard, he straightened the rows of glasses on the shelves. The task seemed to calm him.

"There was a problem at the agency," Sloane explained.

"Adele told me, when she showed up here."

Sloane's heartbeat raced. "Are you leaving me?" *If you are, just say it.*

"What?"

"I know about Harper Kennedy." Her throat closed behind the name. She inhaled quickly. "I read your conversations on your computer. You didn't log out. Who is she, Jason?"

. It seemed as if the lines in his face suddenly thickened and the tone of his skin shifted to gray. She had seen him like this only once before, when Roseanne passed.

"She's nobody," he said.

"You've been talking to Nobody for months. You told her you weren't married. Why would you tell her that?"

"I don't know," he said, momentarily shocked. His expression quickly reverted to sadness.

"It wasn't Heather from the plant who recommended *The Fountainhead,* was it," said Sloane. "It was Harper."

"Harper first. Then Heather."

"You're not having a secret relationship with Heather, too?"

"No."

"Does Harper work at the plant?"

"No."

"Is she real?"

His eyes expanded, and Sloane's hands formed fists.

"Jason, how human is Harper?"

Until that moment, she didn't understand the power of silence. *Say something, Jason. Talk to me.* Tears streaked her cheeks. She felt sick.

"Are you leaving me?" she asked again.

Jason met her eyes. "I don't want to."

His words had a weakening affect. She reached for the wall.

"I love you," he said.

It wouldn't be enough. She could tell by the way he avoided meeting her eyes that he knew it, too.

"What about Harper?"

"I told you I love you and you respond with a question about someone else?"

Someone with whom he had a secret relationship. She pushed her glasses into her face. She didn't want Harper to be like the flickering light above her desk, the one she ignored and got used to. Her voice deepened. "What about Harper?"

His body seemed to shrink. "She was someone to talk to," he said, looking away.

Sloane's bottom lip quivered, but she didn't back down. "Why did you tell her you weren't married?" *Because you don't want to be anymore?*

"I guess I was afraid she'd stop writing. I was lonely. I missed my wife."

"How could you miss me when I never went anywhere?"

"You did go somewhere. You stopped talking to me. You stopped listening. You stopped wanting to be together."

"I thought you didn't want to be with me," she said. "You know, because of . . . everything."

He turned sharply. "What's everything?"

You know.

"Sloane, you don't get to decide how I feel."

Anger filled her. "How am I supposed to know how you feel if you don't tell me? All the time you seem so content or indifferent. You haven't talked about your mom since her funeral, or acknowledged what it means that you're still working at the plant, and I have no idea how you feel about the very likely possibility that I'll never make you a dad because I can't." Her voice cracked.

"Why didn't you ever ask?" he said, innocently.

Sloane pressed her face into her forearm so that the sleeve of her sweater absorbed her tears. "I was scared what your answers would be," she said.

"So instead you made them up because you thought your answers would be better?"

"Not better." She was sure they weren't. "Easier, maybe. I was in control of them at least."

He fiddled with a loose handle on a cupboard. With a finger-nail, he tightened a screw.

"You didn't have to wait to be asked," said Sloane. "You didn't have to go and tell Harper things instead of me."

Jason rubbed his knuckles.

"I thought I was doing you a favor," she finished.

His chin snapped forward. "A favor?"

"If you didn't want to touch me, I thought you would appreci-ate it if I gave you . . . my permission . . . not to. I never meant to give you my permission to have an affair."

"You thought I didn't want to touch you?"

"Look at me," she said, turning and spreading her arms wide. She didn't suck in her belly; she let her body hang natu-rally. To expose the irritated patches of dry skin on the inside of her elbows, she rolled up her sleeves and rotated her arms. She rubbed her belly, drawing his attention to its emptiness. "Look at me," she said again.

He was. He hadn't taken his eyes off her. "I think you're beau-tiful," he said.

She wrapped her arms around her body. "I'm not."

"To me you are."

"You're delusional."

"Maybe you're the one who is."

"I don't look anything like her."

"Like who?"

"Harper."

"How do you know?"

"All the Harper Kennedys on Facebook are beautiful."

"That doesn't mean you're not."

"I turn blue!"

"Do you? Because I've never seen it. Have you?"

"In high school—"

"A bully called you a Smurf and you believed him."

She stuttered. "Well . . . I'm a secretary. I was supposed to be a graphic designer."

"You stopped applying. Adele told me. And you're great at your job, even though you want something else."

"Roseanne never got to be a grandmother because of me."

"Because of us."

"You never talk about it."

Frustrated, he slid the sugar jar the full length of the counter. "*We* never talk about it."

"Was it only chatting?"

"What?"

"With Harper, was it only words between the two of you?"

She stepped back, panicked by his silence. *Have I already lost you?* The pulse in her chest was like a fist punching her heart.

"Jason," she pressed. "Have you met her outside the computer?"

His chin dropped. "I was going to," he said. "I wanted to."

"But you didn't?"

He shook his head.

"Why not?"

He touched the back of her hand. "Because she isn't you, Sloane." With a thumb, he swiped at her cheekbones, erasing tears. "Listen to what I'm saying: I only want you."

"Then how do you explain Harper?"

"It felt like I couldn't have you. Like you didn't want me."

"That wasn't true."

"It felt true."

"I've never stopped loving you, Jason."

"You stopped trying."

"Because I kept failing!"

"You can't fail at trying, Sloane. You just stopped."

Did she? *Maybe I did.* It didn't condone his affair, but Sloane couldn't ignore the effect of her own actions. Did he feel betrayed, too?

"It isn't an excuse for what I did," he said, "but Sloane, I only ever wanted you."

She looked away.

239

"Instead of trying to figure out why I love you," he said, "maybe you should decide if you love me."

"I do! I know I do." Sobs clogged her throat. "I just thought I didn't deserve you anymore. You know, because—"

"What?"

"Because—"

"*What?*"

"Nothing."

"Something."

"It's just that you—"

He grabbed her hand and pulled her forward. "Talk to me, Sloane."

"You never said it was okay," she cried.

"What didn't I say was okay?"

"That things didn't turn out the way we planned."

He gently squeezed her shoulders, encouraging her to stay with him. "Sloane," he said, his face inches from hers. "It's okay."

He kissed her forehead and the warmth of his lips produced another round of tears. She wept and Jason held her tightly.

"It's okay," he said again.

Don't let go.

He didn't.

Finally, she lifted her head off his chest and discovered his face was wet, too.

"You're allowed to be angry with me," he said softly.

"I am." Then, "You're allowed to be angry with me, too."

He pulled her into him. "I am."

"I think I'm more angry with myself than I am with you," she admitted. "It's easier to be mad at you."

He played with the fitness tracker around her wrist.

"Did you love her?" she asked.

"It wasn't about love. It was about not being lonely."

Sloane stifled a sob. "I'm responsible for your loneliness, aren't I?"

"*I'm* responsible for what I did."

"Because you were lonely, and you were lonely because of me."

At the back of her skull, his fingers danced in her hair. His lips traveled gently across her forehead. "I think I understand why you pushed me away."

Sloane looked up, her nose gracing his chin. "You do?"

"You were lonely, because of me. I didn't talk to you about my mom after she passed, and I stopped talking to you about a baby. I thought talking about it would only hurt you, and I didn't want that. But not talking about it hurt you, too, didn't it? At least when we talk about it, we hurt together."

"I don't want you to hurt because of my failures."

"If I hurt a little, then maybe you hurt a little less, which makes me hurt a little less. You get that, don't you?"

For a moment, she was silent. "Do you really want a cat?" she asked.

"What?"

"You told Harper you wouldn't mind a cat."

"No, of course not, you're allergic."

"Would you want a cat if I wasn't, or if we weren't together?"

"Sloane, stop. Don't do that."

"What?"

"Ifs."

"It's just that you never told me you wanted a cat."

"Because I don't. Because you're allergic. And I don't not want to be with you."

"Then why did you tell Harper you wouldn't mind a cat?"

"For the same reason I told her I didn't have a wife. I was trying to be someone else. Maybe so it wouldn't feel so wrong. Look, Sloane, I know you probably have a lot of questions, and you have every right to ask them, and I'll answer as honestly as I can, but asking a 'what if' question is just avoiding asking a question that really matters."

In Jason's arms, Sloane thought of Randy. *Damn it, Randy, I think you were right.*

"Jason?"

"Yeah?"

"Remember when you proposed to me and you said you knew everything was going to be okay because we love each other?"

"I remember," he said.

"I didn't understand it then. But you meant everything'll be okay because we'll always be trying to be okay. I never meant to stop trying."

He smiled. "You're the smartest person I know, Sloane Sawyer."

"I'm sorry," she said.

"I'm sorry, too. I know I need to earn your trust back."

"And I need to earn yours." She pressed her cheek against his chest and slithered her arms around his waist. "In a video game," she said, "how many times can a player earn a one-up?"

He kissed the top of her head. "It doesn't matter," he said. "We're not playing a video game."

Sloane squeezed him harder. "I don't know where to begin," she said. "I feel so lost."

"This is nice, isn't it?"

She whispered, "Really nice."

As he danced with Sloane in the kitchen, he asked, "How's Stephie?"

With her sleeve, Sloane wiped her face. "We're not best friends anymore. We haven't been for a long time. I told her about the night Benjamin died."

"I'm sorry. I know how important she is to you."

"I've spent so much energy worrying about her when I should've been focused on you. You're the most important person in my life."

She kissed his neck. He groaned and she kissed him again. She couldn't remember the last time she had initiated foreplay for a purpose other than earning a checkmark on a fertility calendar. Maybe she hadn't lost herself entirely. Maybe there was hope for her yet. She reached for his face and her thumbs slid into his dimples. He grabbed hold of her wrists and peeled her hands away.

"I know we still have a lot to talk about and to figure out," he said seriously. "I'm not trying to—"

Sloane planted her lips on his mouth. His hands slid down her arms and lingered on her hips. His fingers tenderly clawed at her sides, her sweater bunching and crawling up over her waist. For a brief moment, she tensed. If Jason didn't love her hips, then why was he touching them and getting hard?

Like brushes, his fingertips painted over her skin. She kept waiting for his hands to reject her, but even when he passed over the dry patches on the inside of her elbows, and then the extra flesh around her waist, and then her fetus-shaped ears, his passion didn't waver. It took a conscious effort for Sloane to bury her thoughts and let Jason have his own.

"Do you want to?" he whispered, his hot breath filling her ear.

"Yes," she said. *Yes.*

"I don't want you to think it's all about this," he said.

"I don't," she whispered back, taking his hand and leading him upstairs. "But we can start with this."

Chapter Forty

IN THE MORNING, Randy's truck was gone from the driveway. The key had been taken from the mailbox and in exchange was Sloane's cell phone. She scrolled through her messages. Last night Jason had texted a dozen times and called twice. He really had been worried. There was also a text from Roma.

Boarded! See you tomorrow.

Tomorrow was today. It was Friday, and she had to be at the agency early to make sure everything was ready for the Brownwood pitch. She hoped Joan wasn't furious about the chairs or the revised PowerPoint. She also worried about the booking of the meeting room at the Juniper, another initiative she might be reprimanded for.

In the car, Sloane yawned. She and Jason had stayed up most the night, sleeping a little and talking a lot. Lying next to him, looking into his eyes, she had realized how much she missed him—the intimacy, the telling, the listening. She had bottled up her emotion for so long, dubbed over his words with her own internal dialogue, and rejected his touch—all for him, she had thought. It would take time to break her habits and to heal from the sting of his secret relationship, but she was determined not to waste her second chance. She would work to reject the ironic comfort of failure and take back the leading role in her life. She had encouraged Jason to stay in bed and to also consider "calling in" for his graveyard shift at the plant, so they could spend another night together.

Joan wasn't in her office when Sloane arrived at her desk. She suspected Joan was meeting with other executives before the pitch. Sloane checked her email and voicemail to ensure Joan hadn't left an urgent message and then proceeded to the boardroom. She confirmed that the catering order was correct and tested the laptop and screen. As she was leaving, Lenore entered, her eyes glazed over. Her lips were moving, as if rehearsing her part in the presentation.

"Good luck," said Sloane and quickly got out of Lenore's way.

When she returned to her desk, Sloane's phone was ringing. It was Reception. Daniel Brownwood and three other employees from Brownwood Industries had arrived.

Kendra Jamieson was wearing a white blouse that looked like the same one she'd worn in the photo on the Brownwood Industries' website and her personal Facebook profile. Sloane was speechless when she shook her hand. Daniel Brownwood was a short man with dark hair and a goatee, and when he touched Sloane's hand it was so fast it was more of a slap than a shake. The two others were Alex O'Hara and Janet Stone, both about Kendra's age and recent hires at Brownwood Industries. "Welcome," Sloane said.

"Let's see this place," said Daniel, with what Sloane interpreted as a skeptical smile.

She led the group to Human Resources where Gary took over the tour. Daniel stopped to chat to the occasional employee. He didn't seem to notice the desks with folding chairs; it helped that Sloane and Adele had been selective in which ones got them. In Creative Services, Daniel spoke to Irving. The two men shook hands and Irving was able to make eye contact for a respectable amount of time. Sloane was impressed. She was able to snatch a streamer from the corner of a cubicle, overlooked last night, and scrunched it up in her hand unnoticed. At least she hoped so.

Joan was in the boardroom, along with Ravi Duvelle from Research, Peter Kwan from Creative, Barb Moore from Media Planning and Buying, and Lenore Robinson and Sara Cooper from Account Services. Lenore offered coffee and water and Joan closed the blinds over the glass walls. Only briefly did she make eye contact with Sloane before closing the door.

For the next hour, Sloane kept busy. She changed the ink

cartridge in the photocopier and ordered enough pens to last the remainder of the year. Pens were always being left behind on sales calls. If she was about to be let go, the account managers likely wouldn't notice her absence until after Christmas, when the supply drawer had been depleted and the "low ink" warning flashed on the photocopier. She called Manning Office Supply to confirm no further delays were expected around the arrival of the chairs. She then made the appropriate calls to Security and Cleaning, and then to Oasis Rentals, to arrange for the pick-up of the folding chairs. She asked for the owner and expressed the Kaye Agency's gratitude for Randy Goff's help in a business emergency.

She focused on the flickering light above her desk. Maybe the question wasn't whether to ignore it or to accept it, but rather how could she make it better. She had failed Jason by her lack of effort, not by her lack of success. Inspired, she emailed a work order to Maintenance. It was so easy to do.

After that, she spent some time thinking about what effort meant. It didn't always have to be in the form of a grand gesture; sometimes a simple token could yield the same result. From inside her desk drawer, she texted Jason.

Thinking of you.

It seemed everyone in Account Services looked over when the boardroom door opened. Both Joan and Lenore walked Daniel Brownwood and his team back to Reception.

Joan didn't return to Account Services right away and neither did Lenore. Sloane hoped her boss was with Finance, drafting the new contract for Brownwood Industries, and not with Human Resources, signing termination papers. Either way, Lenore was probably throwing up in the bathroom.

A new email arrived in Sloane's inbox. It was a meeting request from Joan Dawes, sent from her cell phone. It was for a conversation with Sloane at eleven. She was sure it could mean only one thing. *I'm being fired.* She fought off her initial thoughts: What if she lost her job? What if she couldn't change?

Was Jason really going to stop writing Harper? Instead, Sloane focused on positive feelings: She was qualified to get another job. She could make changes in her life. Jason loved her and wanted to be with her. She worried that focusing on the positive ignored the fact that she had almost lost everything. But holding onto the past didn't help either. She had at least learned that much.

She emailed Adele: "Is Joan with Gary?"

Adele replied: "No. Gary's at the gym. Legs day. Helps him to relax. Hear anything about Brownwood?"

Sloane imagined Gary doing squats in front of a mirror during his fifteen-minute morning break. Then she thought of Jason, remembering how it felt to be naked in his arms last night. It was the feeling that caused her to smile at her desk. Jason wasn't a fantasy. He was real. She emailed Adele back: "Nothing yet."

To pass the time before her meeting with Joan, Sloane clicked through the proofs in the Creative Services drive. Irving's design for the Letterfield Recruitment campaign was stunning. He had cleverly omitted the outline of a single letter in the logo. *Genius.* She regretted not getting to know him better. She realized that she would much rather talk to Irving about typography and color palettes than listen to Gary go on about gym exercises and health supplements. Gary was the perfect character in a fantasy, but in real life, it was Irving she wanted as a friend. Maybe she could understand why Jason might pick her over a narrow-hipped, award-winning career woman with perfect skin and a fertile uterus. He preferred Sloane. Maybe it was as simple as that.

At exactly eleven, Joan returned to her office and immediately started typing on her laptop. Sloane knocked hesitantly and then plunged into an explanation the moment Joan made eye contact. Maybe Sloane could save her job. "About the Brownwood account. I booked the meeting room at the Juniper because I didn't think you really wanted to have a meeting with Daniel in the office on Regina Kaye's birthday. It was last minute and the hotel manager wouldn't waive the additional fee for booking less than twenty-four hours in advance. I didn't want to push him too hard on the price because I was worried he wouldn't rent me the meeting room at all. Really, considering the value of the Brownwood account, I figured the rental cost of the room was trivial in comparison, which seems ridiculous, since the cost equaled a month of my rent." She took a breath, and then continued. "About the chairs. We had only twelve hours to solve the situation. I know the ones we borrowed from other departments were mismatched and the folding chairs weren't ideal, but I thought it was the best option, under the circumstances. And I added slides to the presentation, but you didn't have to use them. Am I being fired?"

Joan unfolded her hands. "No," she said, dryly.

"Oh." Sloane caught her breath. "Good. Then I'd like to ask if I can use some of my downtime at work to do graphic design." She didn't know the next time she would have the attention of her boss, so she was taking advantage. "I've already done some design work for the department," she explained. "I made a poster for Lakeside Motors' charity barbeque. It didn't have any revenue attached to it, but Mark said his client remembered it when it was time to commit to their next year's spend. I did the posters for the staff Christmas party. There could be other stuff I could do, if I had the right software installed on my computer."

Joan squinted.

"If it were officially part of my job—designing things for the department that Creative Services doesn't have time for—I could get better at it," said Sloane. "I know I could. I'd like to try." She looked away, but kept her feet planted. She turned her hands upward, so that the sweat pooled in her palms rather than dripped onto the floor in Joan's office.

"All right."

Sloane's chin traveled forward. "Pardon?"

"If it keeps you engaged."

You're saying yes?

"I wouldn't want to lose you to boredom," said Joan.

Sloane seemed to have lost her ability to blink. "You don't want to lose me?"

"You're surprised."

"It's just . . . You barely talk to me."

"Which allows me to focus on my job."

Sloane knew she was staring, but she couldn't seem to stop.

"Which is motivating the account managers," said Joan.

"Right," said Sloane, recovering. *Exactly. Of course.*

"It's a compliment that I don't have to spend my time talking to you," said Joan. "You understand that, don't you?"

Sloane had never looked at it that way before. If it was how her performance was being measured—how Joan expressed her satisfaction with her work—then Sloane was an exceptional employee. She could count on her hand the number of times Joan had spoken to her directly. But it didn't feel like a compliment. Not talking to someone seemed a poor way to compliment their outstanding work. It certainly didn't make Sloane think she was excellent or indispensable. Perhaps it was how Jason felt when she didn't talk to him. Was Sloane like Joan to Jason? *I don't want to be like Joan.*

Realizing she had hijacked the meeting, Sloane asked, "What did you want to speak to me about?"

Joan returned to her laptop. "The Brownwood account is still with us."

"We did it?" said Sloane. "I mean, you did it?"

"That is all," said Joan.

It was the closest Sloane was going to get to a thank you.

Six steps from her boss' office, she returned to her desk. Almost immediately, her work phone rang. It was Adele. Still processing her conversation with Joan, Sloane answered. "Good morning. Account Services. Sloane Sawyer speaking."

"Did you hear?"

Sloane leaned forward, closer to the phone. She actually had an answer. "Brownwood's still with us," she said.

"But did you hear how Joan did it?"

Sloane spoke quietly, as if the information were top secret; the tone of Adele's voice made it sound like it was. "Tell me," she said.

"It was the campaign for the Crawford Foundation."

Sloane was quiet.

"Did you hear me?" said Adele.

"Mmhmm."

"That campaign cost us money! 'The length of my skirt isn't a measure of my consent.' The one with the young girl with the big eyes."

"I know it," said Sloane.

"To think she could impress them with a two-week campaign for a non-profit."

"Did she?" asked Sloane. "Impress them?"

"Get this," said Adele. "They loved it."

"Really?"

"The new marketing manager told Brownwood she'd like to try working with the Kaye Agency on the company's rebrand."

"Oh my God." Sloane couldn't believe it worked.

"I don't know how Joan does it," said Adele, "but she really is brilliant at her job. Lunch today?"

Sloane's mind was reeling.

"Sloane?"

She shook her head. "Yes, lunch today. I'm inviting Irving," she added.

"Fine," said Adele, without hesitation. "Invite Irving."

"Really?"

"Sure."

For the first time, Sloane wondered if Adele had ever had a problem with Irving.

Distracted by her inbox, Sloane opened an email from Joan. It was addressed to the IT department with Sloane cc'd: "Creative Services software to be installed on Sloane Sawyer's computer, asap. Charge to my account. JD."

"Sloane?" prompted Adele.

"Huh?"

"I said, I've got something to ask you in person. I can't wait for lunch. Will you meet me now, in the lunchroom?"

Adele was already in a booth when Sloane entered the lunchroom. Dangling from her wrist was an emerald beaded bracelet.

"I thought you hated green," said Sloane, sitting across from Adele.

"It was either this from Lawrence's mom or the ring from his grandmother. His grandmother's been divorced twice, and his mom's been married for forty years, so."

As if lassoing something behind her, she twisted her hair into a rope, and then flipped it over her shoulder. She scratched at the birthmark on her chest.

"What did you want to ask me?" said Sloane, checking the time on her phone.

Sitting up straight, Adele placed her palms on the table. "Will you be my Matron of Honour?"

Sloane leaned back. "Me? Really?"

"Yes."

"Are we even friends?"

Adele squinted. "I see you more than anyone."

"At work."

"So?"

"I just thought . . ."

"What? I don't have much time for friends outside of work. Between Lawrence and Eva—"

"Exactly. What about Eva?"

"What about Eva?"

Right. It'd be weird to ask your ex-boyfriend's girlfriend. But still, they seemed really close. Unless Adele had been using her friendship with Eva only to remain in Travis' life.

"Do you even like her?" asked Sloane. "I mean, if she wasn't Travis' girlfriend, would you still want to spend so much time with her?"

251

"Girlfriend?" Adele laughed out loud.

"What's so funny?"

"She's not his girlfriend."

"She's not?"

"No."

"Who is she then?"

"His daughter!"

"Eva's his daughter?"

"Yes!"

"Eva's a kid?"

"Eleven."

How had Sloane missed this? Had she only assumed Eva was Travis' girlfriend?

"You're friends with your ex-boyfriend's eleven-year-old daughter?"

Adele laughed again. "I'm the mother of my ex-boyfriend's eleven-year-old daughter."

Sloane's mouth popped open. Adele had been spending her weekends and taking days off work to be with her daughter. It suddenly made sense. She remained friends with her ex-boyfriend to be in Eva's life, not the other way around. All those lunches together, how could it never have come up? Or had it, and Sloane just hadn't been paying close enough attention? Like she hadn't been paying close enough attention to Jason.

I've been focusing on all the wrong things. On all the wrong people.

"You said she was the reason you and Travis broke up," said Sloane, trying to make sense of it.

"She was," said Adele. "It was different with a kid around. Travis took to it better. We were so young. I told you, I was someone else back then. Nineteen and scared. I almost threw it all away. But I changed and Travis forgave me, and I get to be a part of Eva's life."

If I change, will Jason forgive me?

"That's why Lawrence has to want a kid," said Sloane. "Because you already have one."

Jason and Sloane didn't. What reason would he have to give her a second chance?

"She's baking her first cake on Sunday all by herself," said Adele, proudly. "For my birthday."

"I'm sorry. I didn't know she was your daughter," said Sloane. "I should've asked you more about your past."

"I kind of liked it that you didn't."

"So I wouldn't judge you for it."

"A lot of people do."

"A real friend would've asked and not judged."

"Well, how about we be real friends from now on?"

"Okay," said Sloane. "I'd like that."

"Matron of Honour?"

"Matron of Honour."

Pleased, Adele stood. "Now that we're officially friends, you can talk to me about Jason," she said. "I won't judge."

Sloane nodded, "Thanks."

"See you at lunch."

Adele left the lunchroom and Sloane spotted Lenore Robinson speed-walking through Account Services. When she saw Sloane, she diverted and headed for the lunchroom.

"I don't normally do this," said Lenore, standing in front of Sloane, "but I'm going to make an exception." She hugged Sloane. "Thank you."

It was quick, but tight; Sloane lost her breath for a second. "Is Joan going to let you keep the Brownwood account?" she asked, once released.

Lenore shook her head. "She's transferring it to Sara."

"I'm sorry."

"Don't be. I'm retiring. It's time. It was my plan all along. Thanks to you, on my terms."

She smiled, and then hurried off.

Multiple times, Sloane's phone vibrated; over a dozen text messages from Roma.

Honey!

I'm home.
Discovered your father alive.
How are you?
Jason?
Work?
When will I see you?
Tonight?
It's nighttime in China.
Come after work. It'll feel like morning.
You know I'm best in the morning.
How many steps?
I'm making lasagna.
You think your father remembers it's our anniversary?

Sloane gasped. It was her parents' wedding anniversary and she had forgotten to submit the announcement for the Saturday paper! The deadline had passed. Roma would be devastated. Sloane could fix this. *I can try.*

Returning to Account Services, she approached Mark Grier.

"I need your help," she told him. "Can you call your contact at the newspaper and ask for a favor? It's important."

Chapter Forty-One

BEFORE LEAVING TORREN HILLS, Sloane stopped at Grace's daughter's flower shop to finally collect her payment. She wanted to be home with Jason, not driving to Tippett Valley; at the very least, she wanted to have him come with her. When she had texted him the invitation to dinner with her parents, he replied that he was on a roll and wanted to keep working at home, but he had called in for his shift, so Sloane would see him later. She texted him as she was leaving the flower shop.

I can turn around.

It's important to your mom.

Not too late for you to come. She would love it.

Lasagna!

Still in the middle of something.

Working on your video game?

Something more important.

What was more important than that? She couldn't help thinking about Harper Kennedy. Was she the something? Sloane's body tightened. Her phone vibrated.

Not a secret.

A surprise.

For you.

Didn't mean for it to sound like anything else.

When she arrived in Tippett Valley, the smell of the flowers masked the pollution in the air. On impulse, she stopped at 65 Ranger Street. It didn't feel right to visit Tippett Valley without trying to see Stephie. She just wanted to know that she was okay after last night.

Stephie answered the door looking . . . sober.

"Hi," said Sloane.

"Hey."

Flooding her mind were the million things she wanted to say. *Just try.* "I stopped by to tell you how sorry I am," she said. "About . . . everything. Especially Benjamin."

Stephie picked at the paint chipping off the door. "You don't have to keep doing this," she said, her voice uncharacteristically soft.

"Doing what?"

"Trying to be friends."

"But we're best friends." It was a desperate response, and Sloane knew it.

"The teenage versions of us were, but I'm not that girl anymore. I haven't been for a long time."

I know.

"Best friends don't have to be best friends forever. We were when we needed to be."

"Now you've got Randy. He came into your life when you needed him, didn't he? I always felt like he stole my best friend from me."

"The tragedy did that."

"I was fine with the new version of you."

Stephie laughed. "No you weren't. You wanted your best friend back, the one before Benji died. If it weren't for your memories of us, we would never be friends today."

Sloane knew she was right. It felt good to be finally talking about it. "I should've told you," she said. "Back then. Maybe I wouldn't have lost you like I did."

"Maybe either way I was lost."

"If I had told you, you wouldn't have felt guilty all these years."

"I can't fault you for the very reason why we were friends. You never told me the truth."

"This was different."

"Maybe. But I was still a terrible sister, and you had nothing to do with that."

"He loved you," said Sloane. "And he knew you loved him."

"You don't know that."

"Want to know how I do? You were a terrible best friend to me, especially these past years, and I still loved you, and I believed you loved me."

Stephie met Sloane's eyes. "Thanks," she whispered. "You think Kendra believes that, too?"

"I don't know. You could ask her."

Stephie shook her head. "She couldn't forgive me."

"Maybe she can now. You said so yourself, you don't know her anymore. Not the thirty-year-old version of her. You don't know what she'd say." Sloane's eyes dropped. "You think you'll ever be able to forgive me?"

Stephie didn't answer. Instead, she lit a cigarette. Maybe forgiveness wasn't a prerequisite for moving forward. Maybe nothing was, other than the willingness to try.

Sloane heard the sound of a guitar being played from inside the house. "He's not so bad, you know," she said. "Randy, I mean. I understand now why you slept with him. Maybe you should let it be okay. Maybe he's your fate."

Stephie chewed on a chunk of her bangs.

"I should get going," said Sloane.

Walking away, she wondered if she would ever see Stephie again. In some ways, it was comforting to know she didn't have to. She would be okay. *She's got Randy.* Maybe one day they would be friends again. Maybe not.

"Benji had a crush on you."

Sloane stopped. Turning around, she said, "What?"

"He was happy that night," said Stephie.

"What are you talking about?"

"I always thought that what I said to him that night at the party were the last words he heard. That my anger was the last emotion he experienced with someone. It wasn't though, was it? If you were the last person he was with, he would've been happy."

Sloane shook her head. "I told him to take a shower. He fell in the bathtub."

"A million other people would've told him the same thing."

"But it was me."

"It was you," Stephie said. "Randy says that if the dead rest in peace, then sometimes so can the living."

Sloane was sure the sadness of a loss never goes away, but then she imagined Benjamin smiling as he turned on the shower that fateful night. A brief sense of amity between heartbreak and joy came over her. It didn't make Benjamin's death less tragic or her guilt any lighter, but for a fleeting moment a star sparkled in an otherwise blackened sky.

"Stephie," she called out.

On the front step, Stephie took a long drag from her cigarette.

"What did Benjamin take from your room that day?"

She exhaled the smoke slowly. "Your ear."

Chapter Forty-Two

AT THE SAWYERS', Roma entered the kitchen waving a handheld fan, a souvenir from China.

"Sloane!" she cried, embracing her daughter. "Hasn't it seemed like I've been gone forever? Your father said it felt like fourteen days, which is exactly the length of time I've been away. It feels like longer though, doesn't it? Are those for me?"

"Happy anniversary, Mom. Welcome home."

Roma accepted the flowers. "They're lovely. Edward! Come say hi to your daughter. Where's Jason? Tell me everything, Sloane. What did I miss?"

"He's working on something at home," she said. "And you missed a lot."

"Really?"

"A lot can happen when you're gone forever."

Roma smiled, seemingly pleased.

"I thought you'd be tired," said Sloane, "after such a long flight."

"Oh honey, I slept for thirteen hours on the airplane. It was like a cradle!"

"What was China like?"

For the next thirty minutes Roma talked uninterrupted. She described the Chinese landscape, the people, the culture. At the table, Edward was subtle about it, but Sloane noticed he had dozed off. Her mind had drifted too, wondering what Jason was doing at home. Under the table, she texted Stephie.

www.brownwoodindustries.com
You can't fail at trying.

When Edward started to snore, Sloane cut off her mom.

"Should I get out the scrapbook," she said loudly, waking her dad, "so it's ready for tomorrow's newspaper clipping?"

"Oh, yes!" said Roma, glowing.

When Sloane returned from the living room, she observed her parents from the hallway. Roma and Edward were two imperfect human beings in an imperfect marriage. What kept them together?

"Dinner's ready!" Roma bellowed, as she pulled the lasagna out of the oven. "Sit, sit!"

At the table, Edward remained standing. He shifted his weight from side to side, avoiding eye contact with both his wife and daughter.

"I wasn't very good at school," he said. "I failed a lot of tests. Math, science, English. There seemed to be a test every week, didn't there?"

Embarrassed for her dad, Sloane cringed. Why was he talking about high school tests?

"There are a lot of tests in a marriage," he went on, pulling on his collar. "I failed a lot of them, too." He smiled, giving his family permission to laugh. Then he stood incredibly still. "You're wrong if you think that means you've failed at marriage." He looked to Sloane, as if he knew private details about her relationship with Jason. It occurred to her that maybe her dad and husband talked. "I failed high school because I stopped showing up for tests." Edward's eyes shifted to his wife. "Thirty-two years and I'm still showing up for yours."

Roma looked confused. Sloane touched her mom's arm and the fitness tracker dropped out of her sleeve. Roma's face lit up. "Honey, you're wearing it."

Sloane slid the band past her elbow. With a serious look, she encouraged Roma to refocus. "Mom," she said, "Dad is trying to tell you he loves you."

Roma's eyes expanded. She smiled and swatted at the air. "Oh, Edward," she said. "I love you, too."

Their marriage was worth celebrating.

Edward sat and Roma reached for Sloane's arm to reposition the fitness tracker.

"Mom."

"I know. You don't want me to touch you."

"It's not that." She practically forced Roma to take her hand. *Say it out loud.* "I love you, too, Mom."

Roma squeezed Sloane's fingers. "I know," she said. "I know."

It was dark when Sloane turned onto Truman Avenue, but she could still see it from a distance. Instead of pulling into the driveway, she parked on the street in front of the house. Jason was sitting on the step. He stood when she got out of the car.

"What is this?" she asked.

He shrugged, coyly.

"Jason, we have a fence."

Lining the front lawn were short, white pickets.

"But—when did this happen?"

"Today. I just finished."

Sloane couldn't believe it. "You built it? Mr. Yin said it was okay?"

Jason nodded. "He helped."

"We can't afford this," she said.

"Mr. Yin bought the paint and the wood was free. I picked out the good pieces."

Sloane's breath caught. The Harringtons' fence.

"You like it?"

Tears raced down her cheeks. She reached for Jason's face and her thumbs slid into the craters of his dimples.

"Jason."

"Yeah."

"How do you feel about not being a dad?"

Acknowledgments

Thank you—

Tena Laing and Kathryn Hogg for your willingness to read early drafts of this novel. The generosity of your time and your insightful feedback was greatly appreciated.

Jennifer Murray for answering my many questions about goldfish. (Note: in some cases, I chose to take fictional liberties—as this is a work of fiction—in the portrayal of the character). Thank you for responding to my texts sent at ridiculous hours.

My parents, for always supporting me, especially with my art. And particularly for The Camp brainstorm session that helped shape a very important thread in this novel.

Stephanie Fysh for your valuable manuscript evaluation.

Lynn Duncan and Kilmeny Jane Denny from Tidewater Press for believing in me and this book. These two women are powerhouses who I admire greatly for their passion, expertise and kindness.

The many family and friends who support me in little and big ways. You all contribute to my ability to do what I love: write.

Lastly (though first in my heart), Christopher Imrie for listening to me talk through plot and character development, reading excerpts from my manuscript, providing feedback, giving me a hug when I needed one and encouraging me to keep going when I wavered. You live with me—and love me—through it all. You are my rock, my podium, my favorite human being.

P.S. Billie, thanks for keeping my feet warm when I write, and for reminding me when dinner time is, and for insisting I take a break from writing to go for a walk. Every writer should have a dog like you.